ISBN 978-0-282-50870-8
PIBN 10854221

1 MONTH OF
FREE
READING

at

www.ForgottenBooks.com

English
Français
Deutsche
Italiano
Español
Português

www.forgottenbooks.com

Mythology Photography **Fiction**
Fishing Christianity **Art** Cooking
Essays Buddhism Freemasonry
Medicine **Biology** Music **Ancient
Egypt** Evolution Carpentry Physics
Dance Geology **Mathematics** Fitness
Shakespeare **Folklore** Yoga Marketing
Confidence Immortality Biographies
Poetry **Psychology** Witchcraft
Electronics Chemistry History **Law**
Accounting **Philosophy** Anthropology
Alchemy Drama Quantum Mechanics
Atheism Sexual Health **Ancient History**
Entrepreneurship Languages Sport
Paleontology Needlework Islam
Metaphysics Investment Archaeology
Parenting Statistics Criminology
Motivational

ARGONAUTS OF THE SOUTH

By

CAPTAIN FRANK HURLEY

Author of "Pearls and Savages"

*Being a Narrative of Voyagings and Polar
Seas and Adventures in the Antarctic with Sir
Douglas Mawson and Sir Ernest Shackleton*

WITH 75 ILLUSTRATIONS AND MAPS

G. P. PUTNAM'S SONS
NEW YORK AND LONDON
The Knickerbocker Press
1925

The Knickerbocker Press
New York

Made in the United States of America

Dedicated

TO MY COMRADES

IN PERIL AND ADVENTURE AND TO THE MEMORY
OF THOSE OF THEM WHO MADE THE
SUPREME SACRIFICE IN THE
CAUSE OF SCIENCE

FOREWORD

IN this book of Antarctic voyagings I have endeavoured to portray the adventures of those with whom I went exploring in two famous Expeditions, and, if possible, to enable the reader to live through and share in our experiences.

Of scientific detail there is little; those in search of such information should consult the admirable official records in which it is fully set forth.

I have tried to tell of the wonders we saw; of the dangers we faced; of the glamour of being the first to penetrate the unknown; of our successes, and of our failures, —just as glorious—and to picture as far as words can the incredible beauties, as well as the awesome desolation, of that vast unpeopled continent—Antarctica.

The story, which covers a period of five years' wanderings, is true. May it bring back the thrill of adventure to the old and kindle the flame of emulation and achievement in the young.

My most grateful thanks are due to Lady Shackleton for permission to include in this book, the photographs which I took as Official Photographer to the Shackleton *Endurance* Expedition; to Sir Douglas Mawson for the use of the pictures I made while with him; to

Messrs. Sandell and Hamilton, comrades on the Mawson Expedition, for the two photographs of sea-elephants.

I am also indebted to the firms of William Heinemann and Andrew Melrose for the short extracts from Sir Douglas Mawson's *Home of the Blizzard* and Captain John K. Davis' *With the "Aurora" in the Antarctic.*

CONTENTS

ILLUSTRATIONS

ARGONAUTS OF THE SOUTH

ARGONAUTS OF THE SOUTH

INTRODUCTORY

YOUTHFUL DAYS

Then take this honey for thy bitterest cup—
There is no failure save in giving up;
No real fall so long as one still tries,
For seeming set-backs make the strong man wise;
There's no defeat in truth save from within,
Unless you're beaten there, you're bound to win.

MARCUS AURELIUS.

DAWN was breaking over the Blue Mountains as a long heavily burdened freight train, outward bound from Sydney, was laboriously toiling up the steep gradients, to the way-back western towns of New South Wales. Heavy snow had fallen overnight, and the gaunt gum trees stood like white-shrouded sentinels, mutely regarding its passing. The crystalline daybreak was biting cold, and as the sun came peeping above the ridges, shedding a glow of warmth over the frigid white landscape, a boy's head peeped out from beneath a tarpaulin that covered one of the cars, and surveyed the rumbling chain of snow-covered trucks. Observing none of the train's crew in sight the investigating head was followed by a body; a young stowaway clambered out and stretched his shivering limbs to the sunbeams.

The youthful adventurer was woe-begone and weary in mind and body. The events of the past months which had decided him rashly to desert the comforts of the parental hearth, the tribulations of a night spent among rolling barrels and bales of merchandise beneath the icy tarpaulin of a shunting freight train, and contact with the strange hostile world into which he had precipitated himself, were in their cumulative effect, temporarily overwhelming. But the sun, rapidly rising in the sky, dispersed gloom and mist from slope and valley; birds took to wing, rabbits scampered gleefully, and all Nature began to rejoice in the newly born day. The stowaway found the morning gladness irresistible. He, too, sang, and deciding that the boldest was the wisest course, waved greetings to the wayside station officials as the "through freight" rattled noisily on. His audacity succeeded admirably for a time. Officials on duty never doubted his right to travel and waved heartily back!

All went well as far as Mount Victoria. Doubtless the veteran Master at this point had been "had" before. The return "wave" here came from the signal arm which brought the train to a jerky standstill with a clatter of bumping trucks.

The platform had been overrun some distance, and the command "Down out o' there and come here" was bellowed raucously through a megaphone. The boy's first impulse was to escape, but numerous navvies at work repairing the railway line in the vicinity cut off all retreat. There was nothing for him but to obey. He clambered down—and the long line of trucks rumbled away on their Western journey, minus the juvenile passenger. The hour was still early, and only two officials were seemingly in charge of the station; the Master and a junior who winked and smiled maliciously at the young miscreant, as he, with trepidation, followed the surly principal into his office.

"What were you doing on that train?" gruffly queried the Master.

"Going for a ride, Sir!" replied the boy with such dignity as a crumpled collar, dirty face and tousled hair would allow him to assume.

"Going for a ride? Where to?"

"Please, Sir, to the Ironworks at Lithgow to get a job."

"What's your name?"

"Frank Hurley, Sir."

"How old are you—you young rascal?"

"Thirteen, Sir."

"Have you any money to pay your train fare?"

"No, Sir!" and the boy proved the truth of the reply by turning out his pockets and revealing his financial assets as nil.

Further embarrassing interrogation was interrupted by the junior who, scenting an easy victim, began

shadow-sparring at the woe-begone urchin,—my way-
ward self in juvenile days! Maybe it was a reminis-
cence of the old man's own boyhood that sparkled his
eye and appealed to his sporting instincts, or perhaps
he visualised his own son in a similar predicament.
Without more ado he said, "I'll give you a fighting
chance, you young imp. Put up your hands and let
us see what you are made of. If you can lick young
Johnnie here, I'll let you go scot free."

In playground bouts, I had gained notoriety equal
to my fame for lack of scholastic application, so that it
was with some eagerness that I took up the challenge.
Just how the news spread I do not know, but in a matter of moments, officials, navvies, and casual loungers
crammed windows, benches, and all available space.
Like two fierce young tiger cubs we sprang at one another. Instinctively I heartily disliked the office youth.
The arrogant "serves-you-right" grin with which he
had greeted the ignominious end to the train escapade
annoyed me. Science played a minor part in that wild
rough and tumble. Urged on by the spectators, who
seized the opportunity to make bets, we fought. The
officials cheered their favourite, whilst I was goaded by
the navvies with threats of terrible chastisement if I
lost.

For ten violent minutes we fought and then I managed to land a heavy winding blow that won me the
battle and my freedom. I was carried shoulder high
to the navvies' camp, to breakfast with my newly made

enthusiastic friends. Old Bill Jones, the foreman, offered me a job on the line, but this being not in my plans, which I disclosed, I received sound advice and directions instead. Bill gave me five shillings which "the boys" had collected, and I went on my way rejoicing—feeling that the world was not such a bad place after all.

Waiting outside the station gate, to my surprise, was Johnnie, not offering fight this time, but a boy's hand shake, and all it means, and a sixpence. "Take this, you might want it!" he said.

With a light heart I swung away from Mount Victoria, along the undulating road that wandered through my native mountains, to the town of Lithgow some twenty miles away. It was August, the month of early spring, and the tender foliage of the gum tree forests clothed the mountain slopes from peak to gully-creek with crimson, russet, and emerald. The snow was vanishing beneath the cloudless sun and every watercourse was gurgling a merry tune. In a near-by treetop a number of laughing Kookaburras were making the gullies reverberate with cackling merriment. They seemed to be laughing in sheer rapture at the happiness of the morning. How delightful it all seemed to me, rejoicing as I was in recent triumph and uncurbed freedom. These were the Blue Mountains that had ever lured me from the home attic window, when at sunset I had gazed over the roofs and smoking chimneys to the far-off irregular skyline, and in childish fancy, followed the sun as he descended to a mysterious world beyond the horizon.

It was glorious to be walking, liberated from the discipline of the schoolroom, where the previous day—alas! nothing new!—I had been severely chastised for truanting.

Towards evening, tired, hungry and friendless, I came to the last ridge that looked down on the town of Lithgow. The Valley was heavy with smoky haze through which town lights glimmered murkily. Flames and fiery glow belched from blast furnaces, smelters, and refineries, seeming to set the very clouds ablaze with their flaring. The atmosphere was heavy with choking sulphurous fumes; I seemed to have left the paradise of the woods behind me and to be descending into Vulcan's Inferno.

I wandered along the streets of this city of coal and iron, examining eagerly the enticing attractions of café windows, grasping tightly in my pocket my worldly possessions—five shillings and sixpence. At length I came to a homely house, on which was displayed the sign "Board and Residence." In answer to my knock a motherly woman opened the door. Doubtless my weary demeanour evoked her sympathy, for I found myself shown to a comfortable little room. Next morning I got a job at the ironworks as a fitter's handyman at a pound a week!

At last I proudly felt myself to be of some worth in the world, and that night, l wrote to my parents giving

Frank Hurley

an account of all that had happened and asking forgiveness. My father was more kindly disposed than I had even hoped. He wrote a letter of excellent advice and intimated that although it had been his and my mother's wish that I might mend my ways and eventually take up the study of law, they would abandon their hopes if I truly felt that I could content myself in a vocation which I had chosen of my own free will. He concluded by remarking that if I could tackle all life's problems with the optimism and determination I had recently shown, there was nothing I might not achieve. "Let 'Find a way or make one' be ever your motto," he wrote.

For two years I subdued my inclination for roving and progressed rapidly at the ironworks, for I had a natural aptitude for the trade. I might have been there still had it not been for a contract aboard a vessel which caused my employers to send a gang of engineers to the docks at Sydney. My inclusion in the party affected the whole course of my future career.

Aboard the vessel, boylike, I mingled constantly with the seamen, listening intently to droll experiences and stories of foreign lands. They sounded so good to my ears, that all my resolutions crumbled, and I made up my mind to follow a seafaring life at the first opportunity. Instead of returning to the ironworks I went home;—it was nearer the sea.

For the next two years I followed occupations varying from clerical routine to aeronautics! Nor were my nights left unoccupied, for I attended engineering classes and brought some consolation to my parents by winning "Merits" and "Awards." But I grew more restless than ever. I was like a ship tossing idly on turbulent tides without control. Every wind of fancy drove me where it listed and I was heading for the rocks of disaster.

Then I found a new toy. A fellow worker induced me to purchase his camera and to take up the study of photography. Soon I became so deeply absorbed in "this new fad" as my friends called it, that everything else fell into neglect. From the time I first gazed wonderingly at the miracle of chemical reaction on the latent image during the process of development, I knew I had found my real work, and a key, could I but become its master, that would perhaps unlock the portals of the undiscovered World. Not long after, I chanced to make the acquaintance of a man of experience and ability as a photographer. He proposed that we should enter into a business partnership. I was astonished at the understanding and toleration my father displayed towards the proposition; he even financed it.

Under the tuition and stabilizing influence of my mature partner, I flourished. Business progressed rapidly, and I worked hard mastering the complex process of the craft.

We had been established two years when calamity came. My father died suddenly, and my partner, a little later, was stricken with illness and compelled to relinquish active work in the firm. The death of my father not only deprived me of my dearest companion but also cut off financial support, and I found myself in charge of an extensive business without adequate capital. For eighteen months I endured the strain and then I felt incapable of continuing any longer.

One night I returned to the studio in a gloomy block of buildings, inexpressibly depressed, for I had resolved to give up. The bitter word—failure—had never found a place in my lexicon before, but physically and mentally I was on the verge of collapse.

As I laboured up the dark stairway with heavy heart, I reflected on what seemed to be my wasted efforts. How utterly hopeless the future seemed and how futile and barren my ambitions! To stumble blindly in the dark—and fail—seemed to be my lot in life! And then —as groping my way, I turned the landing, suddenly the blackness was pierced by a silvery beam that shone through a window and flooded the stairway with light. An eerie sensation crept over me. I was very young and highly impressionable. Moreover I was in an over-wrought and nervous state, readily responsive to any suggestion wise or unwise. For a moment I stood stock-still. Surely this heaven-sent moonbeam was an omen.

However ridiculous it may sound to staid old and sensible folk, I felt transformed. By the time I gained the top I was determined that nothing should turn me from my determination to achieve success.

On the morrow I set about rallying my remaining forces for a stubborn fight. It lasted for a year. Then gradually the barbed entanglements of adversity were penetrated and the turning point won.

Success begets success, and now that business was flourishing, fortune presented me with the opportunity which I had been awaiting for years.

Doctor Douglas Mawson, now Sir Douglas Mawson, was then organising his Expedition to the Antarctic, and among the vacancies on his staff open for competition was that of Official Photographer. In this I saw the possibility of applying my abilities and realising cherished dreams. I sent in my credentials and determined, even though I had to stowaway aboard the Expedition's vessel, to secure the post.

Nearly every Australian youth and man who could claim intimate or distant associations with camera craft, applied; but I had achieved a reputation which placed me among the "possibles." One evening Doctor Mawson telephoned to me to meet him at the railway station upon the eve of his departure for Adelaide. Feeling that such an interview would necessarily be brief and unconvincing, I determined to travel aboard the "Limited" Express, and get the Doctor entirely to myself. When he arrived on the platform he discovered that I was also a passenger!

For a hundred miles I talked, with all the fervour I could command, to convince him that even if I failed in one occupation, I would surely make good in another.

He listened patiently. In later days, talking over the incident, he informed me that it was not so much my enthusiasm as my initiative in boarding the train that induced him, two days later, to send me the telegram—"You are accepted!"

Three simple words, but they threw open the golden door of adventure for me!

CHAPTER I

THROUGH THE "ROARING FORTIES"

"For we're booming down on the old trail, the out trail,
We're sagging South on the Long trail, the trail that is always new."

KIPLING.

THE adventure began at Queen's Wharf, Hobart, Tasmania, where all the members of the Expedition were assembled and busily engaged sorting out a vast confusion of merchandise and equipment. Doctor Mawson, the leader, had his coat off and sleeves rolled up with the others, and was checking as his men marked the cases with coloured bands and stacked them in orderly dumps marked, "Macquarie Island," "Main Antarctic Base," and "Western Base." In addition to its contents, each case was branded A.A.E. —Australasian Antarctic Expedition.

The Expedition's vessel the *Aurora*, looking very trim in fresh paint, was berthed alongside the wharf, loading. The square rig on the foremast and the schooner rig on main and mizzen, classed her as unusual, and a closer investigation of the sturdy wooden hull and steel-shod prow suggested the nature of the work for which she was built.

Sir Douglas Mawson, D.Sc., B.E., Commander of the Australasian Antarctic
Expedition.

Aloft, sailors were bending on sails and overhauling the shrouds. They sang as they worked, a chanty as old as ships, which greatly entertained the constant stream of sightseers.

The *Aurora* was built in Dundee in 1876 and remained, after long years of ice navigation with the Newfoundland Sealing Fleet, a sterling tribute to honest craftsmanship. The hull, constructed of stout oak timbers, sheathed with greenheart and lined with fir planks, had been further reinforced with heavy beams, and a massive "cut away" bow armoured with steel plates. Her carrying capacity was 600 tons, her length one hundred and sixty-five feet, her breadth thirty-five feet, her depth eighteen feet. The compound engines, situated aft, developed one hundred horse power. Captain John King Davis, her master, and second in command of the Expedition, was twenty-eight years of age and had already gained wide experience in Polar navigation.

Davis led on sea and Mawson on land. Both possessed an inflexible spirit in danger and a rare ability to inspire and encourage. They were equally human and generous and thought of their men first and themselves afterwards. These rare traits, drew from each of us the best and went far towards making the Expedition's plans a success. Briefly these plans were, to explore the unknown portion of the Antarctic Continent lying directly south of Australia in what is known as the Australian Quadrant, to conduct oceanographical observations in the waters of that part of the world, covering as large an area as possible. The first party was to land at Macquarie Island, midway between Hobart and the Antarctic, the next at the main base in Adelie Land, and a third, at a point a thousand miles further west along the Antarctic coast. The three units were to spend a season in scientific work and exploration and twelve months later all were to be collected by the *Aurora.*

It was impossible to compress the vast bulk of coal, stores, and machinery into the bunkers and hold, so the decks were piled high with hut timbers, wireless masts, cases of benzine, boxes of food and endless sundries. The bridge even was encumbered with scientific instruments and meteorological screens. Even these found temporary use on the voyage as hen coops, for a number of fowls coming aboard at the last moment were thrust inside and, as it eventually transpired, had the only dry place above decks.

Sharp on scheduled time at 4 P.M. Saturday, 2nd December, a midsummer afternoon, to a fanfare of whistles and cheers from enthusiastic Hobart folk, moorings were cast off and we headed slowly out into the channel.

Never had I seen the "city of strawberries and cream," as we called Hobart, look more beautiful than it appeared as we passed down the Derwent.

Launches, gay with fluttering bunting, followed in our wake. Over the town lay a purple mist merging

SOUTH POLE

EN M
FR WI
LA
eard.

SĒA
c¹/e
SHACKLETO
REGION
h Orkney
60

ARCOT LA
cander I La
taide I
HAM LAND
h Shetland I

into a marvellous blue where the deep green slopes of Mount Wellington sweep gradually up to a precipitous basalt dome. Near the summit of the Mount a smoke signal was ascending to windless skies. As we proceeded, the silvery limbs of the eucalyptus trees which clothe the slopes on either side with rich green forests, stood out in crisp detail and were reflected in the unruffled turquoise waters.

Further down stream we took on board thirty-eight Greenland sledge dogs, and then all hands turned to, to stow and make secure the confusion of equipment that encumbered the decks. By the time this was done, dusk had fallen and it was not until eight o'clock that the *Aurora* cleared Storm Bay and headed south. South! South! Southward Ho! My young heart leapt within me.

Behind us the contours of the Tasmanian coast lay faintly limned against the waning afterglow. Our small party gathered on the swaying poop—for the weather outside the harbour promised badly, and the *Aurora* was lifting to a heavy swell—straining eager eyes across the leaden waters to catch a final glimpse of home shores and to read the farewell messages flashing out from Signal Hill.

Adventure—if tussle be adventure, was to come quickly.

The freshening breeze which greeted us as we drew away from the shelter of the land, gradually strengthened through the night, and by morning had increased to a full gale.   Most of us were embarked upon our first deep sea voyage and the heave and flounder of our heavily laden vessel in the rough seas evoked mixed feelings.   As we laboured south the storm continued with increasing violence, for we were now entering the "Roaring Forties."   Our little vessel staggered to the crest of mountainous seas and plunged heavily down long troughs.   Would the hoary swells that rose in threatening green surges forty feet above our decks crash on board to sweep away the stacks of building timbers and wrench from their lashings the cans containing six thousand gallons of benzine stored on the poop, and flood us with inflammable spirit?   It seemed crazy stowing and on the top of all the hamper, the sledge dogs, the very embodiment of misery, shivered and whined as driving sprays showered over them.

Each spuming crest seemed to hiss out a wrathful threat of destruction as it attacked the vessel.   As we waited, grimly expecting each moment to be engulfed,— up, up, up the oncoming surge our vessel reeled until in triumph she gained the foaming summit, and there poised as if exulting for a brief moment betwixt clouds and gulf below, before sliding down, down, down,— into the green abyss and, heeling over, it seemed she must be flung on to her beam ends and founder.

This struggle of man against the elements seemed to a landsman's eyes uneven enough by day.   But when black night fell and beetling clouds obscured every star, then, regarding the faint outlines of our ship with its dim decks reeling though the chaos of waters and listening to the fearful drone and siren shriek of the tempest in the rigging, the crash of the waves and the forlorn whimpering of the unhappy dogs, a man could well fancy that he heard Nature's cynical commentary on a hopelessly unequal strife.

And the "Roaring Forties" were to roar still more loudly. On the fourth day, the engines were slowed down and the *Aurora* hove-to. The seas came tumbling aboard almost continuously. One huge breaker flooded the waist of the vessel and tore the large motor boat from its lashings. Floating on the deck, rolling to and fro with every sway of the ship, for a while it looked as if the bulwarks must be battered out of the vessel.

Frank Wild and several of the sailors got to work, waist deep in swirling waters, and seizing an opportunity when the bows became wedged between a deckhouse and the bulwarks, passed a line around the stern of the motor boat, and at great peril to themselves, held on until others had lashed the boat down securely. This prevented the deckhouse door from opening, and two of the crew, who were inside at the time, were imprisoned until the boat could be withdrawn. Hot food for them had to be passed through a porthole.

Conditions appeared to be going from bad to worse. An enormous sea stove in the massive case containing an aerial tractor and drove the machine out at the opposite end. The pumps became choked and half the bridge was torn away by a towering breaker and swept overboard. Fortunately the officer on watch happened to be at the opposite end of the bridge at the time.

It was during these times of anxiety that we saw Captain Davis at his best. Through long days and nights he never relaxed his vigil and thanks to his masterly handling of the vessel we rode out the storms without the loss of any of our valuable deck cargo.

On the eighth day the skies cleared and the weather subsided. The wind had blown the last notes of this Overture to Adventure. Welcome indeed as was the abatement, still more gladdening was the joyous cry of "Land!" All tumbled on deck in the drear dawn to gaze south over the grey expanse of waters to where a faint ashen streak loomed through the mists. Our first objective—Macquarie Island—lay ahead.

Viewed from the sea, Macquarie Island appears dismal and desolate. The ironbound coasts rise abruptly from foaming reefs to an undulating plateau whose height varies from six hundred to a thousand feet above sea level. Set in latitude 55° south, the island is the crest of a submarine mountain that rises from the ocean's bed to a height of nearly 18,000 feet. The section of this mountain which appears above sea level is approximately twenty-one miles long and three to four miles in average width. Gales, blizzards and rainstorms rage without intermission. The island is entirely destitute of trees, but in the less tempest-thrashed sites, tussock grass and a coarse plant called Kerguelen Cabbage thrive luxuriantly.

By noon we lay off Caroline Cove, a boat was lowered and a reconnoitring party under Doctor Mawson was despatched for the shore. As it was my good fortune to be the official photographic recorder, I was always given the privilege of forming one of the pioneering party.

The flat prospect from the sea had appeared uninviting but this impression was entirely modified as we rowed inshore and saw the bold contours of the rugged coast in more imposing perspective.

Soon we were passing through a narrow entrance, scarcely one hundred yards wide, which flowed into a vast basin walled in by fantastic shapes of jagged bluffs and dome-shaped rocks. Wherever there were pockets of earth on cliff or slope, verdant clumps of tussock grass had rooted and stood out in colourful contrast against the umber and brown rock.

As we rowed in wonderment over the glassy surface of swaying reflections, we scared flocks of gulls, petrels and cormorants from their nesting places, and these, circling the great heights, roused the echoes with raucous plaints, resenting our intrusion of their sanctuary.

CHAPTER II

THE HOME OF THE PENGUINS

Along its solitary shore,
Of craggy rock and sandy bay,
No sound but ocean's roar,
Save, where the bold, wild sea-bird makes her home,
Her shrill cry coming through the sparkling foam.

DANA.

PICTURE an irregular-shaped basin of deep green waters with green rugged peaks rising to cloudy mists in the sky above, and a little strip of grey shingly beach crammed with penguins! The boat was beached and the grotesque creatures came crowding around to peer inquisitively at us.

Enchanted with the novel surroundings, quickly I busied myself with the camera. Hunter the biologist drew from his pocket a small mouth organ, and sitting down, began a lively tune. The penguins gathered round, fascinated. They displayed no fear and pecked inquiringly at the bright tags of his boots and my camera fitments. Satisfied seemingly that we were merely a superior order of penguins they nestled down and began dozing off to sleep!

But unexpected adventure awaited us.

As Hunter and I rambled about, composing pictures, we came to a dark cave and, venturing inside, were greeted with a fierce bellowing and snorting from the dark, dank, dripping interior. We fled as quickly as our legs could carry us, and pursuing our flying heels came a huge ponderous creature, tumbling, flopping, and grunting, so close as to scare us thoroughly. Evidently more scared himself, a bull sea-elephant charged wildly ahead, through a fleeing crowd of penguins, which scattered squawking helter-skelter down the sloping gravel into the water. Having regained this safer element, the amphibian whirled about, puffed up his short trunk and opening wide his huge mouth roared defiance back at us.

We laughed heartily over the unexpected encounter, for although these huge animals attain a length of twenty feet and weigh up to four tons, they are quite harmless.

Lying on masses of kelp thrown up by violent weather, we came on large numbers of them—quaint creatures, "pups," "cows" and "bulls" snoring away contentedly, heedless of our invasion.

When disturbed, they opened their big velvety eyes, peeped blinkingly at us, and then as if trying to shut out some horrible nightmare, hurriedly closed them. As if a gradual dawning of danger crept into their dull minds, they would awaken again and, with furtive peep, renew the scrutiny. At last, feeling that danger really was near, their look of enquiry changed to wild-eyed fear. Then their whole bodies began to shiver and as fast as their ungainly motions could carry them, they wheeled about and made off to sea.

The whole place was a glorious picture, made up of complex and beautiful details. Every cranny, ledge, and tussock that composed it, when closely investigated, disclosed the homing place of some feathered creature. These, not knowing man, betrayed no fear. I felt that had I sufficient plates and films, I could live here for the rest of my life! How helpless I felt to portray even a glimpse of it all in a few hours. I must have more time: I must return. But how was this to be done?

According to plan, the *Aurora* was to proceed immediately to the opposite end of the island to discharge equipment and stores for the shore party. In addition wireless masts were to be erected. This was expected to take a fortnight. What could I not do in that time if exempted from other duties! While I meditated, a juvenile subterfuge—for remember, I was still very young—suggested itself.

I took one of my indispensable lenses from its case, wrapped it in waterproof and hid it beneath a rock.

As evening drew on, the party reassembled and returned aboard. Early next morning the *Aurora* sailed for Hasselborough Bay. The work of discharging stores was at once begun.

Then with simulated dismay I discovered the "loss"

of the lens, and reported it to Doctor Mawson. I received a verbal trouncing for my apparent carelessness and was ordered to make ready at once and set out on foot to walk overland to Caroline Cove! It can be imagined with what suppressed eagerness I made preparations to obey.

The veteran biologist of the Expedition, Mr. C. T. Harrisson, was chosen by the leader to accompany me, and one of the few "sealers" who visited the island during the summer months and engaged in the sea-elephant and penguin oil trade, Hutchinson by name, volunteered to go with us and scout out the way.

Heavily burdened, we left the Sealers' Hut, Harrisson with a huge collecting box strapped to his shoulders, while I carried a heavy camera, and Hutchinson the supplies in a waterproof case. In addition we were each hampered with oilskins, cumbersome seaboots and a waterproof "swag" containing a blanket.

We made our way along a narrow shingly beach, the Southern ocean noisily churning the pebbles, at the base of steeply rising cliffs verdured with waving tussock grasses. Out to sea the sun was shining brightly but as the cold mist-laden winds reached the highlands they precipitated a drizzling rain.

The atmosphere reeked with decaying sea-elephant carcasses, which were strewn about the beach in large numbers. The sealers in pursuit of oil had stripped off the blubber and left the rest to decay. Large numbers of carrion birds gorged the offal and reluctantly took to wing as we passed by. As if to add its toll to this grim scene, the ocean had cast up broken spars and splintered remnants of a wreck.

An hour's walk brought us to the "Nuggets" beach where the sealers had a penguin oil refinery. When this outfit was in operation, between 150,000 and 200,000 birds were killed and passed through the digestors annually. Happily this wicked slaughter is now closed and the island has been proclaimed a sanctuary by the Commonwealth Government.

I was averse to going further that day as the sun had broken through the mists, and was shining brightly upon such a scene as I might never again have the opportunity of photographing. Penguins had congregated in thousands on the grey beach, reminding us of a scene at a popular seaside resort. Many were enjoying themselves in the surf, while crowds looked on; but the majority preferred to assemble in little coteries as if to gossip over the latest scandal of their community.

Flung high and dry on the sands in the midst of this strange setting of penguin festivity, lay the remnant of a sealing vessel—the *Gratitude*.

The penguin colony proper lies in a sheltered valley behind the sea cliffs that face the beach. The only thoroughfare to it is by way of a shallow creek, and along it, an endless stream of birds splashed their way from dawn till dark. An orderly traffic was maintained, the birds going to the sea kept to one bank, and those returning home, glutted with small shrimps for their hungry chicks, kept to the other. The rule of the road was seldom broken, for a traffic jam would quickly happen and end in indiscriminate confusion and fighting. The rookery may be likened to a city,—the heart of it lying in the valley bed and the suburbs scattered over the slopes, but linked by shallow watercourses and tracks. The area of the "Nuggets" rookery is approximately ten acres. Some idea may be gathered of its intensive settlement from the numbers of its population which is in the neighbourhood of five hundred thousand. During the breeding season, when each pair fosters a chick or two, the number crammed into this confined area must aggregate three quarters of a million.

We camped for the night in a deserted hut, belonging to the sealers, built among the tussock grass down by the sea. It was a rough shack—a rectangular structure of iron with a few small windows looking over the sea. The inside—gloomy, oily, and smelly—comprised two rooms, one where the hands slept in wooden bunks and a larger one with a long table and stove where they fed. A fire soon made it cosy and cheerful and Hutchinson sang a chanty as he fried penguin steaks and penguin eggs which he took from a large barrel of pickle in a corner. We ate by the light of a candle glow. The dancing flames from the stove made strange shadow-shapes, and lit up the smoke-grimed walls and memorial tablets, which those who had been here before had carved from wreckage. As we loitered over the meal Hutchinson spun yarns about the place, tales of wrecks and sea tragedies. Outside the sea was noisy; a gale was blowing up, and sleet and hail fell tinkling on the iron roof.

We drew closer to the fire, Harrisson piled on drift wood which burnt with weird green flames, and these lit up the bearded features of the story-teller with an uncanny flickering. In this eerie setting the stories told became vivid pictures and presented to my impressionable young fancy, visions of cruel scenes, of stricken ships and men struggling with the sea.

Hutchinson had a close knowledge of the history of the island.

"It was a sad day for this place," said he, "when Captain Hasselborough brought his brig to anchor in the same bay as where the *Aurora* is now. That was right back in 1809 in the days when Macquarie was Governor of New South Wales. That's how the island came by its name; Hasselborough called it after him. Seals! When he landed here the whole place was alive with them!

"The noise he made about it when he got back to Sydney set a whole fleet of sealers racing out, each bent on getting rich quicker than the other fellow. They slaughtered every flipper that showed itself, not even sparing new-born 'pups.' It was a wicked business. One vessel, by the way, the same name as yours, the *Aurora*, carried back 35,000 pelts in one season.

"In five years they clean wiped out every seal.   Then laws were made to stop them from killing any more!"

"Were any of the sealers wrecked or drowned," I queried?

"Wrecked!   Why the reefs are ships' graveyards and the rocks tombstones!" he replied.   "Even when Hasselborough came here over a hundred years ago he found bits of ships, but no men."

The wind shrieked with the voices of ghosts round the house and lashed it with rain.

"A wild night outside," said Harrisson, feeding more wreckage to the flames.

"Oh! it's the usual thing here.   It's a hell of a place for weather," replied Hutchinson.   "Why, even that wood you're stoking up the fire with, came from the *Jessie Nichol*.   She was cast up on the rocks scarce a mile along the beach, on such a stormy black night as this.   Three were drowned, and mighty lucky were the others to get away.   The kelp—that long snaky seaweed—grows very thick along the rocks near where the *Jessie* was wrecked.   God help the man who gets tangled up in it.

"The *Gratitude* or what's left of her, which lies outside on the beach, belonged to the Company who runs this penguin oil business.   They've lost three ships.   The *Clyde* was the last one to come to grief—only a couple of months ago.   She was to have taken us back home, that's why we are all marooned here now.   That reminds me, I must tell you about the *Eagle*, it's the saddest story of the lot; went to pieces during a gale on the West Coast. Nine men and a woman saved themselves after a hell of a struggle. They lost everything and the ten of them all lived together in a cave for two years. What a hell of a life for a woman! bad enough for men to live on sea-elephants and penguins all the time, but for a woman . . .

"The cave is littered with bones and, inside you can see all round the mouldy grass that they slept on for beds. There's a cross too, to the woman, poor soul. She died the very day relief came."

I listened as the thrash of the rain storm beat a wild din on the hut.

"Sealing is not all the big adventure it's cracked up to be," said Hutchinson—"darned rotten grub, cranky little cockleshells of boats, seas swarming with icebergs and reefs and cold Davy Jones always waiting to tuck you up in his locker below. Some of the old sailors used to say this was the port of the 'Flying Dutchman,' and that he lures ships to destruction on these reefs. Anyhow, there's enough wrecks to make one mighty superstitious about it. The *Lord Nelson*, *Beucleugh*, *Caroline*, *Countess Cimento*, and I guess a whole lot of others never heard of, are all scattered about the reefs. It's an evil place."

So we talked in the fire glow, while the wind, the sea and the rain made desolate noises. Finally we went to bed, but sleep for me was impossible. The strange environment, the storm outside, Hutchinson's haunting

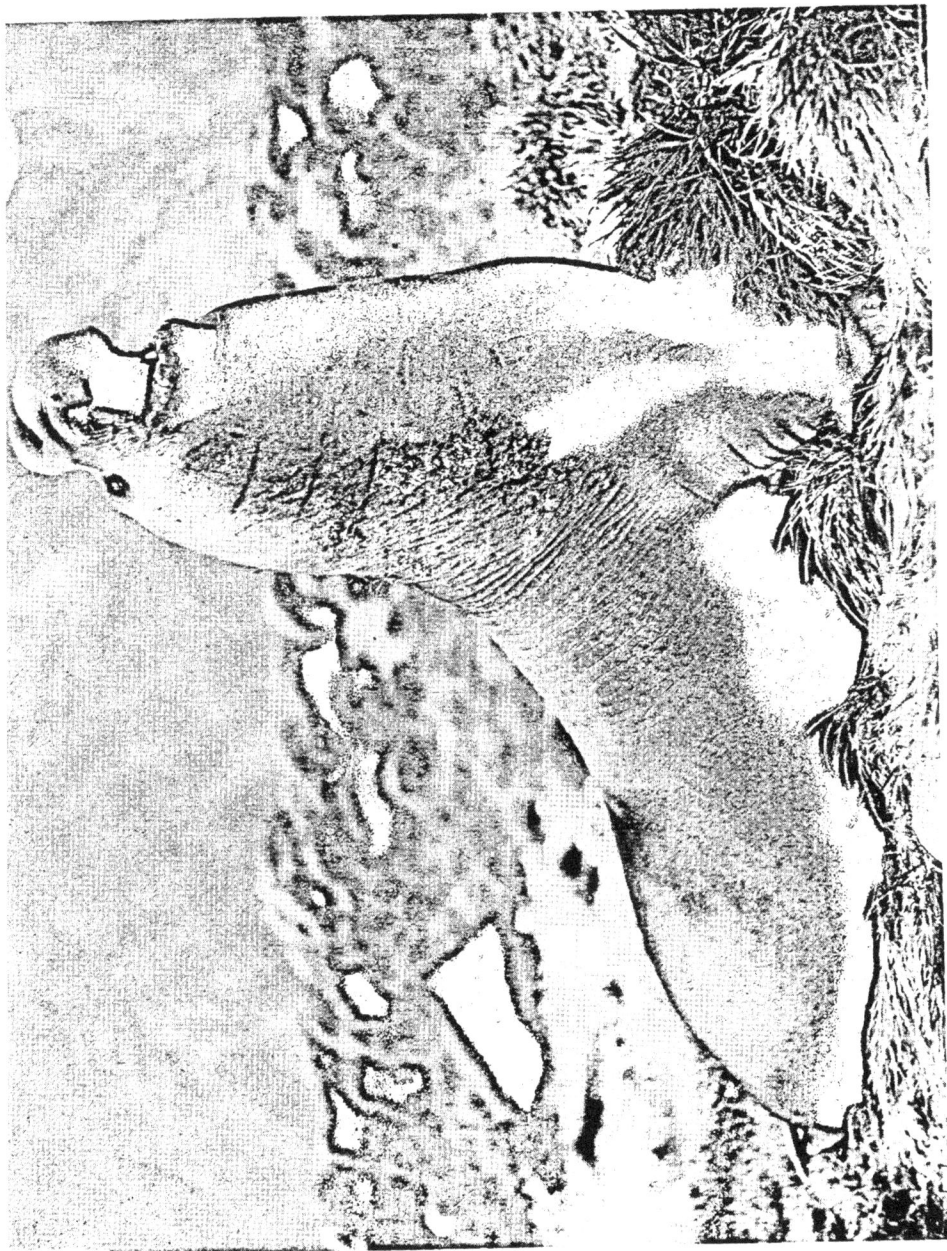

An Enraged Bull Sea-Elephant in Fighting Attitude.

stories, the hard boards, kept me restless. But this was not all. When our voices were stilled and the fire died, swarms of rats sneaked out. They scampered over our blankets and held such revelry that Harrisson climbed from his bunk and rekindled the fire.

We relieved each other at the end of three hours' watch and managed to get some rest in the intervals. Hutchinson told us the rats had come ashore from the wrecks and now infested the whole island.

At the first loom of dawn we bestirred ourselves and after breakfasting set out in the drizzling rain along the beach, which was already astir with penguins, on our way to "Three Brothers" Point. We passed by the scattered remnants of the *Jessie Nichol* and, in the evergreen tussock grass nearby, three graves marked by lifebuoys.

Before reaching the "Three Brothers" the coast became so impassable that we were compelled to climb the cliffs and take to the highlands. The going was treacherous with peaty swamps and we had to step from clump to clump of tussock grass to avoid sinking in. The plateau was barren of all vegetation and littered with lakes and tarns. These were apparently very deep and diverse in shape and size, the largest being about two miles long.

These lakes, of glacial origin, were overflowing with crystal waters that rippled to the cliff edge. There the waters fell precipitously to the sea, tumbling down ravines in noisy cascades.

It was a bleak inhospitable spot, made the more desolate by heavy mists which prevented us from seeing more than fifty yards ahead and baffled us greatly, for we frequently found ourselves on the shores of a lake, not knowing which way it extended nor which was our best way to get around it. Probing the mist through this watery maze cost us a great deal of time, and the day being all too soon spent, we feared the darkness of night would add to our dilemma, so Hutchinson suggested that we had better go down to the coast to try to locate a refuge. This was easier said than done, for occasionally we came to the brink of sheer precipices with no other prospect than a dense gloomy mist and the sound of the surf on the rocks far below.

Precariously we groped a way down and reached a wide coastal flat closely overgrown with tussock grasses. These were our salvation for the whole place was a foul bog only to be crossed by stepping on the clumps. In the darkness we moved with the utmost caution for if we lost our balance on the yielding grasses we would drown in the mire.

We reached the wave-beaten shingle thankful for solid land beneath our feet. The night and mist shut down like a wall; it was useless to venture further. We were weary, hungry and wet to the skin and to increase our misery, steady drizzling rain fell. There was not even a rock to shelter us from the biting sea breeze and envying the sea-elephants who were snoring comfortably on the beds of kelp, we decided to follow their

example.   Selecting the choicest location, well above
tidal reach, we drove the sea-elephants from their lairs
by pelting them with pebbles.   They made a great
snorting hubbub and at first attacked one another,
each thinking that the assault came from his neighbour.
When, however, we added our shouts to their confusion,
they fled to the sea in alarm and left us in undisputed
possession.   We found their beds very wet and slimy,
yet preferable to the cold knobby pebbles of the beach.

First of all we laid a sodden blanket on the kelp,
huddled ourselves together on it, and then stretched
the other blankets and oilskins over us.   But we did
not sleep.   The cold crept in and made our bones ache
with cramp.   Furthermore, we had to be on the constant alert to drive off the sea-elephants, which were
about in large numbers.   Not that they would have
attacked us, but we were in constant peril of their ponderous bulks charging down and rolling over us in the
darkness, for all night long they were in continual un-
rest, fighting and flopping about from place to place.

It can be imagined with what relief we welcomed daybreak.   We were very stiff and limped painfully along
the shingle.

We had covered barely half a mile when we were
attracted by the din of a penguin rookery.   As we
rounded a headland, to our bewildered gaze, there lay
before us a wide expanse densely packed with myriads
of birds.   On the opposite side, scarcely four hundred
yards away, stood a small hut!   We made our way

through the penguins, who pecked viciously at our legs, and reached the haven. The sealers had long since abandoned the site owing to the exposed nature of the coast and the danger in landing stores and taking off the oil. The place was dilapidated and weatherbeaten but, to us, it was a palace.

During our ramble we had observed four different varieties of penguins, Kings, Victorias, Gentoos, and Royals. The Victorias and Gentoos have numerous small rookeries scattered along the coasts, but the Royals are the most prolific and constitute the vast colonies. The rookery, at whose edge stood the hut, was about sixteen acres in area and contained as near as we could estimate a million Royal penguins!

The scene was one never to be forgotten, a writhing congestion of birds that maintained a raucous din. The drizzling rain which falls almost incessantly converts the rookeries into vast slushy areas of filth.

The nests are little more than mud puddles, but this does not affect incubation, for in due course from the eggs are brought forth healthy young chicks to add to the bedlam. What mystified me was that sense or instinct which directed the parent birds when returning from sea with food for their young and enabled them to find their families in the heart of the mêlée. Frequently the parents had to force their way through several hundred yards of indignant neighbours and run the gauntlet of malicious pecks before reaching home. But they did this unerringly, never hesitating as to direction until, quite exhausted, they reached their off-spring. Even then there was no respite, for the voracious young at once assailed the parent, clamouring for food, and there was no peace until they got it. The young are old enough to care for themselves by the fall of the season, and, in April, when the chill winds of winter romp up from the south, the colonies leave the rookeries and go off to sea. In three days' time not a single bird may be observed. Whence they migrate is a matter of conjecture but it is believed they lead an aquatic life until September, when they return to the old haunts even as if working to an exact day in their calendar.

We rested until the forenoon and, as Caroline Cove lay but a short walk over the hills, we shackled on our loads and climbed up the steep cliff to the plateau. From the summit we gained a wonderful bird's-eye view of the South End rookery which we had just left. It extended over a wide flat, bounded by the cliffs and the sea.

Near the descent to Caroline Cove we came to a rookery of giant petrels. These ugly carrion birds were reluctant to leave their nests, and vomited an evil-smelling secretion at us when we ventured near. When frightened they ran clumsily along the ground, with outstretched wings trying to gain flying buoyancy, but most of them were so heavy with overfeeding that they had to disgorge part of their food before they could rise into the air.

I found my lens, and though my inclinations were strong to tarry at Caroline Cove, Hutchinson warned me not to delay as banks of mists were rolling shorewards from the south. Our nearest shelter en route was at Lusitania Bay on the opposite side of the coast.

Though we made all possible haste, darkness overtook us by the time we reached the cliffs behind Lusitania Bay but we were guided by the shrill croaking and whistling of the King penguins which have a rookery close to the refuge hut.

In the dark we groped our way down the cliff, exercising great caution as the stones came away at the least touch and the foothold was rotten and slippery. We reached the bottom where my right foot jammed between two boulders and falling I wrenched my ankle badly. The pain was so intense that I could scarcely move, but with Harrisson's assistance I made my way slowly across the boggy flat to the shack. In the meantime Hutchinson had hastened ahead and got a cheery blaze going. When we entered he was cooking luscious slices of sea-elephant's tongue, which smelt so good that for the moment the anticipation of a hearty meal dulled our physical aches. The hut was falling to pieces, for the oil company had long since vacated the site, the depletion of the numbers of penguins rendering it no longer profitable.

Through the night my foot caused me great pain and by morning had swollen so that I could not put on my boot. Harrisson improvised a makeshift by binding the foot up in canvas, and this enabled me to limp along.

Before turning homewards we examined the rookery, which comprised all the remaining King penguins alive on the island, about 4,000. The rookery differed from the others as the birds did not make nests but each supported a single egg on its feet and incubated it in a kind of pouch. Our approach scared them and they shuffled clumsily away but we never dreamed that the stiff movement was caused by egg-carrying until Hutchinson caught one of the birds and drew an egg from its pouch.

The birds are about three feet in height and weigh upwards of thirty pounds. They are by far the most beautiful of the penguin family, the plumage being very handsomely coloured. On either side of the neck begins a band like burnished gold which gradually merges into a metallic greenish yellow lustre on the upper breast and fades to a creamy sheen at the lower part of the body. The back is an exquisite shade of grey-blue. The young are covered with a heavy brown furry plumage which does not moult until the second year. The parents, in consequence, have to feed their young for two years and unlike the other penguins they do not migrate from the island. The birds are grotesquely human and strut about with stately dignity, bowing politely and talking to one another upon meeting.

The return journey of seventeen miles over boulders,

through bogs and up and down cliffs was greatly retarded through my disabled foot and the added en-
cumbrance of Harrisson's scientific collections. I
counted every step of that rough distance and felt that
I was surely doing heavy penance for the subterfuge
which had been the origin of my tribulations. At last
the anchored *Aurora* came into sight—never was a
destination more thankfully reached. But we had been
exploring and had shaken hands with adventure in
an unknown land.

CHAPTER III

And now there came both mist and snow,
And it grew wondrous cold:
And ice, mast high, came floating by,
As green as emerald.

COLERIDGE.

NOW it was up and away for the icy South. By Christmas Eve the work of discharging stores and equipment for the Macquarie Island station was completed and we bade farewell to our comrades Sandell, Blake, Hamilton, Sawyer, and Mr. Ainsworth who was in charge of the party.

Doctor Mawson had promised a day's holiday to those proceeding to the Antarctic and sailed the *Aurora* round to Caroline Cove so that we might spend Christmas Day ashore.

The *Aurora* was navigated through the treacherous entrance into the tiny cove, and, to prevent her swinging at her moorings and bumping the shore, a stream anchor was run out abeam and made fast to the stern.

We turned in, with the night peaceful, the waters calm, and in high anticipation of a memorable day on the morrow. It was.

39

We were awakened by a horrible pounding and grinding. We rushed up on deck into a grey drizzling dawn, with black cliffs looming all round and a foaming sea driving into the Cove. During the night a north-westerly storm had broken without warning and the incoming swells and wind had caused the vessel to drag the main anchor and drift on to the rocks. The engines could not be started for fear of stripping the propeller blades. Fortunately the stream anchor held. The cable from it was taken to the forward capstan and we warped the vessel, inch by inch, from danger. Once clear of the reef the engines were opened up and we headed for the open sea. There were to be no final junketings on land.

Christmas Day marked the beginning of a turbulent week of gales and rough weather, but we had grown heedless, and the excitement of sailing uncharted seas gave a zest that overshadowed all discomforts. Day after day we strained our eyes over the swells and furrows, eager and impatient to gain the first glimpse of the ice. Adventurers from a land of sunshine, ice and snow were to us quite unfamiliar phenomena.

The first glimpse came one day when the breeze was blowing chill and bleak from the south, driving up great banks of mist that hung in forbidding veils—screening the realms of the known from the regions of the unexplored.

Suddenly it grew calm. No breath of wind stirred; the sails hung limp and an ominous hush fell over the

sea. Gazing at the grey curtains of fog from the deck of our ship, so tiny in the surrounding vastness, we felt like Argonauts whose quest had led to the World's brim. Slowly we crept on, filled with wonder and expectancy. The growl of surf, like breakers grumbling on a reef, came to our ears. All hands mustered on the fo'c'stle head and peered in the direction of the sound. Through a rift we made out the glimmering sheen of a colossal berg. The sea was blustering in its caverns and dashing high up its walls.

We hailed the first Antarctic outpost with cheers that re-echoed as if in sardonic welcome from the ghostly cliffs.

Then a pleasant alluring sound as of wave-rustled shells came through the mist. It grew louder and closer. Soon the *Aurora* was cleaving a crystal sea of small ice, clinkily hustling the floating fragments as she steamed slowly on her way.

As we proceeded the ice grew bigger and the vessel shivered under the shocks of collision with heavier pieces. Thrilling navigation to us, this new experience of ramming a ship through a sea of "floating rocks." "Hard a-starboard! Steady!" Then "Hard a-port!" The two men at the wheel were kept busy. The steering chains rattled in their channels—the engine room telegraph clanged noisily in the still cold air while the ice scrunched along the vessel's sides.

Out from the mist came strange groanings, squeakings and gurglings as the pack heaved and rubbed in the swell.   The ice grew too heavy and as we could not see ahead, Captain Davis brought the *Aurora* out in search of a more favourable opening.

When the mists cleared away unexpectedly, a scene that held us breathless was unfolded.

Fleets of crystal gondolas drifted on blue canals that wound through what seemed to be the ruins of marble cities. A mammoth berg, two miles long, rose up ahead, dominating the wonders of this glacial world. Unfamiliar birds flew past, snow petrels, spotless as the snows, fulmars and tiny Wilson petrels that flitted above the waters like swallows. Occasionally the silence was interrupted by the loud blasts of whales blowing in the leads and jets of vapour shot up as from fumaroles.   Large numbers of Weddell seals and sea leopards basked on the floe in the warm sunshine, and little groups of Adelie penguins squawked, peered and wondered at the strange sight of a ship.   The dogs took active interest in the passage of the vessel through the ice.   The sight of seals excited them to frantic yelping and they strained at their chains in vain efforts to leap to the attack.

Perched aloft, or dangling from the bowsprit, I found unlimited subjects for my camera—in fact everyone did; shutters clicked on each strange formation, and these were endless. Mertz, aloft in the crow's nest, was in high ecstasy, and entertained us and the denizens of the pack by warbling loud yodels.

For a week we manœuvred through fields of pack-ice

as variable as the weather. At times we ran through open water in sunshine, but more often the surface of the sea was congested and obscured with ice and the sky heavy with clouds. In the grey light the pack lost all its charm and beauty, and became featureless, sullen and sinister. It was then that we sensed the ever-lurking danger and realised how easily the ship might be gripped and held captive, or crushed to death between the massive floes and bergs.

At times we took shelter behind some friendly berg, while the icefields, driven before the press of the blizzards, crushed irresistibly past. During these overcast days, the sky was a wondrous chart. The blink from the icefields was reflected stark and white, while pools of open water smirched the clouds with patches of smoky hue. This curious phenomenon was of great assistance, for by the signs in the skies we were able to read the face of the sea and navigate accordingly.

On the fifth day after entering the ice a bright gleam in the sky to the south signalled our approach to the Continent. Every eye, telescope and glass was trained on the horizon and as we sailed closer, a white line gradually rose above the pack. It grew higher; then ice slopes assumed contours and finally we sighted vertical cliffs rising from the sea. We had reached the coasts of Antarctica at last!

The *Aurora* was headed into a wide lane of ice-free "land-water" and we skirted dazzling ice-walls on which the sun was glaring. We scanned every yard of the mighty barrier in the hope of finding a possible landing place but not so much as a foothold offered for over one hundred miles.

It was a wondrous wall. The golden radiance of the midnight sun, glinting on its face of light green, transformed the icy coast into cliffs of fiery opal. The most matter-of-fact mind thrilled before this spectacle of beauty and mystery.

We entered a wide bay. Wild was the first to pick out rocks on its shores. A few tiny black specks could just be distinguished in the ice at the head of the inlet, whence a gradual slope ascended to the inland plateau.

The bay was roughly twenty miles wide at the entrance and Doctor Mawson named it "Commonwealth Bay"—a fitting appellation for the scene of the activities of an Australian Expedition. The *Aurora* was headed in and as the distance diminished to our great delight we observed that the ice sloped down to the water's edge and appeared to offer a possible landing place. The whaleboat was lowered and manned by Doctor Mawson, Wild, Bickerton, Bage, Kennedy, Madigan, and myself.

Even the beauty of recent scenes waned before the glamour of this landing. The sun shone brilliantly as the boat moved over a watery mirror reflecting the cloudless sky, among tiny ice-capped islets resembling giant mushrooms and wedding cakes. We had come to a fairyland of ethereal blue and silver. Nor were fitting denizens for this enchanting scene lacking. Quaint

Coasting Along the Barrier Cliffs of Adelie Land.

and highly interested penguins played, dived, and plopped about the boat in fearless welcome as we rowed over the unruffled waters.

Such was our first acquaintance with the Mackellar Islets, so named by us after a staunch friend of the Expedition. We entered a beautiful miniature boat harbour skirted with marble-white ice and drew up alongside a crystal landing place. Doctor Mawson leapt ashore—the first man to put foot on Adelie Land. We all wanted the honour of being second and jumped excitedly ashore in a bunch—I slipped and fell—gaining the honour of being the first man to "sit" on Adelie Land. Actuated by curiosity the penguins waddled after us in a most amusing and quaint human-like way.

High exaltation swelled our hearts as we inspected the site and for the first time the virgin solitudes rang to the cheers and voices of man. The inspection disclosed several ridges of rock facing the seafront from which the ice sloped up in a gentle gradient—ideal for sledging parties setting out for the interior, and in many other ways the site appeared a desirable one. Doctor Mawson decided to establish his Winter Quarters upon it. Owing to shoals the *Aurora* could not be brought into the boat harbour, so Captain Davis sailed her to a safe anchorage beneath the ice cliffs about a mile distant. The discharging of the cargo at once began. Two whaleboats were used for lightering, the motor boat towing them between the *Aurora* and the boat harbour. Though hampered by occasional brief but severe gales, the vast quantity of stores, coal briquettes, hut timbers, equipment, twenty-nine dogs and eighteen men were landed in ten days without mishap—save for the temporary loss of a single case. Doctor Mawson eventually rescued this case from the water by diving in after it. Several of the party emulated his example, but we soon voted diving and swimming too chilly an amusement.

Time was moving on. The programme called for the establishment of a Second Base somewhere about a thousand miles along the coast under the command of Frank Wild. The *Aurora* was to transport this second party to the scene of its operations and then return to Australia. Next year she would come back to pick us all up again. A year! How much might happen in a year, not only to us but to those at home. The day of parting came. It was with strange feelings that we watched the *Aurora* steam out of the Bay and become lost to our sight. Our link with home and civilisation was broken. We were isolated in icy solitudes.

We soon forgot our loneliness in work. We built a temporary shelter from cases of foodstuffs and briquettes, in which to live until the hut was erected.

Doctor Mawson selected a site on a rocky flat, and building operations went on under the supervising eye and able hand of Hodgeman, the cartographer and architect. The Leader's Antarctic experience induced him to take no risks of our home being swept away by blizzards. He had personally designed the hut and had seen it erected before leaving Australia. The timbers had all been numbered and marked and we had only to reassemble them. Doctor Mawson left nothing to chance. His motto was: "Be prepared for every contingency in Antarctica. If the worst does not come so much the better; if it does, then you are prepared."

The foundations were blasted from the solid rock and filled in with many tons of boulders. We, who were inexperienced, thought the precautions excessive. The weather was brilliant; to us it did not appear possible that a region of such peaceful calm could ever be assailed with raging hurricanes. I shall ever remember those first few weeks in Adelie Land. The novelty of everything—the glorious sunshine, the high spirits of all, made our sojourn like an old time college camp. We worked hard, ate heartily, and slept better.

Most of the party had "seen" carpenters' tools before; but they were enthusiastic beginners, and bruised fingers, cuts and splinters were regarded cheerfully as part of the job. In spite of lack of experience our home went ahead magically. Many amusing incidents happened.

Doctor Mertz was sitting astride the outer ridge cap, nailing it down, and the learned bacteriologist, Doctor McLean, was "tacking" on the thin ceiling lining with four-inch nails directly beneath.

Suddenly Mertz sprang into the air with a wild yell, lost his balance,—slid down the sloping splintery roof, clutched a stay that held the kitchen stove pipe and took the chimney with him in a headlong dive into a snow dump.

Everyone rushed to the rescue—to be in the fun—with cries of "championship"—a term adopted to crown maladroit achievements. Investigation displayed two inches of bristling nail which had been driven through the ridge cap by the scientist below, and had caused the puncture which the aggrieved Mertz was rubbing. The collapse of the chimney had overturned the kitchen range and the saucepans and contents lay mingled over the floor. Forthwith a large leather medal was cut and presented to the chief actors to commemorate the occasion. Good humour characterised those days in which each man grew to know his fellows.

The hut was nearing completion when the short-lived Antarctic Summer broke and the first blizzard tested the quality of our work. The wind was comparatively mild—60 miles an hour—but it warned us that our smiling environment had a sinister temperament as well.

We fortified the windward side of our home with stone barricades and heavy cases, and made ready for what evils the future might send. The calm spells between the blizzards grew shorter and the blows longer and stronger, until during the second month there was no respite from ceaseless hurricanes and rivers of snow that swept madly and relentlessly from the Pole. As time wore on, it became evident that the calm week of

"We Scanned Every Yard of the Mighty Barrier in the Hope of Finding a Possible Landing Place but not so Much as a Foothold Offered for Over One Hundred Miles."

A Gigantic "Mushroom" of the Mackellar Archipelago, Formed by Blizzards Pelting Frozen Sea Spray on to an Exposed Reef. The Mushroom Grows Until the Summer when it Splits up and Disintegrates.

our landing had been an abnormal condition. It seemed as though the wild had adopted the ruse as an inducement to lure us into its solitudes and, once the vessel had departed and left us marooned, to scourge us for our temerity in trespassing into its domain. As records afterwards proved we had landed on the most tempestuous spot on the face of the globe. Within the hut we ensconced ourselves as snugly as possible and made preparations against siege by the Polar Winter.

"Winter Quarters," as we called the hut, was built entirely of timber and comprised two large rooms encircled by a closed-in verandah. Bunks were arranged round the walls of the larger room, and there eighteen men ate, slept, and made the best of life. Just inside the door on the right was the kitchen—open entirely to the public gaze—with its large ever-burning range which maintained the temperature equably at freezing point!

Just behind the range was my sanctum—the darkroom. By the light of the ruby lamp not only was the latent photographic image rocked into reality but latent wit was cradled into song. It served as a lair, in whose concealment surprises might be prepared. From its shuttered precincts the chef would emerge ceremoniously holding aloft some culinary triumph, or the grotesquely garbed actors of "The Its Society for the Prevention of the Blues," would step forth dramatically into the acetylene glare to perform their latest farce amidst uproarious applause. The Annex or second room was in reality a complete hut, but in place of sleeping accommodation it contained workbenches and the wireless equipment. Passing through double doors one emerged on the verandah—a dark tunnel in which were piled rows of tinned foods and stacks of provisions. Half this enclosure was partitioned off from the stores and given up to the dogs. As the season advanced the hut became embedded in a huge snow ramp with only the roof projecting and egress was through a trap-door in the roof of the outer verandah. Both huts were illuminated with acetylene gas and the generator was installed on a platform in the living room to prevent it from freezing.

When we were settled in our Antarctic home each man was handed his clothing allowance and sledging equipment. The clothing was simple, light, efficient and evolved from the experiences of previous South Polar Expeditions. A singlet of pure wool and a suit of heavyweight woollen combinations comprised the underwear. Over these we wore a garment made of camel hair fleece and a woollen guernsey. Each donned a woollen helmet and two pairs of socks. Leather boots could not be used during the winter as they froze stiff, so we discarded them for light comfortable boot-lets—"finnescoe"—made from reindeer fur. A pair of felt or dogskin mitts completed the fine weather dress. During blizzards we wore "Burberry" overalls—a helmet, blouse and trousers made of windproof gabardine. Actually our Polar dress was very little heavier than that which would be worn at home during a severe winter. The body itself builds up a natural resistance to cold and clothes are merely insulation to retard radiation. In the rigours of Polar climate no amount of garments piled on will bring warmth if the constitution is feeble.

As time wore on and the rage of the inclement wild kept us close prisoners for weeks on end, it might be thought that eighteen men cooped up in the darkness of a dingy hut would become subject to depression and irritability, but with us it was not so. All were possessed of geniality and the spirit of toleration—greater attributes to men in our situation than either muscle or genius.

This was a typical day's routine—an extract from my diary.

No one stirs in the darkness of the Hut except the night-watchman who is nearing the end of his vigil. At 7 A.M. he calls the cook for the day. At 7.30 A.M. the night-watchman winds up the gramophone and selects a record according to his mood. A towel is thrust into the horn to subdue the tune to pianissimo. Gentle strains fall on the ears of the sleeper—maybe to produce happy reveries. The sleepers stir and turn in their bunks. It is pleasant to play the day in with harmony—it invariably closes with song. As the hour of awakening draws near, the towel is withdrawn and a lively tune blares gladly, mingling with the wind as it bellows over the hut.

The table is set noisily with much clashing of enamelled plates, bowls, knives, spoons and forks. At 7.50 A.M. the cook and night-watchman combine their voices in a raucous

"Rise and Shine! Rise and Shine!" and make noise vigorously with kitchen utensils. One after another, unkempt bearded men turn out drowsily, dress and take their respective places around the table. Water is scarce so the luxury of the toilette is postponed until the cook who attends to the ice-melter is unwatchful or favourably inclined. At 8 A.M. the cook calls "Breakfast on the table." The meal proceeds silently except for the night-watchman who prates jovially about the night's experiences—of the wind reaching ninety miles an hour, of wonderful auroral displays, dogfights, of the garments he washed and so on. After porridge the night's drowsiness has worn off and by the time the preserved-fruits course is eaten a much more cheerful atmosphere has developed. The night-watchman, tired, has dozed off to sleep. We gleefully revenge ourselves for his disturbance of our slumbers. There is a hush—a signal is given—a whispered "one, two, three!"—and seventeen voices cry jubilantly, "Rise and Shine!" The sleeper awakens with a start.

The table is cleared and all set about various routine duties in the hut or don Burberrys for the sterner tasks that compel them to go outside.

Madigan, the meteorologist, and his assistant Hodgeman—looking like goblins of the storm—are ready to make their morning round of the recording instruments. It is a stiff job. Out through the double-doors into the verandah, there they pause to make sure all is secure, before making their next move.

At once the fiendish clutch of the blizzard grips them and they are wrenched away staggering before its bluster, with garments madly flapping. The two men cannot see more than a yard through the rushing blast of snow and they grope to the lee of the hut. The torrent of drift is so dense that the daylight filters through in a feeble grey flicker. Now there is 400 yards of unsheltered ice to cross. They fight onward, bent double, driving their spiked crampons

The Winter Quarters, Adelie Land. The Hut Lies at the Foot of the Wireless Mast near the Centre. In the Background the Slopes Rise to the Plateau. This was the Way by which Sledging Parties Made their Way to the Interior.

into the ice.   A slip and they may be swept into the boat-harbour.

Both turn sideways and shoulder ahead into the wind. It is like struggling in the grip of a violent undertow.   The hard snow particles and ice crystals pelt like a sandblast and cover their faces with masks of ice.   Blindly butting on, they reach the rocks at the base of the rise on which the instruments stand.   Here the fury of the wind is frightful. The meteorologists are sucked into its eddies and they grip the rocks and crouch low for breath.   They break the ice-masks from their faces but the ice adheres in lumps to eye-brows and beards and rapidly forms again.   Foot by foot, holding on to the rocks as they go, they climb upward and grope about for the screens.   The position is exposed and a slip would mean being hurled to the ice one hundred feet below.   They find the instruments.   The temperature is sixty degrees below freezing point and changing the records is a painful occupation for frostbitten fingers.   In calm the work would be done in five minutes but it takes them under these conditions an hour.   The records are changed and blank papers substituted.   Then they begin the return. "Home" is reached at last.   The icemasks thaw from their faces which throb and tingle with the warmth of the hut and reviving circulation.   The snow-laden Burberrys are left in the outer hut and they re-enter the living room. Their comrades look up and welcome them.

"Hello Maddie!"   "Hello Hodge!"   "What's it like outside?"—all gather round to ascertain the result of the twenty-four hours' blow.   In the peace of the hut, the tussle with the wild is forgotten—it is all part of the day's work.

Within the hut the cook is the man of the hour.   If a member of the proven circle known as "The Unconventional Cooks" he is bound to be popular.   He is a chef with imagination who scorns reference to the pages of "Mrs. Beeton."   He must have qualified for initiation by produc-ing six approved original dishes and as many topical songs.

"An Unconventional" must not only be a master of his art but a minstrel as well. A tough penguin steak, or a leathery seal's liver will often dodge criticism if diners are cajoled with the sauce of good humour.

Chefs in a second category belong to "The Crook Cooks Association," with which is affiliated "The Society of Muddling Messmen." These scorn the culinary art as base routine. They leave the selection of the day's menu to the storeman who brings in an assortment of snow-covered tins—the nearest that have come to his hand. The scientist, uninspired by gastronomy, itching to get busy with his work, vacillates betwixt his microscope and the stove and leaves the thawing out of the tinned foods to the messmen who thrusts them into the oven—and then forgets. Within half an hour there is a terrific bang followed by a hissing fizzle and steam and smells fume the air. There are tumultuous cries in the hut of "Championship!" "Something Burning!" "Crook Cooks!" and so forth, and a rush is made for the oven and tins fatly expanded with steam pressure are hastily withdrawn.

The grandmaster of "the Crook Cooks Association" won his badge of office with a Salmon Kedgeree. The Cookery book says:—one tin Salmon, one pound boiled rice, 3 ounces bread crumbs, cayenne pepper, salt. On serving there were vociferous yells of "Championship." The indignant cook swore that he had followed the recipe minutely and exactly. A scientific analysis was therefore made and it was found that three ounces *each* of cayenne pepper and salt as well as the bread crumbs had been added to the ingredients! Then there was a "roly-poly" that resembled synthetic rubber and turned the knife edge; and "bread" that even the dogs barked at. The "Crook Cook" buried it in shame beneath the snows but someone dug it up and the geologist classified it as a boulder of fossilised bread from the Stone Age. The trophy was placed on the top of a high mound in the hope that haunting the perpetrator, it might extort a confession, but we never found out who "cast" it, though we had strong suspicions.

Not a scrap of food, not even the "Championship" efforts of the "Crook Cooks," is wasted. The dog-bucket, kept beneath the kitchen table, receives all rejected morsels. Mertz and Ninnis feed the dogs twice daily and augment kitchen leavings with Seal meat.

In addition to training the dogs the "dog-men" fill in their time preparing dog rations for the trail. Seal meat and blubber are cut into hunks and desiccated by frizzling on the work-room stove. The resulting odours are strongly resented by all, except the "Crook Cooks." They rejoice, for the unsavoury effluvium submerges effectively their own malodorous frizzlings.

In the thick haze of the work-room Hunter the biologist is busy pickling his trophies and collections. Correll, the mechanic, is fully occupied repairing the recording instruments, for the wind is a mighty destroyer. In the living room McLean is making blood tests and bacterial cultures. Laseron has converted the dining table into a taxidermist's bench and is skinning seals and penguins. Bage, "The Astronomer Royal," is in a quiet corner busy with his slide-rule, computations, and log books. I am general handyman and when not out photographing fill in my time as master of a sewing machine, tentmaker and licensed jester. Webb has the most strenuous job. He goes out in the blizzards at all hours to attend to the magnetic instruments, which are housed in a small hut half a mile away.

The rest pursue many employments. The unexpected severity of the climate has necessitated extensive alterations in our sledging equipment and clothing. Tents are being remade, sledging rations compounded, weighed out and packed in calico ration bags. On days when the blizzards moderate, sorties are made to gather specimens and data. These collections give the scientists ample work until the next lull.

The day's work nominally ends with the setting of the evening meal. The meal progresses cheerfully with yarns and comments on the day's work or the cook's efforts. After dinner there is no dearth of willing hands to help the cook and messman.

Gramophone selections or Stillwell playing on the harmonium will bring back thoughts of home with many old favourite tunes.

So the day ends and the night-watchman—each takes turn —comes on duty at 8 P.M. He attends to the meteorological observations, stokes up the kitchen range and attends to his personal affairs—generally a bath and clothes washing.

So ends the account I made when these happenings were our daily routine.

Birthdays were eagerly looked forward to as affording splendid excuses for festivity and song. One of the "Unconventionals" was then in duty bound to spring a surprise.

While Mrs. Beeton was the faithful but, alas! frequently dishonoured ally of the "Crook Cooks Association" Mr. Whittaker of Almanac fame was the staunch friend of the Superior Society. An "Unconventional," when birthdays were scarce, would turn up the pages of historic events to find something that could be worthily celebrated. On one occasion "The Anniversary of the Lighting of London with Gas" was commemorated with tremendous enthusiasm. It was fortunate indeed that we had the capacity to extract fun from trivial daily happenings and misadventures. Thus was the gloom which might have been engendered

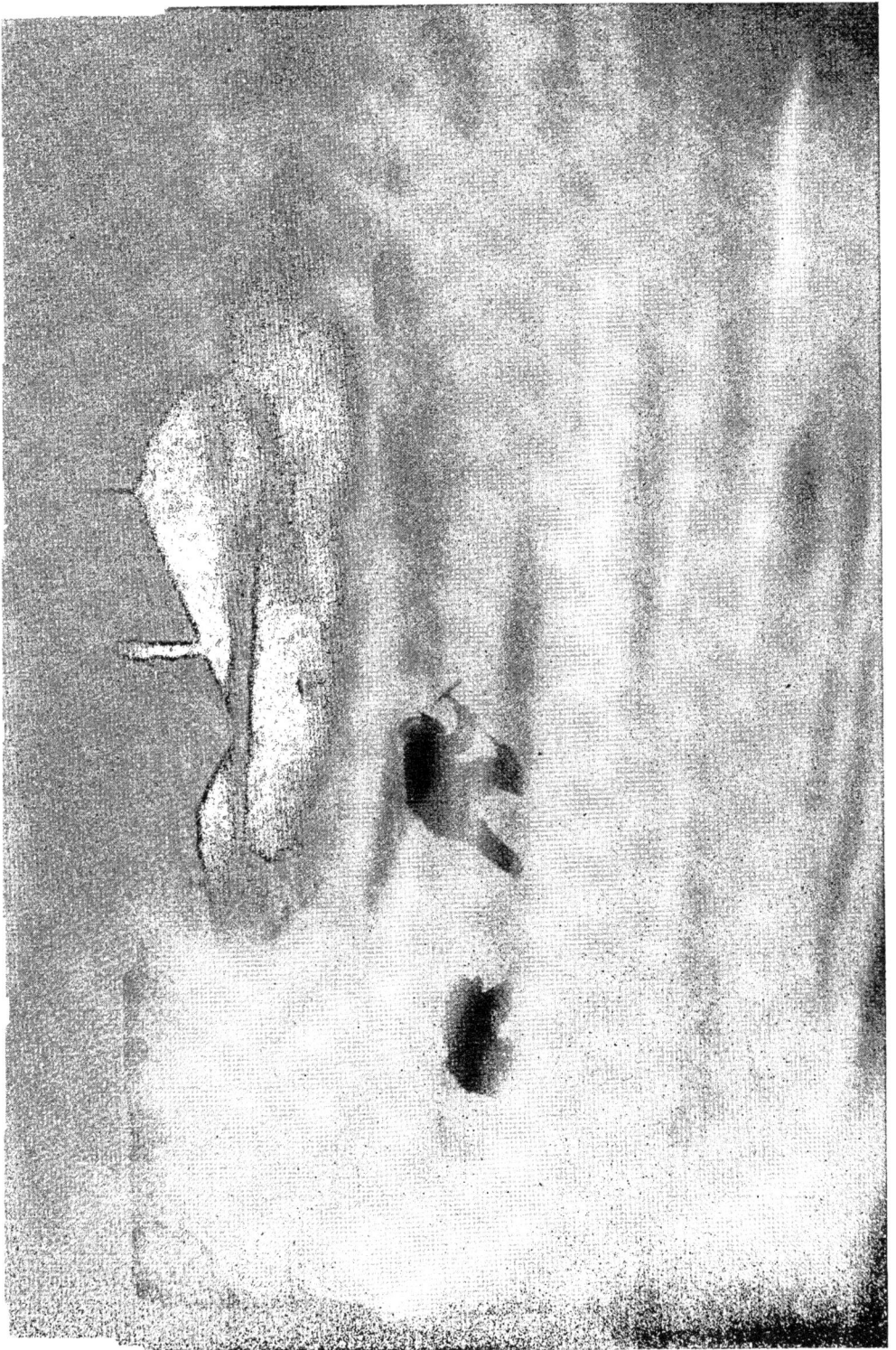

under the strain of the long dismal confinement to the hut, mitigated. We had to be "wise enough to play the fool."

But the awful climate outside the hut seriously hampered my own operations for no conditions could have been more unsuited for photography.

I was determined, however, to make the blizzard itself a subject for a moving picture. To illustrate the pace and force of the wind I built a shelter from blocks of ice, and under its lee photographed the meteorologists as they fought their way to and from the recording instruments, and other members of the party as they struggled about, bent—very literally bent—on their duties. Frequently my fingers, which I had to withdraw from the mitt to turn the handle of the cinema camera, were frostbitten, and often, in moving from point to point, I was swept away by fierce gusts. On one occasion, when the wind attained a velocity of 120 miles an hour, I was lifted bodily, carried some fifteen yards with my camera and tripod which together weighed 80 pounds and dumped on the rocks. I was reduced to crawling on all fours, and finally had to call in an assistant, who followed close on my heels, dragging the tripod, while I went ahead with the camera. We would return to the hut with our faces masked with ice, through which we breathed with difficulty, and which we removed with painful care.

At the close of Winter, the weather took a turn for the better, and we actually had a calm spell lasting for forty-eight hours! The temperature stood at sixty degrees below freezing point, so that the sea, undisturbed by the high winds, rapidly froze. The second day, the sea-ice was two and a half inches thick, and just firm enough to bear my weight. It was an uncanny yet fascinating sensation walking over the bosom of the sea on the young ice; and I at once realised the opportunity it afforded to take a series of pictures under the coastal ice-cliffs. Thither I turned my steps.

I was filled with awe as I stood beneath those mighty ice-walls, which towered a hundred and eighty feet above me. The silence, and the sense of my insignificance, in that region of the gigantic was sharp and depressing. I had just erected my camera, when, without warning, the ice gave way beneath me. In an instant I was floundering in the sea. I threw my arms out, and saved myself from being swept beneath the ice, but the thin sheet, once fractured, would no more than barely support me, and broke every time I tried to climb out.

My predicament was desperate. I was two miles away from Winter Quarters and there was no help. The suck of the current was dragging me beneath the ice and I had horrible visions of killer whales and sea leopards. My muscles were contracting and my limbs growing numb. Fortunately I espied a heavy piece of ice that had fallen from the cliffs and was frozen in some fifteen yards ahead. Pushing my camera along on the ice, I broke my way towards it. By good fortune I found a hand-grip, and laboriously I drew myself out—a half frozen, but a wholly wiser, man.

But my troubles were not yet at an end. Looking up in the direction of the Barrier Cliffs, I saw that the horizon was clouded with scudding snowdrift. The wind was coming, and at any moment the ice might break up and drift out to sea. Snatching up my camera I went for dear life across the thin ice as fast as my stiffly frozen garments would permit. My heart jumped each time the ice bent beneath the added pressure of my pace, but I reached the rocks and safety. A few minutes later I saw the ice which I had crossed, break up and drive out to sea. Through the rising wind I hobbled back to the hut. My clothes were like armour; my trousers like stovepipes. But if I expected condolences, I got none. I was received with ironical cheers and much persiflage from my comrades who had little sympathy for my recklessness. My camera had to be restuck, and my results were minus.

So, slowly passed the long darkness of the Polar Winter. I cannot describe the infernal conditions that raged permanently outside the hut as other than hellish. The ceaseless roar was like the rushing of a hundred freight trains tearing along at one hundred miles an hour. We attained varying degrees of accuracy in guesses at its velocity from its roaring note. Wagers were made in Antarctic currency—chocolate—while the meteorologists computed the hourly wind average.

The most boisterous day and wildest month was

July, when we noted "Snow drift thick as a wall outside with an 85 miler." Subsiding slowly through the seventies and then suddenly regaining strength, it rose to a climax about midnight on July 5th—one hundred and sixteen miles an hour! For eight hours it maintained an hourly average of 107 miles, and the timbers of the hut jarred and wrenched as it throbbed in its mightier gusts. These were the highest wind velocities recorded during the two years' observations in Adelie Land and probably the highest sustained velocities ever reported from a meteorological station. The mean hourly average of the wind taken over the two years' observations was 50 miles an hour.

During the hideous darkness the highly electrified atmosphere manifested the phenomenon of St. Elmo's fire. The ridge and projections of the hut were outlined with a bluish "brush" glow and the meteorological screens became highly charged with static electricity. If touched, a violent shock was experienced and electric sparks half an inch long could be drawn from the metal instruments. When moving about in the dark our forms were outlined with an uncanny glow like a faint aura.

The close proximity of Winter Quarters to the Magnetic Pole made it a splendid station for the observation of the Aurora Australis and many magnificent displays were witnessed. When the winds were not laden with snow, we would crouch in the lee of the hut and look up through the darkness to the sublime won-

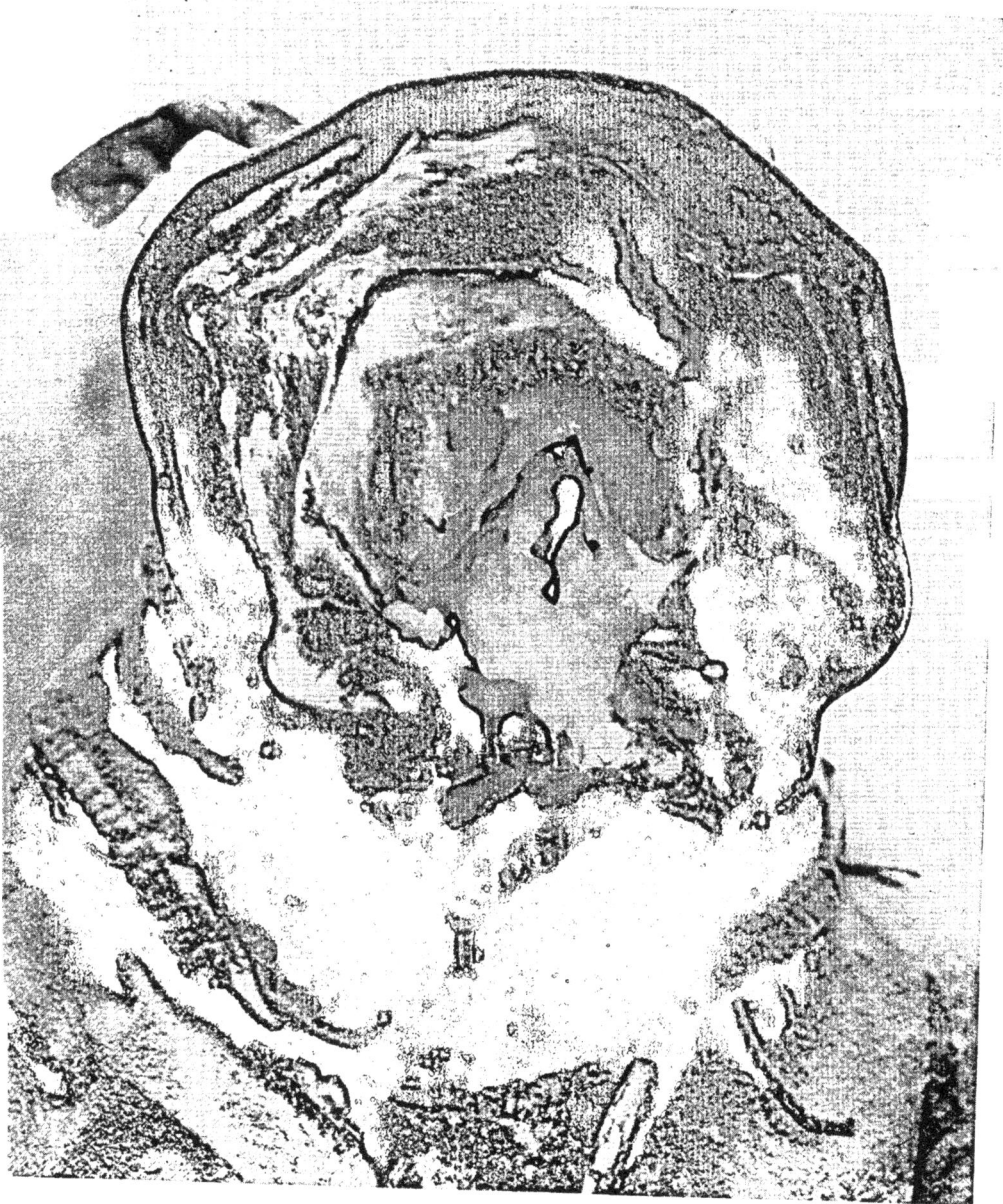

hotography in the land of the blizzard was fraught with many problems. The w pelting on to the face would rapidly cover it with a mask of ice and the snow t found its way into everything.

An Adelie Penguin Ready to Defend her Chick. Fluffy Down is still Adhering to the Upper Part of the Young Bird while the Lower Half has Assumed Adult Plumage.

ders of the skies. At times the whole heavens were
draped as with diaphanous folds of gently swaying pale
green gossamer. Then the tint would rapidly flush
with rose or violet. Coruscating streamers of light
would ripple over the curtains and the whole waving
veils of the sky danced in shimmering green. It
seemed as if the vault of heaven was about to rend and
we were to peer, affrighted, on undreamed-of glories of
God. Then the light would wane and the curtains
fade and, in their place, nebulous arcs and arches of
light, green and violet, would span the skies. Flame
shapes would shoot up from the south as if the plateau
were on fire. It was a mystic, incommunicable sight
that transcended even the splendours of the Polar dawn.

With the passing of Winter and the growing hours of
daylight we looked forward optimistically—not to a
calm, but to an abatement in the weather that would
permit of active field work. Thankfully we noticed
that the blizzards were less charged with snow but the
wind was still inexorable. Mid-October ushered in
returning life. Seals came ashore and the first penguins put in an appearance. It was a cheery sight.
They made direct for their old rookery and after giving
it a preliminary look-over returned to the blizzard-
swept sea, no doubt to report to their fellow migrants.
Next day the birds began to hop ashore in twos, threes
and groups. A few days later what had been a bald
expanse of guano-covered rocks teemed with active,
chattering birds. It was a great comfort and pleasure

to us to observe these companionable creatures returning and we found much diversion and entertainment
studying the quaint antics and the routine of their
rookery life.

Mostly the new arrivals were females. To them apparently was allotted the task of home making. Building materials—odd pebbles and bones of previous
penguin generations—were scarce, and much thieving,
squabbling, and henpecking went on over their possession. During an unguarded moment a bird would
steal a stone from another's nest. If caught, a severe
chastisement of vicious pecks was meted out, in which
the neighbours with righteous indignation enthusiastically participated. The more artful builders seized
these opportunities to add many pebbles to their
homes. The birds had a strenuous time building their
nests in the winds and during hurricanes they would
stop work and shelter behind the rocks. During the
housebuilding boom, the male birds made frequent calls
to the rookery, noting the progress, and waddled among
the nests, obviously appraising their merits rather than
those of the ladies who had built them. Then a process
of selection began; the birds possessing superior nests
were quickly mated, and I observed that there appeared
to be some reluctance to take a lady who was without
a home, or who possessed only an indifferent one,
merely on her face value. Afterwards we noted occasional rare females, who for some unguessable reason
had neglected to take their part in the homebuilding

activities, lurking on the outskirts of the rookery,—superfluous penguins, homeless and lonely, pathetic in their isolation.

After mating, a brief courtship began, the birds displaying their affection by muffled croaking and guttural crooning. The eyes are encircled with white rings which enable the bird to register a wide range of comically romantic expressions.

The Adelie penguin lays two eggs. These are held on top of the webbed feet and kept pressed against the warmth of the lower breast. The eggs are incubated under the most harassing conditions, the birds never daring to leave the nest for fear of the eggs freezing, despite the severe blizzards which at times entirely bury them with snow. Rearing a penguin family in Antarctica is an arduous task that requires the combined and incessant care of both parents. Not only have the young chicks to be protected from the harsh climate and fed, but they have also to be defended from the fierce Skua gulls that are ever on the alert to swoop down and carry off strays. We frequently observed these predatory creatures attack the mother and while one engaged her attention, another would pounce down and carry off the chick. It was a pitiful sight to see the bird return to the nest and find her chick gone. She would utter long lamentations in which the nearby neighbours joined. Eventually she would try to console herself by sitting on a stone or by kidnapping a neighbour's chick.

The young grow very rapidly, and are veritable gluttons, always clamouring for food. They quickly change from brown fluffy balls to pot-bellied gourmands, exceeding their parents in girth. When the young have attained this stage they are placed in a common nursery with a guard of elders round the margin. Truants are driven back by pecks and vigorous smacks from the flippers. The principal food of the Adelies is a small shrimp which is very abundant in these waters. The young bird feeds by placing its beak within its parent's, and swallowing partly digested food regurgitated by the older creature.

The moulting season converts the young into the most grotesque caricatures imaginable. The brown down moults in clumps allowing the adult plumage to show through in patches. Frozen snow mats the feathers and they hang bedraggled and give the birds a weirdly unkempt and ludicrous appearance. But when the moulting is completed the transformation is as startling as when a moth emerges from the chrysalis. One can scarcely conceive that the spruce and elegant young flapper with breast of white and silver sheen and back of glossy slate plumage was but lately an ugly, begrimed and shapeless ball of tousled down. Then the birds take to the sea, and in a few days the rookeries are completely deserted.

While these penguin domesticities were entertaining us, preparations were going ahead for the serious work of exploration.

During the Spring several sledging parties set out to lay depots and make preliminary investigations of the plateau. They experienced frightful weather. The greatest distance covered by any party was a bare fifty miles—nothing in comparison with the journeys that our programme demanded, yet they returned badly frostbitten and with their equipment ripped and damaged by the blizzards. They reported conditions on the plateau as utterly impossible and unfaceable. We chafed and ached under the despotic reign of the blizzard. We could only wait, hoping that with the approach of Summer the climate might grow milder and more propitious.

CHAPTER IV

THE FLIGHT FROM THE MAGNETIC POLE

Have you suffered, starved and triumphed, grovelled down, yet grasped at glory?

ROBERT W. SERVICE.

E VEN in the early days of summer, the weather showed little signs of improvement, and it became evident that the sledging programme would have to be executed in circumstances of extraordinary severity.

Mawson, however, was not the man to be daunted by blizzards. Courageously cheerful himself, he fired all of us with his spirit. It was incredible too how the human organism responded and adapted itself to these hellish conditions. The body developed new muscles and powers to resist the intense cold; the mind, confidence and determination. Our slogan ran: "that the worst might be infinitely worse."

Parties of three were selected to form sledging units, each with its own mission in the great Unknown. I was chosen to accompany Robert Bage, who was in command, and Eric N. Webb, magnetician, on a sledging journey with the object of reaching, if possible, the South Magnetic Pole, conducting on the way magnetic, meteorological, and general exploratory work. We took advantage of a comparative calm early in November to set out with provisions for nine weeks. We were due back on January 15, at about which time the *Aurora* was to pick us up for the return home.

Five miles from the hut, on the crest of a long, steep grade, lay Aladdin's Depot, at which we completed the packing of our sledge, and here we were "fare-welled" by Dr. Mawson, Mertz, and Ninnis, who were loading sledges and preparing their dog teams before setting out on their eastern journey. Little did we think as we shook hands when parting that it was the last farewell to two of our comrades.

At seven o'clock we set off in serene calm and sunshine to pick up our supporting party at "Eleven Mile" depot. There are few forms of physical exercise better calculated to rub the edge off a "greenhorn's" keenness and, incidentally, to prove his mettle, than hauling a sledge, with a load of eight hundred pounds, over an uneven uphill surface. However, despite the over-weighted sledge, the lack of training and the stubborn uphill going—to say nothing of the many crevasses into which we plunged waist deep—we made the distance, and met our complementary trio. Three extremely weary men crept into the sleeping-bags that night, and three very stiff men crawled out in the morning,—to find the wind freshening and snow beginning to fall. Three miles marked the limit of our march that second day in the blizzard's teeth. Each party pitched its little tent—and it is no mean performance to pitch even a little tent in a wind that is choked with snow and blowing at seventy miles an hour—got out of our frozen Burberrys and into our sleeping-bags. In the tent there was scarcely room to move, but even so, it was necessary to shout in order to be heard above the roar of the blizzard.

For nine months our company had listened to its raging voice—now whining high, now groaning low—from the security of the hut, and in that time the fine days could be counted on the fingers of one's hands, but now, pushing out into untrodden territory, we lay beneath the frail shelter of a thin drill canopy, whilst the wind bellowed over us at eighty miles an hour and filled every crevice with snow drift. Drifting snow! How soft it sounds. But "drifting" is a misnomer, for when snow "drifts" before a blizzard it resembles a sand-blast. Its flying particles will polish a metal surface till it shines, will cut into a board like coarse sand-paper, and will wear ice projections to smooth and shining knife-edges. These tiny particles, bombarding the eyeballs if goggles are left off, burn like sparks of white-hot metal, and cause an agony worse than snow-blindness.

The weather conditions during the first week of our march may be gauged by the statement that whilst we were scheduled to average twelve miles a day to reach our goal and return in safety, yet for the first week the total distance we covered was but thirty miles! We fought against a wind that varied in intensity but never ceased and we trudged on an up grade to an elevation of 3500 feet above sea level in those thirty miles. One or two extracts from my journal will convey an idea of the nature of the going.

14 November.—Through the night the wind blew up to 70 miles per hour and although our light tent is pitched in the lee of our supporting party we had grave apprehensions of it being blown to shreds. It is now 9 A.M. and the wind is bellowing at 80 miles an hour! The thin tent threatens to rip at any moment, whilst the seething drift pelts like a sand-blast. It will be fatal to have our thin calico walls rent by the terrific conditions, yet it seems impossible they can hold out much longer. Remained in our sleeping-bags until 3.30 P.M. It took us nearly two hours to put on our frozen garments and get the few necessaries off the sledge outside to make "hoosh." We all got badly frostbitten, and were glad to return to our sleeping-bags. If one once gets cold it is a hard job to warm up again and much of the value of the food is wasted; so we find the bags the best and only place. Oh! for a fine day so that we might dry our fur mitts and sleeping gear. At present when they come under the influence of our body warmth they are little better than wet rags and when we take them off they freeze almost brittle! Our supports although in a tent a few yards away, have not been seen or heard the whole of the day. Yet thank Heaven we are as well off as circumstances will permit for as we say on the trail, "It might always be worse."

15 November.—I am so disgusted with the weather that I force myself to make this entry: That we spent three hours patching our tent—a stitch every five minutes— Our fingers are painfully frostbitten—that the wind is between 70 and 75 miles per hour—that it is drifting dense snow and the temperature is 48 degrees below freezing point—that we wonder if the plateau will be blown away and ourselves with it. We cannot leave the tent.

16 November.—The weather moderated at noon and we made a speedy start. What a change! All day the weather improved and we made 5¼ miles, over hard sastrugi polished with drift and wind. At 6.30 P.M. heavy nimbus clouds came rolling up from the South and as another storm threatened a halt was made. Tents were erected in a dead calm! What a striking contrast to the blizzard's eternal roar. Every sound seems frozen. Our voices ring strangely in the awesome silence, while our ears, so accustomed to the continuous din, ache dully. Our tent is limp, for not the gentlest zephyr stirs. What is going to happen? What a place of excesses, and how welcome to us wind-battered toilers this cessation comes. Yet we lie vainly wooing sleep till Bage in desperation puts his head out of the tent and shouts to our supports an order to pelt our tent with snow. Anything to break the infernal silence!

17 November.—The calm lasted for a few hours only. This morning we hauled in very light drift, but the sun and the distance were hidden by dense hazy clouds. The light was so diffused that it was impossible to discriminate rise from hollow, even the sastrugi which were large and numerous were quite indiscernible. This was due to the even pall of light casting no shadows, so that the entire surface looked even and blank. We had many falls, stumbling and tripping over the unseen obstacles, but covered 5½ miles, bringing the total up to date to 30 miles and a week gone.

But with the turn of the week came a dramatic change in the weather. We had toggled up in our sleeping-bags cold, wet, and miserable, with the old familiar howl of the fifty-mile blizzard for lullaby. But imagine our waking, to find the midnight sun shining out of a clear sky across the clean-swept icefields! No breath of wind was stirring; the head rang and the ears ached with the roaring of past tempests, now mentally audible in the literally painful silence. But the contrast did not end there. Anxious to make distance while the sun shone, we packed the sledge and started off. Soon the Burberrys were doffed, the jackets of fleece shed, and then clad only in our underclothes, we plodded along through that which at home we would have called a sweltering summer day. Nothing would have been more welcome than a feast of ice-cream! Those with even a rudimentary knowledge of temperatures will appreciate the record that the black-bulb thermometer registered 116 degrees in the sun and the spirit-bulb 40 degrees below freezing point in the shade.

At 67½ miles, instead of at 100 as originally planned, we built a snow mound ten feet tall over a depot of food and surmounted it with a special indestructible flag vane twenty feet high. We named it "Southern Cross" Depot and then said "Good-bye" to our supporting trio, who were soon out of sight on their homeward journey in the low scudding drift.

Now we would put our backs into it and raise our daily mileage! But alas, the wind rose again and we spent the first day in our sleeping bags waiting vainly for it to drop to a point at which travelling would be not comfortable, but possible.

It was an "occasion" too. Webb had reached another mile post in the journey of life and insisted on celebrating. He produced three crushed cigars, treasured for the event! Bage unpacked the small "perk bag"—more precious than the chamois pouch of any trader in diamonds. There was something strangely solid about that receptacle of our delicacies. The truth was that the lid had come off a tin, and powdered milk had sifted through the contents of the bag. The drift snow, which would penetrate a burglar-proof safe, had done the rest. Almonds and raisins, chocolate and sultanas, were all mixed and solidified. However, we cut the bag open and consumed the amalgam with relish, and through the rolling clouds of smoke from the cigars, we told stories of other birthdays—some happier and some far less happy.

Here we were, cold and hungry, days behind our schedule, miles behind our ambitions, held fast by an iron hand when we were aching to be up and on the move. Yet nine months in the hut and the nine days on trail had taught us that there is something far more satisfying to the soul than mere creature comforts, something better even than achievement, and that is the fight! We turned over—we had "turned in" many hours before; our feast had been enjoyed as we lay in our bags—with the expressed determination to take the trail on the morrow and defy the elements to do their worst! And surely on the morrow they did their worst!

We left "Southern Cross" Depot. The drift cut our faces and the wind split our lips. After a long uphill struggle against the blasts, we came to an area of very bad sastrugi and snow ramps. The sledge was frequently overturned and the wind increased, but still we plodded on. The sledge was blown sideways, and its windage, added to the heavy load, made it almost impossible for us to keep it moving. At last came a point when we could not do even that. After a great deal of trouble we managed to erect our tent, and the wind strengthening even more, forced us to build a shelter of snow blocks. At midnight we struggled into our bags and lay awake listening to the wind roaring past at 75 miles an hour! The tent was however effectively protected and safe for the time at least. With stiff fingers I scrawled at the end of the day's record: "Sledging under these conditions is—hell."

Thus we won a few grudged miles each day till the century mark was passed, and on the 29th November we observed the sun at actual midnight for the first time. His wheel rim just skimmed the horizon and rose again to shine on the toils of another troubled day.

During this sort of weather the end of the day's march is not the end of the day's toil. First, a level camping site has to be found. This is difficult owing to the surface being gouged deep with sastrugi furrows. Large blocks of névé then have to be cut from the surface and built into a "break-wind," generally some fifteen feet long, three feet thick and five feet high.

This in a high wind and drift is a cruel and lengthy business, but it takes the viciousness out of the wind and though laborious in erection is well worth while. The tent is erected, a matter for experience and strength, in the lee of the shelter. The flounce is heavily weighted with snow blocks and there stands "Home," flapping and frail, yet a heaven-sent relief after battling all day against the blizzard.

Each takes turns cooking. First, I go inside. Bage and Webb then carefully unstrap the sledge, holding tightly on to everything lest it be torn from their grip and whirled away. The floor cloth is passed in and spread. Then follow the sleeping bags, the Nansen cooker with its inner and outer compartments filled with snow, then the "ditty" bags, each of a different gay colour. It is a great relief to look at them after the eternal white—they contain dry sleeping garments. Then the Primus stove is put inside and the rations in small calico bags each containing a week's supply. The sledge is anchored with the ice-axe, lest it be blown away in the night. Bage and Webb whisk the snow from their clothes and finnescoe footwear and come inside, immediately tying up the funnel-shaped door behind them. By now, after several false starts, I have managed to get the Primus stove going and my tentmates are taking off their outer windproof Burberry blouses and trousers, changing their socks and putting on dry finnescoe. All this in the faint green light filtering through the flapping tent fabric, and a

"Southern Cross" Depot sixty-seven and one-half Miles from Winter Quarters on the outward Journey to the Magnetic Pole.

continual shower of rime crystals produced by the ascending warmth from the Primus and our condensing breath.

Soon steam begins to issue from the cooker, and the pemmican ration, a mixture of powdered dry beef, lard and ground plasmon biscuit, previously measured out, is tipped into the boiling water. After a few minutes "boil up," blissful "hoosh" is ready. The cook scrapes the "hoosh" pot scrupulously clean and the water, which by now has thawed from the snow in the outer compartment of the cooker, is poured into it. While the water is boiling the meal goes on. Topics of the day and the prospects of the future are discussed. The hot hoosh soon sets the blood a-tingle and we become downright cheerful. Steam again issues from the cooker, the cook measures out a ration of cocoa compound, a mixture of cocoa, sugar and glaxo, tips it into the water and turns out the Primus. The cocoa is poured into the same hoosh mugs, a sledging biscuit is nibbled and as it is necessary to conserve every calorie, if not already in sleeping-bags we hurriedly wriggle into them. Nor is anything wasted, not a crumb nor a drop of Primus kerosene.

The reindeer finnescoe, very damp from wear during the day, are moulded into shape, and with the grass padding which forms an insulating inner-sole are hung up on a line so that they may freeze into shape. Our woollen helmets, saturated with frozen breath, have also to be "shaped," and woe betide him who forgets to mould his mits, for in the morning back and palm will be frozen together as hard as metal and it will take half an hour to get them on.   The outer Burberrys are spread on the top of the sleeping-bags, where they soon become as stiff as boards.   As cook, I am last into bag and my comrades squeeze together to enable me to wriggle down, for the three of us barely fit the tiny tent. Bage enters the meteorological observations, which have been taken every four hours on the march, and Webb writes up his magnetic reports.   Both work out our geographical position from sun "shots," and Bage plots the day's traverse on a small squared chart. Finally our wet socks are pushed up under our jerseys, so that they may be less wet for the morrow,—we snuggle down.   Bob (Bage) is always last, his calabash pipe pokes from the opening of the sleeping bag and whiffs of pungent fumes escape.   The pipe is smoked, and after the last "Good night," the "swish, swish," of the everlasting drift lulls us to sleep.   If the weather is fine in the morning we are out early, but if it is bliz-zardly—the trail has to be faced just the same—there is no shirking.   The one whose turn it is to cook is first up; the others lurk in the warmth of the bags until hoosh is ready.   Then comes the ordeal—taking off the warm sleeping clothes; putting on the frozen stiff helmet—Bage and Webb do this slowly but I prefer pulling it on with a jerk—changing dry socks to damp; donning the stiff Burberrys and frozen footgear and making ready for the trail.   Bags are rolled up, chattels collected and packed in their respective places on the sledge. Before striking the tent Webb takes a set of magnetic observations which is a miserably cold job. The wind shelter is converted into a high mound—it will form an excellent landmark on the return journey —and then we buckle on our harness for another bout with the wild. Such were our evenings, nights and mornings on this trek south.

On December 1st the monotonous stretch of desolate snow was broken for the first time by the sight of some snow ramps which we turned aside from the true course to investigate. Hauling our sledge across a valley-like depression we mounted a second ridge and an amazing field of huge crevasses confronted us.

The whole place scarred and crisscrossed by enormous crevasses resembled an area cut up into allotments. Many of the crevasses were eighty feet wide and were spanned by great bridges of compressed snow. To take the sledge through this chaos was the next problem. It was my day to lead, so attached to a long rope, I would venture out on to the snow bridges, stamping and jumping to test their holding power. If they survived this test it was fair to assume that they would bear the catlike tread of my mates. Upon crossing to safety, we hauled the sledge across by means of a long line. Several times I broke the snow bridges and went through to my waist but my companions speedily hauled me out again.

We were half way across the field of crevasses and I

was continuing the good work when suddenly I dropped through a deep fissure. There was a sickening sensation of falling followed by a violent jerk. As before, I shouted to my mates, "Right-O! Haul away!" As I began slowly to ascend, to my dismay I discovered that the thin line had sawn deeply into the crevasse lid, which extended well out over my head like a roof. I came up against it with a bump and loudly made the others aware of my predicament. My position, gently swinging to and fro and slowly rotating on the slender line, gave me qualms, but I could not help noticing the unearthly beauty of the abyss into which I had fallen.

I remember that on either side, its walls, about thirty feet apart, were the colour of jade at the top, gradually shading down through sapphire to pure cobalt and then, below, to blackness. The sheer faces were covered with exquisite crystals that scintillated as I moved. Presently I heard Webb's voice and observed his dull shadow stretched full length on the marble-like ceiling overhead. Then his face peered through the opening and he told me they had managed to overturn the sledge, anchor it, and make the rope fast, and that he was going to chip away the overhanging snow. I called back, mocked by a hollow echo from the depths, "Don't chip through the line." The position was dangerous for both of us, as there was great peril of the broken lid collapsing under our combined weights. The chippings and crystals showered down on me but I did not hear them strike the bottom below. Then

Webb announced he was going back to help Bage to haul. I succeeded in swinging round so as to face the direction of the pull and this enabled me, when I was drawn up level with the surface, to get my hands out and assist. Soon I emerged with the thought that there were worse places even than the plateau surface. It was a tremendous relief when we put miles between ourselves and the "Nodules" as we christened the place.

So we progressed on our journey, fighting constantly over treacherous surfaces and harassed by snapping breezes and snarling blizzards. Yet so happily constituted is the human mind that when five weeks of pitiless wind were followed by a single day of calm, impulsively I wrote:

(*Dec. 19.*)—I take back all I have said about the harsh weather . . . today was heavenly, calm and cloudless . . . all day we have been marching over a vast white plain, three tiny specks of life in the solitude of a vacant Continent. As we plod onward we are appalled by the vastness of it all. Day after day, week after week, nothing but Snow—Snow—Snow, and the interminable barrier of the horizon. What lies beyond? Months drag by, but only the unattainable ridge and Snow—Snow—Eternal Snow. Sometimes the plateau is as featureless as a stagnant sea; then there are plains convulsed with deep furrows, gouged by the almighty plough of the wind. In times of peace it is silent; so silent as to be terrible. There is no sound but the glide and creak of the sledge runners and the laboured breathing of the toilers.

When the midnight sun, like a fiery ball, rolls along the

northern skyline, the desolate plain becomes a mighty palette where the Painter of the Universe blends His colours. Our long shadows point and our impulses yearn far to the South. Forward we follow them over a frozen sea of magenta ripples and lilac furrows. From the base of the horizon the sky ascends in a glorious dome, as iridescent as mother-o'-pearl.

While the blizzard sleeps, the sun is King. Dazzling and radiant he ascends the sky and the colour vanishes. South-ward we move over a continent of gleaming marble,—so glaring and blinding that we may only gaze upon it through deep yellow glasses.

On December 21st we reached the safety limit of our rations. The Magnetic dip needle stood at 89° 43.5'. What a temptation to go on and raise the needle to the vertical! Only another sixteen and a half minutes— probably under fifty miles. A couple of miles ahead stretched another of the everlasting ridges that had lured us on. What lay beyond? Another ridge?

Although the plateau was bathed in bright sunshine, a strong wind was blowing and the temperature 44 degrees below freezing point. We assisted Webb to build a shelter before taking his observations. I re-corded for him and was mighty pleased when the four hours work was done. It was a vilely cold job handling instruments and the keen and uncomplaining way my comrades always went about it elicited my admiration. After lunch we hoisted the Commonwealth flag in latitude 70° 36.5' South, longitude 148° 10' East, and gave three cheers for the King—they sounded very strange in the vast solitude. Then we packed up and turned homeward in our tracks to the north again.

For six weeks we had fought our way up an undulating slope, hauling in the eye of the wind and had reached an altitude of 6000 feet; now we tackled the return journey with three weeks in hand, two depots to replenish our stores en route, and just sufficient rations to bridge the gaps. The start was brilliant. Rigging a sail on our sledge—forcing our enemy the wind to become our ally—we travelled two and a half miles to our first return camp in an hour. Next day, with our forty-nine square feet of sail reefed down, we covered eighteen and a half miles with no more exertion than walking entails, and the following day passed three old camps in a twenty-mile run.

There followed a patch of trouble, on the way to Lucky Depot, established on the outward journey, 200 miles from the hut, and we were two days overdue when we reached it. We celebrated Christmas Day on the 27th.

I was unanimously voted cook and while Bage and Webb conducted the usual series of magnetic observations I set about concocting a banquet with a double ration, eked out with the "savings" we had accumulated from day to day. This is the Menu of that memorable Christmas, which gave us as much delight as the traditional gorge of turkey and Christmas "duff":

Hors d'œuvre

Angels on gliders.   Made by placing a raisin on the
top of a bar of chocolate previously fried.

Entrées.

Biscuit fried in sledging suet.

Roast.

Frizzled pemmican on fried biscuit.

Piéce de Resistance.

Extra thick and greasy sledging ration.

Sweets.

Plum pudding.   Made by grating up three biscuits
with the bonsa saw.   Glaxo, sugar, 7 raisins, flavoured 3 drops of meth. spirit.   All mixed with
snow and boiled in sock 5 minutes.

The Christmas pudding, about which I had secret
qualms—before sampling—turned out to be a culinary
triumph.   The beverage about which we all had frank
qualms—after sampling—was Bage's recipe,—five raisins boiled up and flavoured with methylated spirit
from the Primus stove.   It was as the inventor claimed
"Stingo," and though the Royal toast was honoured
with the nose held firmly in the left hand, while we
gulped the unholy brew, our sentiments were none the
less sincere, and our wishes no less hearty than the
three cheers for His Majesty with which we followed it.
We thoroughly enjoyed our dinner, and I never knew

a happier or jollier Christmas than this one I spent with Bob Bage and Azzi Webb at "Lucky Depot," two hundred miles up on the plateau.

To celebrate the occasion, and to add a new interest, we made up our minds to lower the Polar record for a day's march with a man-hauled sledge. With a good surface and fair breeze we reeled off a dozen miles between camp-break and lunch, and at the end of twelve hours—with two pauses for food and rest— thirty-three and a half miles stood to our credit. After another two hours' rest, we took to the trail again, and when finally we made camp we had the satisfaction of knowing that we held the record, having covered 41.5 miles in sixteen hours' actual marching and six hours' resting.

But as so frequently happens, easy beginnings have stubborn endings and after these pleasant days once more the blizzard drove down. Though the wind was behind us, we could not see the surface, which was terribly broken, through the driving snow. We stumbled along, constantly falling, the sledge incessantly overturning. We all had painful periods of snow blindness but Bage was most susceptible. New Year's Day brought added tribulations. Bage was suffering terribly and temporarily blind, so Webb and I hauled him on the sledge. The "piecrust" like surface still further retarded us. It would not bear our weight; we broke through at every step and sank to our knees. Worse still, our feet were caught beneath the hard caked surface and the effort to free them after every step fatigued us terribly. Moreover we were compelled to go on half rations, for the unforeseen delay ate into our food supplies disastrously.

When we pitched camp, dead beat, eleven miles from "67½ mile" depot, in heavy snow and a high wind, the ration had to be further decreased. We could not see more than a few yards and it was utterly impossible to try to find the snow mound that marked the depot eleven miles away. It was dreary waiting and our need was growing desperate.

The wind lessened on January 5th and although the sky was heavily overcast and light snow was still falling, we pushed on urgently towards where we calculated the depot should be. But we were baffled. We could not see more than a hundred yards and were forced to camp again to await clear weather.

The sky was still overcast on the following day but Bage managed to get a lucky sun "shot" that indicated that we were on the exact latitude of the depot. We walked east and west, but were unable to see more than a few yards through the curtain of falling snow.

Only a day's ration remained, and on the scant allowance we were beginning to feel deadly cold. Again we pitched camp, gnawed the remnants of a frugal meal, and crept into our sleeping-bags to try to conserve our warmth. I dozed in restless sleep and had a strange dream.

For three months we had lived on a concentrated

sledging ration, its calories scientifically calculated to produce so many units of energy, but otherwise very unsatisfying. Manhauling a heavy sledge against terrific winds, we had become very emaciated. The incessant hunger and lack of variety in food manifested itself in "food" dreams. This endeavour of nature to effect a counterpoise was not new to us. It was a nightly experience and it became our custom to entertain each other by relating these workings of our subconscious minds. Curiously enough, these fantastic food dreams satisfied to some extent our bodily yearnings, for after an imagined orgy we would awaken physically stimulated.

This was my dream:

We were all back in Sydney in the banquet hall of the Australia Hotel. A thousand candles shed a festive glow over a long table, around which were seated the members of the Expedition, all in polar accoutrement, unwashed and with very long beards bleached white. The entire length of the table was set with an enormous silver salver of preserved strawberries. Upon the sea of fruit was anchored a fleet of pastry vessels, each one a detailed model of the Expedition's vessel, the *Aurora*, and upon the syrupy margin sat crystallized penguins. Then a long line of glorious nymphs, each with a steaming bowl of sledging "hoosh" glided in, with a creature fairer than Venus in the lead. As I reached for the bowl she slipped and it broke upon the floor.

I awakened to the roar of a tempest. The blizzard

had broken out with redoubled fury.   Peering from my sleeping-bag the seriousness of our plight burst upon me.

What three insignificant microbes of life we were, I thought, to trespass into these icy regions! Only a handful of food remained, and if we failed to find the depot, a mere mound of snow which possibly had been blown flat by the wind, we were faced with a seventy mile march to the hut.

Huddled in our sleeping-bags we held a council, wriggling close together so that we could hear each other above the swishing snow. Our decision was to wait for the end of the blizzard, remaining in our sleeping-bags to conserve bodily warmth, and try to keep the fire of life smoldering with one-sixth of a ration.

We spoke little, for even talking consumed energy. If the blizzard continued, we might last out five days. The memory of Christmas rankled in my mind. If only we had saved the extra ration. That "feast" haunted me like a crime.

But repining was futile. "To hell with it all, let us die cheerfully," I wrote in my diary. I even found some mental diversion and fought remorse by composing doggerel verses. I append a few lines out of the 500.

I've dined in many places, but never such as these—
It's like the Gates of Heaven, when you find you've lost the
    keys.
I've dined with Kings and Emperors, perhaps you scarce
    believe;

For even they do funny things when round comes Christmas
    Eve.
I've feasted with Iguanas on a lonely desert isle;
Once in the shade of a wattle, and a maiden's winsome smile.
I've "grubbed" at a threepenny hash-house, I've dined at
    a counter lunch,
Refreshed at a slap-up café, where only the "swankers"
    munch.
In short, I've dined from Horn to Cape and up Alaska way,
But the finest, funniest dinner of all was on that Christmas
    Day!

"Pretty rotten," said Bage cheerfully, when I re-
cited the last line.

"Might be much worse," added Webb, quoting our
sledging slogan.

Encouraged by our cheerfulness, hopes grew again.
We agreed that if the morrow dawned clear we would
look for the cache. If we failed to find it, even though
the blizzard continued, we would take our desperate
chances and try to gain the hut. That they would be,
in the strictest meaning of the words, desperate chances
we knew only too well.

Near the magnetic pole area, a horizontal compass is
quite useless, the magnetic field being practically vertical. Consequently, our navigation across the featureless ice wastes was by a shadow compass—a contriv-
ance not unlike a sundial. A reference to our pocket
chronometer for time and an adjustment of the instrument accordingly, indicated the cardinal points, but
when the sun was obscured by the blizzard, and objects

only a few feet away were hidden by driving snow, this was useless.

Furthermore, at the end of the journey we had to locate a narrow pathway one hundred yards wide, through fields of impassable crevasses. If we missed this narrow path, which could only be found by accurate theodolite observations, we would stumble into the crevasses. The hut was at the base of a steep slope, and was not visible until the crest of the ridge immediately behind was reached. We had but one directing influence—the wind itself; even this veered between south and southeast.

The next day broke with a lull in the elements. We hastened from our sleeping-bags, Bage got out the theodolite, Webb and I measured off a base line in order to take the bearings of some distant ice ramps which would enable us to localise the cache. Our observations indicated that the food was somewhere within a mile radius. The mound and the high staff surmounting it should have been visible but they had evidently been swept away by the blizzards. As we scoured the surface of the ice the skies grew overcast, snow began falling and the wind again rose, growing each moment in velocity. We paused and looked at each other in utter dismay. The blizzard was returning and we had failed to find the cache. There was nothing to do except to take the forlorn chance of reaching the hut. We returned to the sledge, cached our instruments, everything except our records, sleeping-bags and tent. Our food supply weighed a matter of ounces. We seemed to feel in the whirling snow the icy breath of death. We did not speak, but gripped each other's hands—none can understand the sensation unless they have been through it—and then off into the blizzard, steering a course 10 degrees east of the wind.

All details had been worked out previously in the tent. Webb would lead the first day, then I would take my turn, then Bage. Bage would keep the time, and after every hour we would rest for five minutes. After eight "fleets" we would pitch camp for ten hours and then strike tent and off again.

So through the wind and snow we fought. The sledge was whirled sideways and constantly overturned. We could not see one another through the dense drift which swept along at eighty miles an hour. At rest-times we crouched in the lee of the sledge, comforting each other with talk that another two miles had passed; "there's only so many to go."

So the first day passed—one of the sternest of my life. We pitched camp, Bage measured to each approximately two ounces of rations, and, so that one might not receive a crumb more than the other, Webb turned his back, while Bage pointed to a ration and asked, "Whose?" We took as much time as possible over the tantalizing morsels—while the blizzard roared without. But we had won through the first day and our spirits had risen.

We slept little, for excitement overcame physical

weariness, and we shivered painfully, for agonizing cold crept into our sleeping-bags. Our fingers and toes were becoming frostbitten.

Punctually on time Bage announced, "Turn out!" With the pain of leaving the little warmth of the sleeping-bags, the mad desire came over us to gorge the last remnant of food and remain where we were—for ever! Then the will took charge and said "out!" It became a compelling force in spite of our physical inclinations.

It was my day to lead. In the chaos of the storm on the end of the hauling line, buffeting, fighting, stumbling, how inexpressibly lonely I felt. My comrades were hidden behind somewhere, tethered to the sledge in the void.

A strange feeling came over me, infinitely comforting. Some indefinable force seemed to be beside me and guiding me on. In a state of high exaltation I knew we were going to win through. The second night we were much happier, for although we were unspeakably cold, we had covered more than half way.

Bage led off next morning. Our jaded bodies, stiff and frostbitten, rebelled, but WILL won, and the march warmed us.

Then came a great surprise. Late that afternoon the blizzard ceased suddenly, the sun came out, and disclosed to our astonished eyes—the sea! The low sun shone over ice-littered water and the icefields around us and lighted all with a delicate pink radiance.

Where were we? According to our computation, the

sea should have been 30 miles away! It seemed impossible that we could be that much out of our reckoning. Perhaps we had been walking three miles an hour and not two as we imagined. The scene was as disconcerting as the blizzard. As we advanced wonderingly we recognised the jutting headlands of Commonwealth Bay. We had struck the right bay, but it was twenty miles across. There was a track a hundred yards wide somewhere on its crevassed coastal slopes that would lead us to the hut. We could not last out another day, for we were now reduced to staggering along. We had to find that tiny track through impassable ice or pay penalty with our lives. We decided to march west for a few miles and try to locate it— a mistake and nearly a tragic one. Soon we were in the crevasses. To add to our plight, the impact of frozen snow particles had inflicted injuries to my eyes that caused excruciating agony. I was rapidly growing blind. Tiny cracks were magnified into terrible chasms and dangerous ones dwarfed into cracks—so that I had no idea of danger or safety.

As we descended the ice grew into a maze of crevasses with yawning pits on every side. To progress was hopeless; we must return and try elsewhere. We were about to retrace our steps, despair freezing our souls as bitterly as the blizzard had frozen our bodies, when Bage stood on a snow bridge and pointed ahead. He just had time to cry "Look!" when the bridge collapsed and with tragic absurdity he was precipitated into the abyss, with a jerk at our end of the towline. Webb crept to the hole to observe our comrade swinging like a pendulum in the blackness. To our intense relief we heard him call back, "All well! The Mackellar Islets!" Rubbish! He was raving! Owing to our weakness, it was with difficulty we hauled him up, and he pointed excitedly to a group of small islets which we knew lay immediately off the hut! Webb corroborated the good news, which I did not believe, as my blindness prevented me from seeing. As we climbed back again up the ice slopes, Bage's eagle eye discerned a stick standing above the surface of the plateau. We recognised it to our unspeakable joy as Aladdin's Cave five miles from the hut! Here was a cache of dog biscuits—food in plenty! We stumbled towards it.

Presently three ghastly objects, looking like dead men returned to life again, stood by the depot and joined hands. Below the surface of the ice was a subcavern excavated many months ago as a shelter. We descended. It was a crystal grotto that beggared Aladdin's mythical palace. The Primus stove was set going, and we had our first meal; but we ate sparingly, knowing two well the reaction of overeating in our present physical condition. We had scarcely finished when a great drowsiness overcame us and we fell off to sleep. The journey of over 600 miles was nearly over.

After a light breakfast we climbed out of the cave into the sunshine of a glorious day. My eyes had recovered but poor Bage was blind again. Ahead lay the track through the crevasses. Had we marched straight ahead without turning to the west the previous day, we would have walked straight on to it! What Hidden Hand had led us through the inferno of blizzard unerringly to this narrow path and what demon had lured us in doubt from this unseen guidance?

As Webb and I marched ahead, hauling Bage on the sledge, never had I seen the Antarctic appear so serene and beautiful. It was a heavenly vision that made one forgive its tempestuous moods. As we descended the long ice slopes the hut came into view, our comrades saw and rushed out to welcome us. As we drew closer, we three, knit together by a great comradeship and affection, our hearts swelling with thankfulness and joy over our deliverance, gave raucous voice to the sledging song that had urged us through many trials and tribulations:

Hauling, toiling, tireless on we tramp,
O'er vast plateau, sastrugi high, o'er deep crevasse and
    ramp,
Hauling, toiling, through drift and blizzard gale,
If it has to be done—then make of it fun,
For we're men of the Southern Trail.

CHAPTER V

A MAROONING AND A RESCUE

THE reunion with our comrades and the safe return to Winter Quarters marked an epoch in our lives. What a grand place the hut seemed! To us, its untidy, grimy, dim interior rivalled the comforts of a mansion. How agreeable to hear the tones of fresh voices and listen to new themes of conversation; how delicious the banquet which Close prepared from the remnants of a meal and a few tins of preserved fruits! How cordially our palates, vitiated by the changeless greasy sledging ration, responded with relish to forgotten flavours! To walk by the sea and to hear the call of home in the prattle of the surf; to loiter among the penguins and be entertained; to look on solid black rock!

Our stern adventures on the plateau and our narrow escape had been a peerless experience, but we had had enough of peril and were resolved never again to venture into those infernal realms where the blizzard reigned King. Happy, contented and rejoiced as we were, the next day was to crown all with fresh excitement and surprises.

We were in the hut, when to our astonishment we

heard the tread of feet and the sound of strange voices in the outer verandah.   In a few moments who should enter but Captain Davis and two seamen carrying bags of mail and packages.   The *Aurora* had returned exactly to schedule, and had sailed into Commonwealth Bay during the night.   As the anchorage was not visible from the hut Davis had been able to take us completely by surprise.   To say the least, it was a sensationally happy reunion—the Great Day we had been looking forward to for many heavy months and had feared we might not live to see.   Letters and newspapers!   The first news from home, friends and the world for over a year!   It is hard to express our thoughts, sentiments and anxieties as the mails were being sorted.

We had now only to wait for the various sledging parties to put in their appearance at Winter Quarters and we would leave this blizzard-hounded desolation for ever and head back for the Sunny North and Home. The thought went to our heads like wine.

By January 18th all the parties except that which comprised Doctor Mawson, Lieutenant Ninnis and Doctor Mertz had returned.   We felt no anxieties, at the time, for the safety of the leader's party, for we knew too well the countless inevitable delays that occur on a long journey where obstacles and incessant bad weather are the daily lot.

But as day followed day and there was no sign of the absentees, we began to fear that some calamity had overtaken them.   Captain Davis instructed Mr. C. T. Madigan, who was now in charge of the Shore Station, to send out a relief party.   This party consisted of Hodgeman, Doctor McLean and myself.   We were instructed to proceed to the south-east as far as possible, to erect a series of snow mounds with rations and directional instructions on each, and to return in five days.   Before this call to duty and action, my resolutions never to tramp the plateau again, vanished: but I was determined to run no further risks of starvation and attended to our rations accordingly.

During this journey, the weather resumed hostilities, employing, it seemed, more subtle tactics for our discomfiture.   The temperature, comparatively high, had the disadvantage of making the icy surface mushy and rendering the crossing of crevasses unsafe.   As we laboured ahead, the blizzards caked us with wet drift and we continually broke through rotten snow bridges and had to be hauled from deep fissures.   Our sleeping-bags and clothes became so wet that in spite of fatigue, we preferred action in the open to the discomfort of resting and shivering in the shelter of the tent.

On the fourth day we were twenty-five miles from the hut and the weather began to clear.   We piled up a huge cairn of snow blocks and cached a bag of rations, with instructions giving the bearings and distance to the hut.   Through the glasses I then swept the horizon —limited to a range of three miles owing to mist—for signs of the missing men, but could see nothing of them. What could have happened? Had they passed us in the blizzard or had some terrible disaster befallen them? With these thoughts disturbing our minds we turned back. With the wind behind us, we made a speedy march, and gained the hut during the evening of the fifth day. But Doctor Mawson and his two comrades had not put in an appearance.

While we had been away, Captain Davis had re-provisioned Winter Quarters and a party had been selected to remain for the second year to search for the missing men, should such a dire necessity arise. Doctor McLean and Messrs. Bage, Hodgeman, Bickerton and Jeffryes under the charge of Mr. C. T. Madigan, formed this gallant little band.

Meanwhile Captain Davis made a final search in the *Aurora* along the East Coast but his voyage proved fruitless and on January 31st he returned to pick up those of us who were returning to Australia. But the Antarctic, it seemed, was reluctant to release us, and determined to give one more taste of its quality. A strong wind was blowing at the time, making the seas too choppy to send off the motor launch, so the *Aurora* was forced to cruise up and down the coast waiting for a lull. But lull there was none. Instead the wind rapidly increased, and for a week, maintained blizzard velocity. At times the gusts rose to ninety miles per hour and, smiting the sea, lashed it white, tore off the crests and whirled them in clouds of spuming fury. We stood in the shelter of the rocks and gazed anxiously across the seething bay to the fighting *Aurora* painfully conscious of the desperate plight of those aboard, and of the perils that menaced them in the reef strewn waters. For hours she would remain lost to sight. Then, as we strained our eyes, we would see her emerging from the driving spindrift, white, encased in frozen spray—a spectral ship looming through the hurricane.

We had absolute confidence that if seamanship could save the vessel Captain Davis and his crew would succeed in riding out the storm. Fortunately the nights had not yet grown totally dark, but in the feeble afterglow, the desolate prospect from our lookout, with the winds shrieking round us, over an inferno of scudding snow and hurtling spray, was enough to make the stoutest heart despair. Could the ship, engulfed in the callous gloom, live till morning? As the light increased our anxieties and fears would be dispelled by the gladdening sight of the little vessel re-appearing through the sea-smoke. Our prayers and thoughts sped with the winds to Captain Davis and his men in their struggle.

On the seventh day, the blizzard suddenly moderated and, as if utterly fatigued by its mad riot, an unruffled calm followed. Davis had won. The *Aurora* steamed in towards the boat harbour and the launch came ashore. Those of us who were leaving for home made our farewells and set off for the ship.

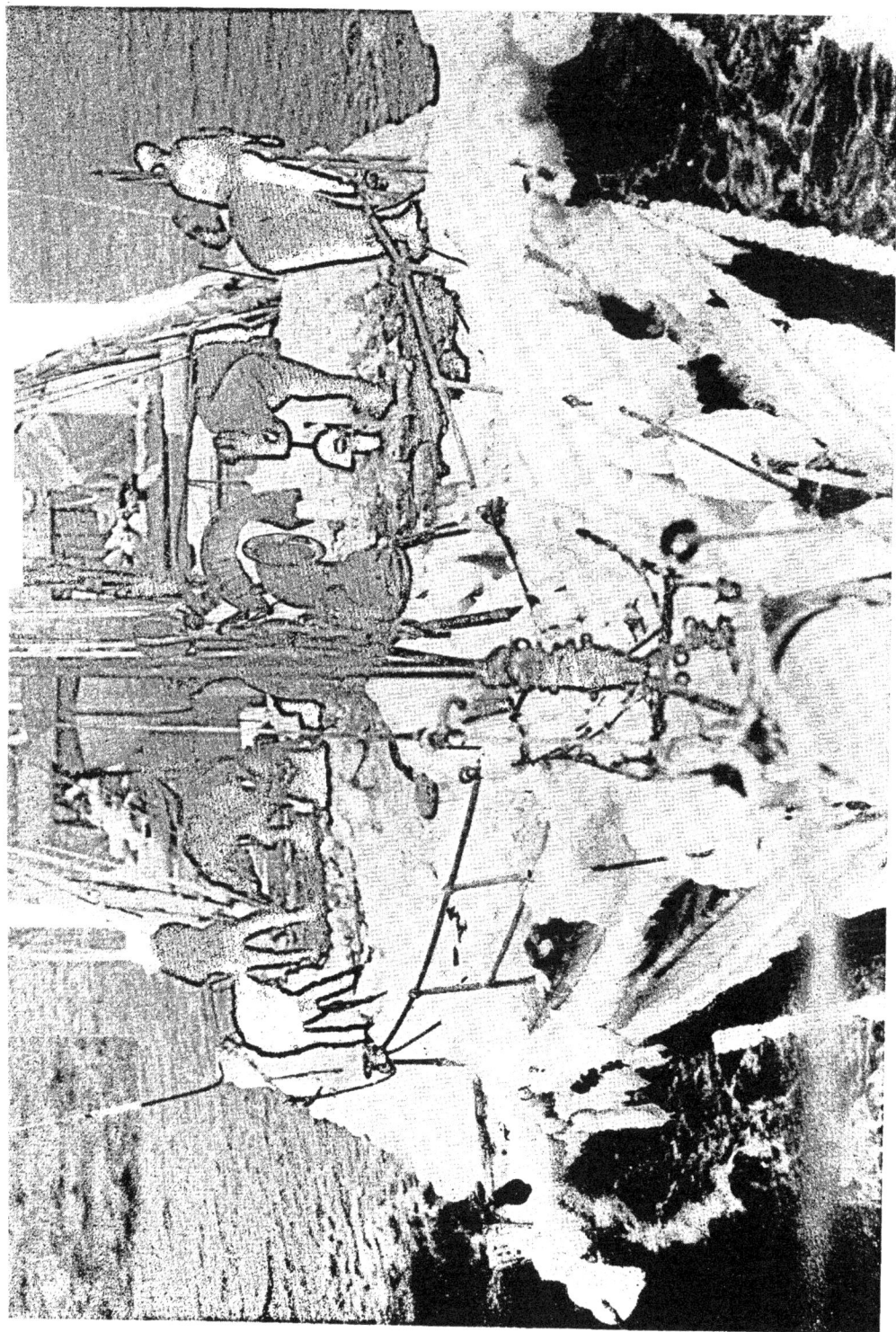

Doomed to spend another year, outcasts in this barren land, our sympathies went out to the six heroic fellows who stood on the icefoot and waved across the growing expanse.

As we drew alongside the *Aurora* we admired her grim iceclad beauty, which told of the rigorous times those aboard had passed through. From masthead to waterline she was sheathed in ice; ropes and spars were draped with icicles that crashed from aloft on to ice-clad decks as they thawed in the warm sunshine. On the furrowed faces of Captain Davis and the crew was written an epic of struggle. Davis did not speak of the ordeal, but I afterwards learned that he had not left the bridge throughout the seven racking days and nights.

"Full speed ahead" was rung down to the engine-room. As we drew away from the land six tiny specks were seen waving from a rocky summit—soon to be swallowed up in the vastness of the solitude.

Our thoughts turned to our missing leader and his companions. They were twenty-four days overdue. What could have happened?

Before us now lay a perilous voyage to relieve the men at our second Antarctic Base—Frank Wild who with his party of seven had been landed a year ago on a precarious floating barrier 1500 miles to the west. The season was far advanced; the vessel's coal supply was running low. If we were to effect the rescue, it would be necessary to steam at full speed day and night to reach the party before the seas froze over and imprisoned the men for another year.

Hannam had rigged up an aerial and wireless receiver on board the *Aurora*, and had arranged with Jeffryes, the wireless operator of the party left behind, to call the ship up at definite intervals.

At 8.30 P.M. the same evening, he received a message from the Main Base.

Mawson returned: Ninnis and Mertz dead: return immediately and pick up all hands.

The news was a terrible shock but the suspense and anxiety of the past three weeks was ended.   The ship's head was turned back at once to the Main Base and we hoped fervently that the favourable weather would continue.   But our hopes were doomed to disappointment.

The *Aurora* re-entered Commonwealth Bay in a freshening breeze which, as we neared the shore, developed into a blizzard.   The pilot-jack, our pre-arranged signal announcing Doctor Mawson's return, was flying off the wireless mast.   But nobody was in sight.   It was impossible to launch a boat in the boiling sea, so once again the *Aurora* steamed to and fro in the lee of the ice cliffs hoping that the weather might quieten even for a brief half hour.   Towards evening the wind became so violent that the ship began to fall away and become unsteerable although the engines were doing their maximum revolutions.   We observed that the wake of the ship was passing its bows at a rapid rate. We were drifting helplessly into the reef strewn bay. With the barometer falling and the blizzard increasing from bad to worse, not only was the safety of the ship and those aboard involved, but possibly the lives of Wild and his men who were depending on the *Aurora* to rescue them. I quote Captain Davis's words on this grave crisis:

I felt that decisive action was necessary. The position was very difficult, as a sense of discipline and obedience to orders urged me to remain, leaving the responsibility on the Leader who had called us back, but duty urged me to take prompt action, and I decided to proceed west for the following reasons:—

1. Dr. Mawson and his comrades were safely housed and fully equipped for the coming winter.

2. Any further delay was seriously endangering our chance of being able to relieve Mr. Wild's party this season. The Navigation of the Western Base (1,500 miles distant) was becoming daily more difficult on account of the increasing length of the nights and the conditions of the ice.

3. The only vessel, *The Gauss*, that had wintered in the vicinity of Wild's Base had been frozen in on February 22nd. The *Aurora* was not provisioned for a winter in the ice.

4. From the records at the Main Base, it had been ascertained that gales often lasted for many days at the close of the short summer season. We had just weathered one lasting seven days.

5. As a seaman, I realised the difficulties encountered approaching Wild's Base the previous year; and also in getting away from it. It was now three weeks later in the year.

I went down to the wardroom and announced my decision to the officers. I invited them to suggest any

alternative measures, but none were forthcoming. At
6.30 P.M. we hoisted the flag and dipped it as a sign that
we were leaving.[1]

We scanned the shore through the blinding spray
and again observed no one. At least our comrades were
saved the mortification of seeing the ship head away
through the storm that doomed them to another year of
exile.

For the next fourteen days we headed west through
a belt of storm, packice and dense fog that hung in a
murky pall over the sea. Under both steam and sail
we hurried with all possible speed, tempting Fate and
taking chances, for if we loitered, the freezing sea might
trap and grip us in its clutch. Wild and his men we
knew would be anxiously waiting; their provisions
would be running low and we were already three
weeks overdue.

During the day it was impossible to see through
the sheeting snow and mist more than a few hundred
yards, and when darkness fell we seemed to be rushing
into black nothing whence shapes of bergs came looming like ghostly apparitions. Two men were sta-
tioned on the fo'c'stle, staring ahead, hailing a warning to the officer on watch, as the ice came dimly into
view. On one occasion a faint blink suddenly suffused
the darkness. The watchers on the fo'c'stle called
"ice ahead," then—"ice on the starboard bow," then—

---

[1] *With the " Aurora " in the Antarctic*, John K. Davis, page 98.

"ice on the port bow," three warnings in as many seconds.

The helm was put hard over, the ship swung just in the nick of time, and hit the ice a glancing blow. It towered in a nebulous wall above our masts and barred the way. We proceeded slowly, following the loom of its shape, hearing the hollow rumbling of the sea in caverns, and the sinister growling of the surf over its foot. We steamed half a mile before the ship could be turned on to course again. The *Aurora* had been heading at full speed for the centre of an enormous berg.

But a region even more dangerous was yet to come— the dread sea of icebergs. As we entered its outskirts, for once the weather was cloudless. Thousands of mighty bergs were grounded on a vast shoal and our way lay through their midst. No grander sight have I ever witnessed among the wonders of Antarctica. We threaded a way down lanes of vivid blue with shimmering walls of mammoth bergs rising like castles of jade on either side. Countless blue canals branched off and led through what appeared to be avenues of marble skyscrapers—dazzling white in the full sunshine. Waves had weathered out impressive portals and gigantic caverns in their gleaming sides, azure at the entrance and gradually fading into rich cobalt in their remote depths. Festoons of icicles sparkling like crystal pendants, draped ledges and arches.

We glided on; the silence broken only by the purling at our bows and the boom and echo of dislodged fragments falling into the waters. We were indeed running the gauntlet; at any moment those unstable walls might cave and precipitate thousands of tons of ice about us. Many of the passages we threaded were mere narrow canyons, two hundred feet wide with precipitous faces towering two hundred feet above our decks. Heavy fog shut down again during the afternoon and in the gloom we were unable to distinguish the pale bergs more than a ship's length away. So well were they concealed in the mist and with such unexpected suddenness did they reveal themselves that it was impossible to avoid collisions and the ship received many bumps. With deepening darkness navigation became so perilous that all waited on deck, ready in case of emergency. It seemed beyond human power to grope a way through this accursed maze in fog and darkness with only pallid shadows to guide us. Yet we moved ahead—miraculously avoiding disaster—as though piloted and protected by a Higher Intelligence.

Glorious dawn came at last and Captain Davis headed in towards the land. We skirted along the sea face of majestic ice cliffs until we entered a bay that marked the site of Wild's Winter Quarters.

As we steamed nearer one of the sailors called out excitedly, "There they are!" Sure enough there was a group of little black specks moving about in the distance; but we could count only seven—there should have been eight.

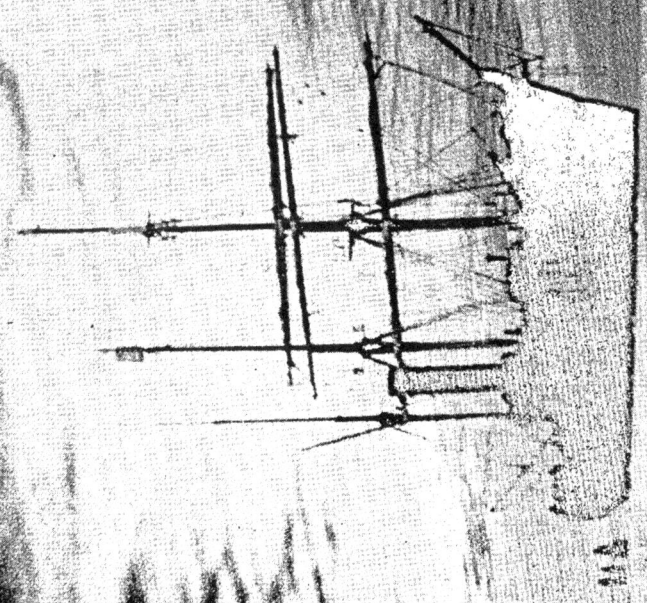

The adventure of Polar Exploration adds considerably to the instabilities of life, and the relieving of a party is always a time of uneasiness and tension.

To our relief we discovered the "seven specks" to be Emperor Penguins: they did indeed resemble a party of men in the uncertain light.

A little later Mr. de la Motte who was on the lookout in the crow's nest aloft called down to Captain Davis, "I can nearly see the hut, Sir." Captain Davis, who always demanded precise and explicit expressions, replied:

"What the devil do you mean, Sir. You can either see the hut or you cannot see the hut."

"I can see a flag at the top of the Wireless Mast, Sir," responded de la Motte.

"Then why the Hell didn't you say so, Sir!"

De la Motte made no reply but there was much chuckling from those on deck. Wild's hut was hidden by the brink of the cliffs and could not be seen from the sea. As we neared the head of the bight we observed men standing on the bay ice beneath the cliffs, awaiting us.

As we drew up alongside the floe, someone on the fo'c'stle shouted, "Are you all well?" Wild cheerfully called back, "Yes, all well, and glad to see you. Is everything right at Main Base?" There was silence —none would speak the bad news. Later when the party had clambered aboard, Captain Davis read the tragic wireless message that told of the sad disaster in Adelie Land.

By evening the scientific collections, stores and miscellaneous gear were embarked and a quantity of ice taken on board for fresh water. A quaint touch was given to the loading operations by the arrival of a large number of Emperor Penguins. They hopped from the open water in "follow-my-leader" procession and waddled in stately file towards the vessel like a queue of inquisitive sightseers. They bowed politely to everyone and everything and took a keen interest in what was going on.

The *Aurora* turned north in the calm dusk, farewelled by our penguin friends who swam and dived about the vessel. Early next morning we re-entered the sea of bergs, but the good weather held, and the Providential Hand, which had already protected us through countless dangers, piloted our vessel safely through ice-packed seas to the great waters that rolled wild and free towards the north.

The homeward passage was rough though joyous. There was so much to discuss and so many experiences to exchange that time and our vessel rolled merrily and happily on.

Like ourselves, Wild's party had contended with a despicable climate, but in spite of all handicaps, they had carried out their programme of research and discovery.

On March 15th we arrived at Hobart, Tasmania,

and so terminated our sixteen months' wanderings. As we sailed up the Derwent, the sunlit scene looked intensely hospitable and inviting. How homely it all seemed—brown rock, green grass, flowers and wooded slopes—above all it was warm and calm. Our bleak environment had almost erased from our memories the charm of a civilised landscape. At last the outskirts of Hobart city were reached; then the town—buildings—people—life. The wharf was crammed with old friends, waiting to welcome us home. As we drew near there was a babel of greetings: familiar faces smiled up from the pier. The gangway was lowered —then the handshakes and embraces! Just how the blood stirs and the heart throbs on such occasions must be experienced to be understood. But mingled with the joy of our return came the thought of the men we had left behind. Our job was not finished until we had returned to rescue them. The earliest date at which it would be possible for a ship to reach Adelie Land would be the beginning of the following Summer.

CHAPTER VI

THE RELIEF OF MAWSON

EIGHT months later found me at Hobart aboard the *Aurora* steaming down the Derwent bound once again to the south. Correll and Hunter, who had been members of the first Expedition, were also on board and of course Captain Davis was in command. The first days were filled with stories of our "holidays" in civilisation. Mine had been unique. An opportunity presenting a dramatic contrast had knocked at my door and a few weeks after my return home to Sydney I had been commissioned to secure a series of moving pictures illustrating the Dutch Indies, a region that by a coincidence lies as many degrees north of Sydney as Adelie Land lies south.

In a few brief weeks I thus jumped out of the Antarctic Circle, to the Equator. A temperature of 70 degrees below freezing point was exchanged for a heat of over a hundred degrees in the shade. The appalling silence of the white and unpeopled South gave place to the clamour of the colourful and teeming East. In Adelie Land one placed a single figure in a landscape to emphasise its vast emptiness; in Java with its population of millions, one fought the crowd that swarmed round the camera when a picture had to be filmed. Yet never in the Antarctic expanses did I feel quite so lonely as when making my way through crowded Java with an assistant who could speak but half a dozen words of English.

Six months were occupied in this Javanese expedition. It was a quaint parenthesis in polar adventures—an interlude which certainly gave me an opportunity to thaw the ice out of my marrow and store up sunshine in my blood in preparation for further Antarctic rigours. Central Java was the nearest approach to an oven that I have ever experienced.

A curious incident had happened on the return journey from Java. We touched at the Papuan township of Port Moresby and on visiting the wireless station I was surprised and delighted to find that the operator in charge was one of the members of the little group we had left behind on Macquarie Island a year and a half before. Moreover, by a strange coincidence he had just managed to catch a wireless message, relayed by the Macquarie Station from Mawson's party in Adelie Land, and had learned that all was well with them. Swifter than the wireless itself my thoughts had sped to the snowbound hut where Mawson and his comrades awaited the return of Summer and the *Aurora*.

Now, we were assembled on that stout vessel, outward bound on our mission of deliverance, the constellation of the Southern Cross before us inspiring hope and guiding us. The white ducks of the tropics had been doffed: the time was come to don the Burberrys and the fur-lined mitts.

We rolled down, under skies that grew day by day steadily more leaden and unfriendly as we moved through the Roaring Forties once again. Yet the seas treated us compassionately—or perhaps it was that we had grown indifferent to ordinary storms and bad weather and even felt a little elated when the elements frowned.

At last the steely blink of the icefields gleamed, and the jostle and scrunch of the pack sounded good to our ears as once more we butted through.

On January 13 we entered Commonwealth Bay. The sun was shining brightly over the glistening slopes that lead up to the plateau as if in welcome, as it had done when first we had glimpsed these shores. We looked towards the distant line where ice and sky combined. Beyond, over a thousand miles of untrodden snow extended to the Pole. Past hardships were forgotten. There came an impulse to tramp again "The vast and God-like Spaces."

One familiar scene after another came into view. But there was a new feature that struck a note of tragedy. A cross stood out against the rising slopes of the inland ice dominating the landscape. It had been erected by our comrades we discovered later.

To Commemorate the Supreme Sacrifice made by Lieut. B. E. S. Ninnis R. F. and Dr. X. Mertz in the cause of Science.

We drew up to the old anchorage in the lee of the ice-cliffs, the whale boat was lowered and we rowed for the shore. Feelings of suspense and anxiety crept into our minds. So far there had been no signs of life. We knew only too well the hazards of a winter in Adelie Land. Anything might have happened. Were we about to raise the curtain on a scene of tragedy? But we banished these pessimistic thoughts for the ship had arrived in advance of the date on which she was expected and moreover the hour was yet early.

We landed and tramped towards the hut. To our relief the door opened, and Dr. Mawson strolled out and saw us. Nothing ever astonished Mawson; he just grinned at us with a sparkling eye. There was no rhetorical flourish in his greeting. "Halloa," he said. "Back again"—as casually as if we had merely returned from an excursion between breakfast and dinner.

Turning he called to those inside the hut, "Halloa, you chaps, the boat is here." It was good to hear his voice. The others came tumbling out. We cannot be blamed if our hearts filled with sentiment and if tears of gladness filled our eyes. Such reunions awaken feelings too deep to be expressed.

The weather continued mild for several days and we were able to make excursions in the *Aurora* to neighbouring rocky outcrops that had attracted the party from Winter Quarters. All these locations without exception were teeming with penguins and bird life. One of them named after Hunter, the biologist, was the site of a huge rookery of Antarctic Petrels. This was the first time one of their nesting places had been discovered. The birds crammed the ledges and crannies in thousands and took no heed of us. Man had never disturbed them before, and they were fearless. It was possible to approach and even to stroke them while they nested.

Meanwhile preparations for the return of the Expedition went forward busily. By December 24th the personnel, dogs and stores had been embarked aboard the *Aurora*. We had intended spending the last Christmas Day ashore but the wish was unfulfilled—a repetition of our experience at Macquarie Island two years previously. From early morning rapidly moving nimbus clouds and snow whirls were observed eddying over the plateau, a sign which portended a break in the weather. The Antarctic was tuning up for a performance. We had not long to wait.

By 10 A.M. the wind swept down in a succession of terrific gusts which attained a velocity of seventy miles an hour. By noon the land was hidden by the flying spray and a terrific hurricane was raging. During a mighty gust, we felt a violent shock and our anchor began dragging; the stock had been wrenched off. The ship rapidly drifted from the lee of the cliffs out into the wind-whipped surges. The towering rollers reached the motor boat and tore it and one of the davits from the ship. The wreckage was cut adrift

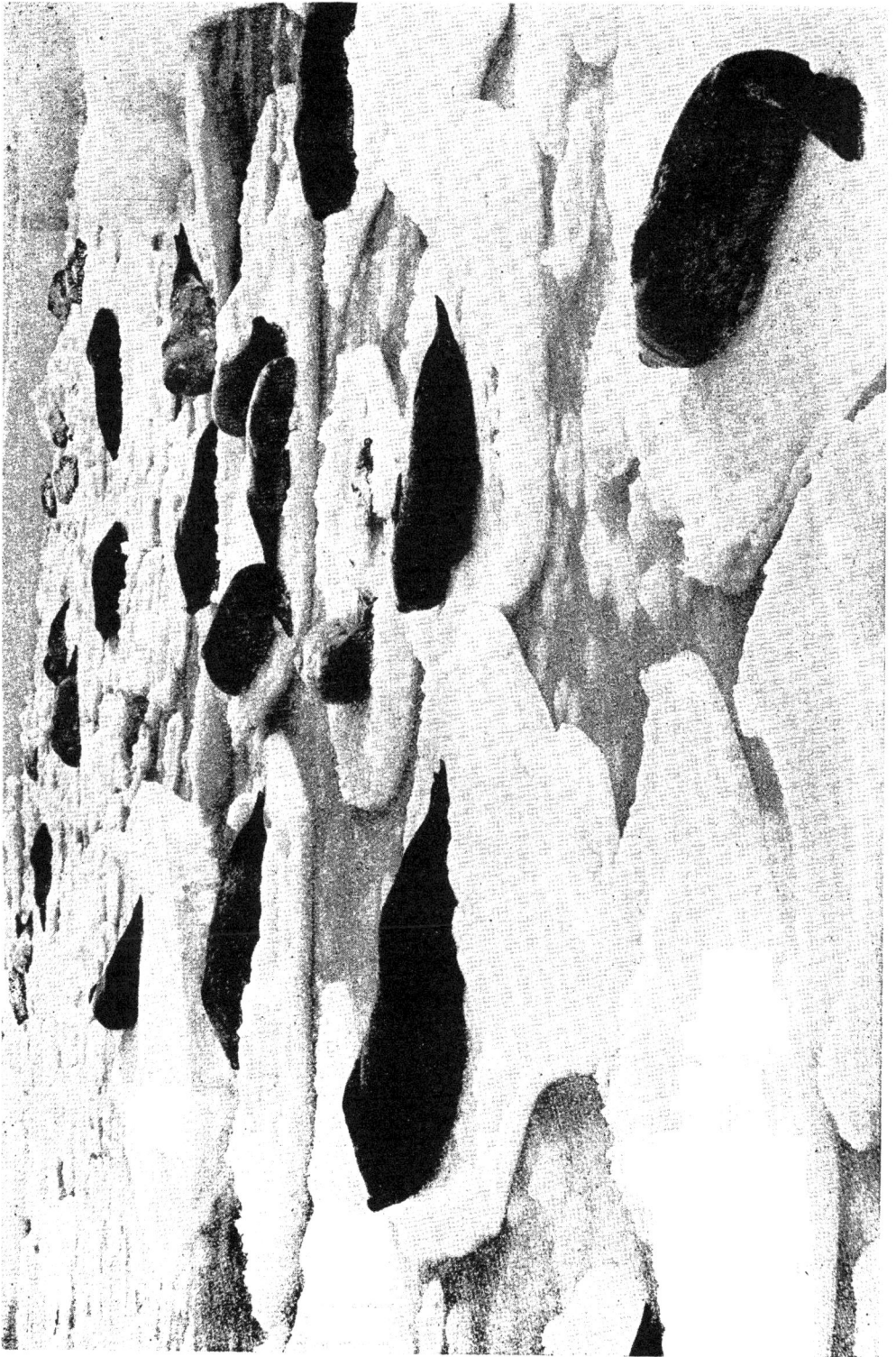

and the motor boat disappeared, the weight of the davit dragging it, nose down, beneath the waves. After great difficulty the anchor chain was hauled in and the sailors on the fo'c'stle head were doing their best to make the anchor fast. It was a dangerous job in the high seas which swept over them, as the *Aurora* dived her bows under, and sheathed herself with ice. We had great admiration for the seamen, who seemed inspired by Captain Davis who always rose supreme on these occasions, although he treated them merely as incidents in the day's work.

As we headed away, the shriek of the wind rose to an awful scream, as though summoning all its furious energies in a crescendo of farewell.

We gained the last glimpse of Winter Quarters and the cross that stood out like a lonely sentinel, telling of the sad toll the wild had exacted. Near the entrance to Commonwealth Bay we ran out of the blizzard though it continued to rage over the land. On several occasions it had been noticed that the storms attained their maximum violence in the proximity of the shore and steadily decreased until, ten miles out, conditions were normal.

An extended cruise was embarked upon in the direction of Wild's old base, the object being to explore and map the coast in detail, and carry out oceanographical research. Though the ice-packs were more scattered, bergs were much more numerous than on the previous voyage. They were of the characteristic table-top type, vast masses of barrier ice that had broken adrift, with vertical cliffs rising high above the sea. Many were gigantic in area; the longest encountered measured forty miles! This stupendous floating island, whose sheer coasts were serrated into bays, inlets and capes, rose to one hundred and fifty feet in height. The sea had eaten innumerable caverns in its massive sides—one, a magnificent gothic portal of deep azure, one hundred feet high, spanned a channel of gently swaying indigo waters that flowed into the gloom of deep recesses.

In the leisure hours of this last cruise we learned something of the privations of those who had remained in Adelie Land during the second year, and Doctor Mawson told us of the tragic fate which had befallen our two comrades Lieutenant Ninnis and Doctor Mertz.

His story took me back in memory to a well-remembered day. After Bage, Webb and myself had taken farewell of him and his two comrades at Five Mile Depot on our outward journey to the Magnetic Pole, the three set out with two dog teams to explore the coast extending to the south-east of Winter Quarters. Their journey was mostly over fields of crevasses and through ceaseless blizzards; but in spite of these gruelling conditions they reached a point three hundred miles distant from the hut. As they continued, the weather and the surface began to improve. Relieved, they imagined they had left the region of nightmare crevasses. Then came a fateful day. The weather was bright and sunny and they started off in the highest spirits. Mertz was on skis well ahead in the lead, breaking trail. Doctor Mawson followed with his dog team and Ninnis brought up the rear with the second team.

Mertz signalled by holding up his ski-stick that there was a crevasse. On reaching the spot, Doctor Mawson noticed a faint indication of a fissure but it did not appear specially dangerous. He crossed without incident. When he next looked round in response to a second signal from Mertz, it was to find that Ninnis and his team were nowhere to be seen. What had happened? Hastening back along the trail they came to a gaping hole. Two sledge tracks led up to it but only one continued on the other side.

I take the liberty of quoting Doctor Mawson's own description as given in his book *The Home of the Blizzard* of the tragedy that had come upon them.

Frantically waving to Mertz to bring up my sledge, upon which there was some alpine rope, I leaned over and shouted into the dark depths below. No sound came back but the moaning of a dog, caught on a shelf just visible one hundred and fifty feet below. The poor creature appeared to have broken its back, for it was attempting to sit up with the front part of its body while the hinder portion lay limp. Another dog lay motionless by its side. Close by was what appeared in the gloom to be the remains of the tent and a canvas tank containing food for three men for a fortnight.

We broke back the edge of the névé lid and took turns leaning over secured by a rope, calling into the darkness in the hope that our companion might be still alive. For three hours we called unceasingly but no answering sound came back. The dog had ceased to moan and lay without a movement. A chill draught was blowing out of the abyss. We felt that there was little hope. . . . By means of a fishing line we ascertained that it was one hundred and fifty feet sheer to the ledge on which the remains were seen; on either side the crevasse descended into blackness. It seemed so very far down there and the dogs looked so small that we got out the field glasses, but could make out nothing more by their aid. . . . Stunned by the unexpectedness of it all and having exhausted the few appliances we carried for such a contingency, we felt helpless. In such moments action is the only tolerable thing, and if there had been any expedient however hazardous which might have been tried, we should have taken all and more than the risk. Stricken dumb with the pity of it and heavy at heart, we turned our minds mechanically to what lay nearest at hand.

There were rations on the other sledge, and we found that there was a bare one and a half weeks' food for ourselves and nothing at all for the dogs. . . . We returned to the crevasse and packed the remaining sledge, discarding everything unnecessary so as to reduce the weight of the load. A thin soup was made by boiling up all the old food-bags which could be found. The dogs were given some worn-out fur mitts, finnesko and several spare rawhide straps, all of which they devoured.

We still continued to call down into the crevasse at regular intervals in case our companion might not have been killed outright and, in the meantime, have become conscious. There was no reply.

A weight was lowered on the fishing line as far as the dog which had earlier shown some signs of life, but there was no response. All were dead, swallowed up in an instant. . . . At 9 P.M. we stood by the side of the crevasse and I read the burial service. Then Mertz shook me by the hand with a short "Thank you!" and we turned away to harness up the dogs.

Before them lay 300 miles of fearful country over which the shadow of death brooded. If the weather continued fine, there was a bare possibility that they might win through.

During four weeks the two men fought their way back towards Winter Quarters, subsisting on the barest ration that would support life. One after another the dogs were killed, the bodies cut up and given to the survivors; the choicest parts were kept and eaten by the two desperate men. As every drop of kerosene for the Primus stove had to be conserved with miserly care, they were only able to half cook the meat, which held very little nutriment as the dogs were almost starved themselves.

Endeavouring to cheer and console one another in their awful plight, the two comrades plugged on over the most hellish land in the world, painfully decreasing the distance until they found themselves within one hundred miles of the hut. Of the agonies of the terrible two hundred miles they had travelled Doctor Mawson hardly spoke, but starvation had reduced them to mere skeletons, the skin was peeling from their bodies, and where their clothes chafed the withering flesh, horrible sores had broken out. Yet, remorseless, the Antarctic was to claim another victim. Poor Mertz could go no further and after a succession of fits, collapsed.

During the afternoon he had several more fits, then became delirious and talked incoherently until midnight when he appeared to fall into a peaceful slumber. So 1 toggled up the sleeping-bag and retired worn out into my own. After a couple of hours, having felt no movement from my companion, I stretched out an arm and found that he was stiff.

Late on the evening of 8th I took the body of Mertz, wrapped up in his sleeping-bag, outside the tent, piled snow blocks around it and raised a rough cross made of the two half-runners of the sledge.[1]

Left alone, his two companions dead, the leader in anguish of mind and body stumbled away to face the last hundred miles—a fearful solitary journey. His rations were nearly exhausted, and his emaciated body almost refused to obey the impulse of his will as he staggered along.

Crevasse lids collapsed and he fell into chasms but, by some miraculous act of Providence, the sledge he was hauling always became locked in the holes through which he had fallen, his sledging harness held and he was able to clamber out.

When he was almost at the last gasp a miracle happened. Again I quote his written words.

I was travelling along on an even down grade wondering how long the two pounds of food which remained would

[1] Mawson's *Home of the Blizzard*, page 259, vol. 1.

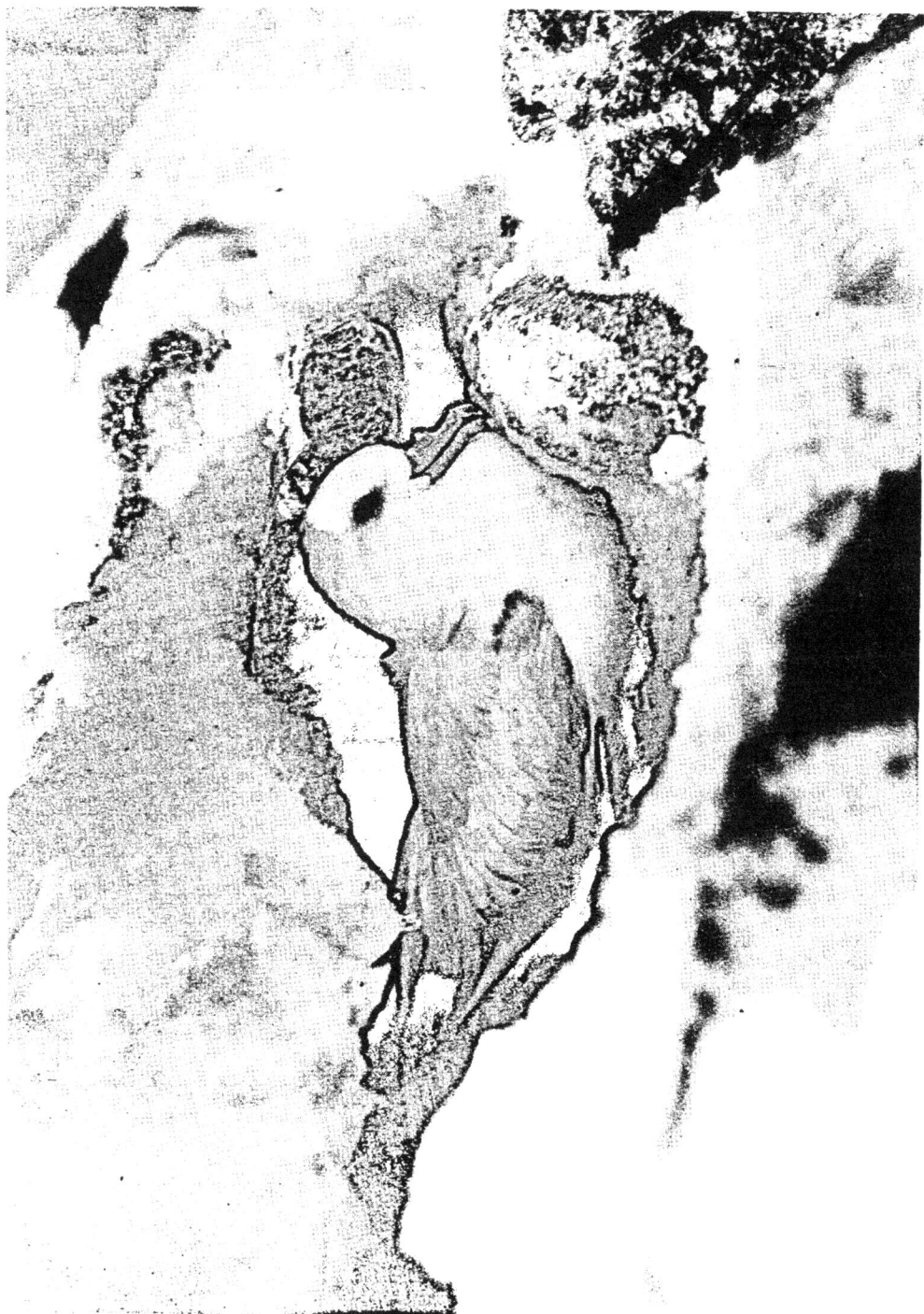

last, when something dark loomed through the drift a short distance to the right. All sorts of possibilities fled through my mind as I headed the sledge for it. The unexpected happened—it was a cairn of snow erected by McLean, Hodgeman and Hurley, who had been out searching for us. On the top of the mound was a bag of food, left on the chance that it might be picked up, while in a tin was a note stating the bearing and distance of the Mound from Aladdin's Cave—(E. 30° S., distance 23 miles)—that the ship had arrived at the Hut and was waiting. . . .

It was rather a singular fact that the search party only left this mound at eight o'clock on the morning of that very day (January 29). It was 2 P. M. when I found it. Thus, during the night of the 28th our camps had only been five miles apart.[1]

As we heard the story from Mawson's own lips well did I remember piling up that cairn. Had only the weather been clear when I swept the horizon with the glasses I would have seen the tent in which he was resting! When we left the cairn a blizzard had started.

What power had directed the lone man, in the hour of his direst need, to that Cairn of Salvation, which could only be seen but a few feet away in the snow drift?

After resting a few days while the food enabled him to regain a little strength, he reached Aladdin's Cave (Five Mile Depot) and late in the afternoon began the descent to the hut. As he drew closer he eagerly scanned the bay for signs of the *Aurora*. Even as he gazed, he noticed far away on the northern horizon a

[1] *Home of the Blizzard*, p. 269.

tiny speck with a trail of smoke behind it. The *Aurora* had departed for home but two hours previously!

Such was Mawson's story first told to us in quiet watches in the brooding silence of the Antarctic while the ship threaded her way through pack and berg-strewn waters.

After three weeks we headed finally for home.

Our last view of the pack was unforgettable. In the glow of the midnight sun it looked ineffably beautiful. As I stood on the poop watching the showers of golden spray dash on the sun-gilt walls of the last outpost—a giant berg—a great longing filled me: a longing to spend a season in the pack to study it in all its unearthly glories and terrible moods. It was an outrageous wish, yet it was to be fulfilled!

Our arrival at Adelaide, Dr. Mawson's home, was a scene of great enthusiasm and hospitality which was tinged for us with sadness by the memory of the two sterling fellows who were not there to participate in it. Adelaide marked the termination and disbanding of the Expedition. It was with deep regret that we said "good-bye" to one another. Intimate association and the stern code of the South had bound us with the ties of a brotherhood. When I turn South again may my comrades be such characters as the men of the Australasian Antarctic Expedition.

No words of mine can do justice to Sir Douglas Mawson, to his judgment in choosing his men, his care for their welfare and the resourcefulness and courage with which he inspired them. Those who lived with him through long tedious months in the blizzard-smitten South looked up to him not only as a leader but loved him as a comrade and a man.

CHAPTER VII

THE ANTARCTIC CALLS AGAIN

Yes, they're wanting me, they're haunting me, the awful lonely places:
They're whining and they're whimpering as if each had a soul;
They're calling from the wilderness, the vast and the god-like spaces,
The stark and sullen solitudes that sentinel the Pole.

ROBERT W. SERVICE.

AFTER life in the vastness of a vacant Continent, civilisation seemed disappointingly narrow, cramped, superficial and empty. A couple of weeks of it sufficed to bring on an attack of wander fever.

Once again the call came from the Tropical North. I fitted out a small Expedition to the little known territory of North Australia and set out on the long trail from Sydney in motor cars, bound for the sun-scorched shores of the Gulf of Carpentaria. Mud, malaria, and mosquitoes constituted our environment for many months.

Man is a discontented creature. When he is hot he wants to be cold and when he is cold he wants to be hot. Often my thoughts wandered back to the white South where the atmosphere, though mightily bleak, was certainly pure. There it was possible—occasion-

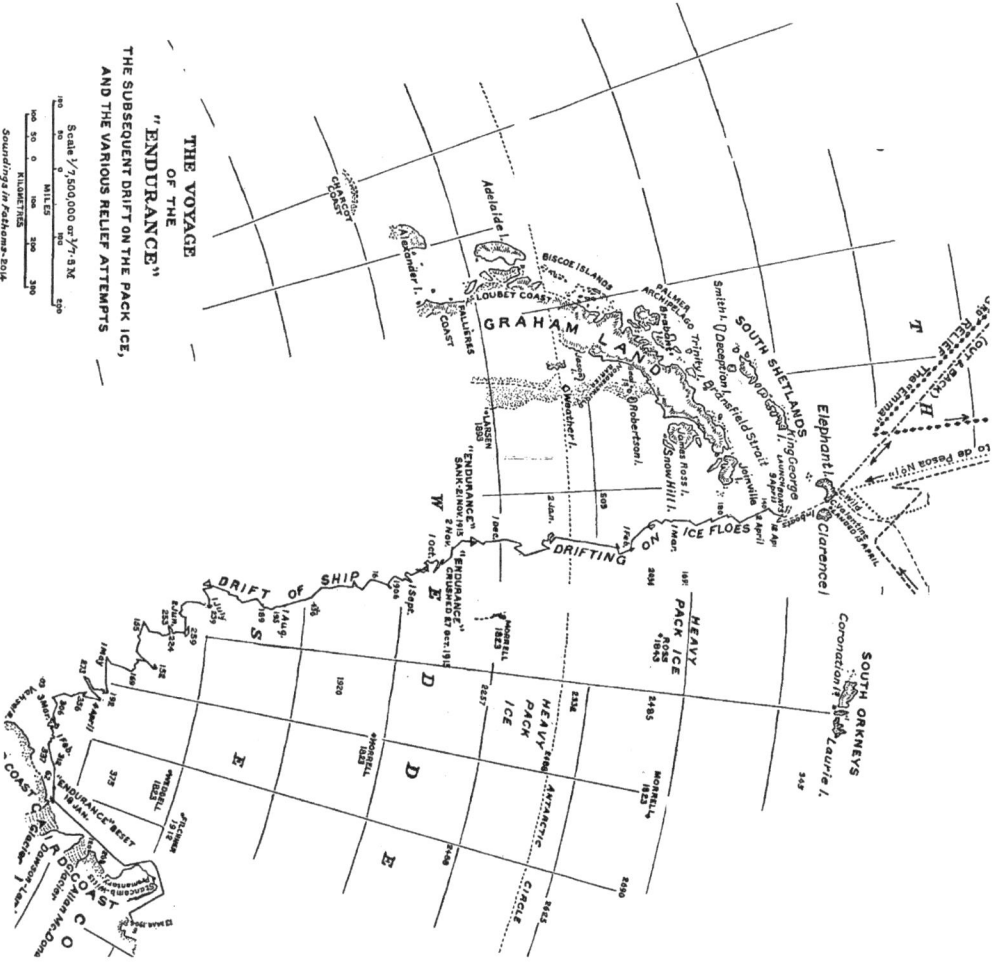

THE VOYAGE
OF THE
"ENDURANCE"
THE SUBSEQUENT DRIFT ON THE PACK ICE,
AND THE VARIOUS RELIEF ATTEMPTS

Scale 1/7,500,000 or 1"/118 M.

MILES

KILOMETRES

Soundings in Fathoms-2014.

ally—to get warm, but on the shores of Carpentaria it was utterly impossible to get cool. Nights and days were like the breath of a furnace and, a great contrast to the sterile South, swarmed with myriad forms of insect life. We were irritated with all sorts of creeping, biting parasites. Sweltering at nights I longed for the South again.

One day I had occasion to run into Burketown—a small remote outpost—for supplies. It possessed a telegraph station and there I was handed a sealed letter marked "Urgent Cable." Opening and reading it, I could only express myself in spasmodic and disjointed exclamations. Good Heavens! A surprise? Nay—a miracle! Could it be possible? It was a cable from London! A cable from Sir Ernest Shackleton, offering me the post of official photographer on his forthcoming Expedition! Would I accept! Would I?—rather!!

It was the work of a few hours to strike camp on the banks of the Nicholson River and commence the return over the rough trail to civilisation. I had no misgivings about accepting Sir Ernest's offer although I had not the slightest idea what the trip might involve beyond the knowledge that it was a Polar Expedition. The spell of uncharted seas, the lure of the South, and the glamour of Polar adventure called irresistibly.

The cable intimated that I should join the party at Buenos Ayres in six weeks' time. It meant motoring back over some two thousand miles of bush tracks and voyaging halfway across the world—a race against Time.

Save for occasional pauses to take on fuel and supplies, I hastened night and day to Sydney and arrived to find that a steamer was leaving for South America in a few days.

Crossing the Pacific, I voyaged by way of Cape Horn, and was welcomed at Buenos Ayres by the members of the Shackleton party who had arrived from England but two days previously. I was forthwith introduced to the Expedition's vessel *Endurance*, where I at once took up my station and began activities.

In comparison with Mawson's sturdy and powerful ship *Aurora*, the *Endurance*, at first glance, appeared light and frail, but, upon going below decks and investigating, I was gratified to find a mighty frame of oak and hull of massive pine and greenheart. She was built by Christensen, the famous Norwegian constructor, originally for tourist work in the Arctic and, in consequence, was provided with more comfortable accommodation than the *Aurora*, which was built for sealing. She was approximately 350 tons burden; barquentine rigged and capable of steaming up to ten knots. The *Endurance*, festive in fresh paint, radiant in her dress of spotless sails, was a creature of elegance and shapely beauty. She was embarking on her first voyage—a bride of the sea.

My first impression of the men with whom I was to be intimately associated for the duration of the Expedition was pleasing and gratifying. They were a genial and lusty crowd of young fellows, mostly from Oxford and Cambridge, and differed from my comrades of the Australasian Antarctic Expedition only in accent and manner.

Frank Wild, my old comrade of the Mawson Expedition, was the second in command, and briefly outlined to me the objects and plans.

From Buenos Ayres we were to proceed to the sub-Antarctic Island of South Georgia and, after re-coaling at one of the whaling stations, the *Endurance* was to push southward through the pack-ice to the head of the Weddell Sea. There a base would be established and the scientific party landed. This unknown quadrant was to be extensively explored, and a party of five members would be chosen to accompany the leader in an eighteen hundred mile sledge-journey across the Antarctic Continent, via the South Pole to the Ross Sea. In the meantime, the *Aurora*, which Sir Ernest Shackleton had purchased from the Mawson Expedition, would sail from New Zealand to the Ross Sea and pick up this trans-continental party. It was a plan that only a daring leader with wide vision and strong faith in his ability to inspire and endure would conceive. Those were the qualities that suggested themselves when I met Sir Ernest Shackleton for the first time, and those were the qualities which were continually impressed upon me as time progressed.

Shorter by half a head than Sir Douglas Mawson, in many other ways he bore little resemblance to my former leader. His square chin, strong face, with its masterly nose, and broad brows, was in sharp contrast to the finely-chiseled features of the Australian, whose high forehead and longish chin made the face appear narrow and thin. They had some characteristics in common. Both possessed the fearless, indomitable will of the born leader. Both were strong men physically and mentally, able organisers and accustomed to having their own way.

In achieving equal results, however, Mawson would expend twice the nervous force and twice the amount of personal energy. Shackleton planned on broad lines, and while exercising the greatest thought for the safety and comfort of his men, delegated the responsibility of carrying out details to others. Mawson also saw far ahead, but planned elaborately and had almost a mania for minutiæ.

Shackleton was an explorer of the type that has carried the Union Jack over uncharted seas and planted it in the heart of unknown lands for sheer adventure's sake. Mawson was first and foremost a scientist, but, not content merely to interpret the data gleaned by roving adventurers into strange lands, had gone to gather them himself. Shackleton grafted science on to exploration—Mawson added exploring to science.

Of Frank Wild, the second in command, one cannot write without admiration. With more actual Antarctic experience to his credit than any other living man, he was a tower of strength to his commander and a capable substitute when the responsibility of leadership fell on him. Wild is not a big man, but for sheer grit, tenacity of purpose and comradeship he would be difficult to match.

The supercargo may have known that twenty-eight human beings intended to travel aboard the *Endurance* but he gave no evidence of the fact. It was rumoured that there was a possibility of the Expedition extending over three years so he took no risks, but took everything else that could be stowed aboard.

Coal and stores filled every cubic foot of hold and bunker; sixty sledge dogs occupied all the deck space; every man's cabin, stacked with scientific impedimenta and indispensables, conveyed the impression the personnel were the least important trifles of the Expedition.

It was a deeply-laden vessel and a high-spirited company that left Buenos Ayres that bright October day and headed for South Georgia, eager for adventure.

The second day out, the boatswain reported to Sir Ernest that while stowing gear in the hold, he had observed a man's foot cropping out from the cargo. An investigation was at once made. The foot was one of a pair and, after hauling on them, a human being was extracted from the darkness.

Sir Ernest, with characteristic Irish humour, regarded the incident as an excellent joke and treated it humanly. At first he feigned austerity. But the youth, undaunted, begged to go with the Expedition in any capacity. Observing that Blackborrow—for that was his name—was an athletic-looking and promising lad, the leader decided to take him South. He became the ship's steward and a loyal and valuable addition to the party.

On the tenth day, we gained a fleeting glimpse of the peaks of South Georgia rising above banks of fog. As we headed for the land we entered a heavy mist that obscured all prospect. Though unable to observe the island, we were literally able to navigate a course by the aid of our noses. There was no doubting that we were drawing closer as the breeze wafted out to us with growing intensity emanations from the whaling stations.

Unable to determine the harbour entrance in the enveloping fog, the siren shrieked incessantly in the hope of attracting a whaler. It was not long before we received an answering blast and a small vessel emerged from the mist and ranged alongside. Captain Michelsen of the *Sitka* piloted us into Cumberland Bay and then into a miniature haven—King Edward Cove—where anchor was dropped off Grytviken, the shore station of the Argentina Pesca Company.

Ashore, before us, clouds of steam were ascending from an extensive collection of sheds to the mists that wreathed snow-clad heights. Numbers of whale carcasses inflated like balloons were moored to a buoy just off the cutting-up platforms or "flensing plan."

Derelict carcasses stripped of blubber drifted about the greasy waters and lay stranded on the beaches in vast profusion.

A noisy welcome tooted from the factory whistles and a noisome one from the floating carcasses that drifted alongside. Our senses divided our impressions of Grytviken. Slimy waters lapped loathsome foreshores, polluted by offal and refuse—the accumulations of years. Viewed through the reeking atmosphere with the nose firmly gripped, even the magnificent inland scenery seemed to grow tainted and lose its splendour. But first impressions are apt to be misleading. We were destined to spend an enjoyable month in South Georgia.

The dogs were landed and chained out on an adjacent hillside under the care of half a dozen of our men, who, for a time, took up their abode in the station hospital. The animals, after their confinement aboard, were exceptionally frisky and broke loose continually, greatly to the consternation of the station pigs which the dogs took a wolfish delight in rounding up.

Although South Georgia belongs to Great Britain, the men engaged in the whale oil industry are mostly Scandinavians—seamen of the hardiest type, willing to risk their lives to effect a "kill" and taking the good and bad in weather or men as it comes. Vikings in feature and physique, they worthily uphold, though in another sphere, the best traditions of the hardy Norsemen.

South Georgia possesses some of the grandest mountain scenery in the world. Its wild coasts rise precipitously to jagged scarps—divided by glaciers—and covered with perpetual snows and mists. Round the irregular shores are many fine natural harbours and beautiful fjords, and on the pick of these are based the land stations of seven whaling companies. The industry is prosperous, well-organised, and carried on scientifically on an extensive scale, over a thousand men being employed during the height of the season. During the year of our arrival no less than 6000 whales were captured, and the value of the oil and by-products approximated a million and a quarter pounds sterling.

I accompanied the whalers on many "hunts," and though scientific methods have robbed it of much glamour and romance and put the odds against the whale, the chase is not devoid of excitement and thrill.

The vessels engaged are similar in dimensions to a fair-sized tug boat, and powerfully engined to speed up to fifteen knots. The whaling gun, secured to a universal mounting on the ship's bows, is capable of projecting a harpoon weighing 120 pounds for about 200 yards. The harpoon, an implement of simple ingenuity, throws out four flukes on entering the whale, making an efficient anchor. A stout manila cable is attached by an ingenious sliding block device to the harpoon, sufficient slack line for the preliminary flight of the weapon is coiled on an inclined table in front of the gun, and the end of this line is attached to a drum of rope which is carried in the forehold. The nose of the harpoon is armed with a deadly detonator —a much healthier proposition for the harpooners, and more humane than the protracted struggle, followed by the slow death inflicted by the steel lances of the boatmen, in days of old.

Before dawn the whalers steam out to the fishing grounds, the effective limits being one hundred miles from the coast. When a swell is running, life aboard is an ordeal, especially for the look-out man in the barrel at the foremast head, as the tubby little craft plunges her bows under and combers sweep the decks. She cruises slowly about till the look-out "spots a blow." The skipper raps out prompt orders to engine room and helmsman, and stands by the harpoon gun. The chase is on, and unless saved by a freak of weather or subtle wiliness, the whale is doomed. No tell-tale periscope was ever so conspicuous as that misty column of expelled breath that the monster blows skyward when he rises to refill his lungs. With the skill of experience, the skipper estimates the probable spot where the whale will reappear and guides his vessel accordingly.

Whales differ in cunning as in bulk, and frequently a "fish" will double back or strike off at a tangent and keep up the grim game for hours; but in the end the relentless chaser gets a chance and draws within shooting range. Carefully the skipper lays his gun, glances at the coiled line, squints through the sights, and pulls the trigger. Away speeds the great arrow, describing a shallow arc and followed by spirals of line, to strike its mark just behind a flipper, and bury itself in the great side. The dull thud of the detonator can be heard. The monster "sounds" in a foaming swirl, throwing its flukes clear of the water. The harpoon line whirrs outboard, while the winchman, with expert eye on the dynamometer, regulates the strain on the rope to a nicety. It is great fishing, this playing of a whale on a line.

The skipper knows roughly how long the dive will take, but no one can tell how long the fight will last. After a while the needle of the dynamometer begins to fall back, the strain on the rope diminishes, the line is winched just fast enough to keep it taut. The whale is coming to the surface. Will he make another burst for freedom? But no: the excitement is over! the bomb has done its deadly work, and the huge carcass soon rolls heavily awash. Hauling it alongside, a tubular lance is driven through the blubber and a stream of compressed air injected to inflate the carcass and prevent it from sinking. The lance is withdrawn, the hole is plugged with oakum, a tow rope is bent around the tail, the flukes are cut off, and the dead whale is taken in tow alongside the vessel.

It is not always so dull at the finish. Sometimes the harpoon strikes just fore or aft of a vital spot, or maybe the detonator proves to be a "dud." Then the whale in its terror and pain dashes off madly, dragging the

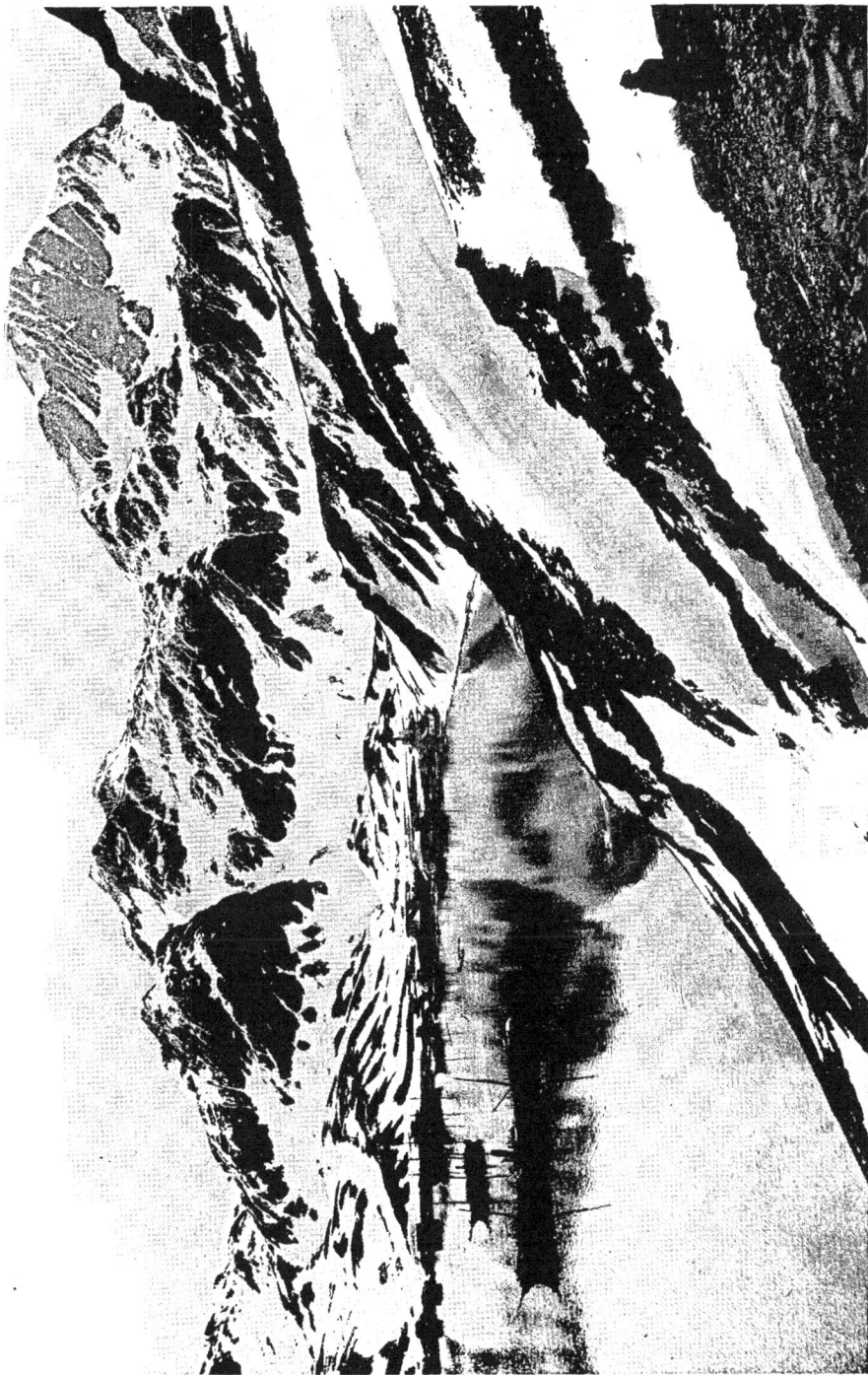

King Edward Cove, South Georgia. The "Endurance" is the Smaller of the Two Vessels Riding at Anchor. Sir Ernest Shackleton Lies Buried in the Small Graveyard at the Right Hand End of the Station.

whaling vessel at a merry gait. But towing an eighty- ·
ton steamboat is fatiguing work, and the giant's
strength soon wanes. After numerous dashes and
fierce attempts to break free, the exhausted creature
is winched near enough for a second shot, or is despatched with a steel lance.

The carcass when towed back to the Station is
hauled up on the "flensing plan" and dissected into
small pieces. These are mechanically fed to digestors
which extract oil under steam pressure. The residue
is made into flesh-meal—a fattening food for cattle—
and guano for fertilizing purposes.

A pleasing phase of our month's stay at South
Georgia was the constant hospitality tendered to us
by the principals and whalers generally. Many con-
vivial evenings were spent at the home of the Manager
of the Argentina Pesca Company, Mr. Jacobsen, who
was ever a staunch friend to the Expedition.

The little house boasted a billiard table, piano and
a charming collection of geraniums blooming in the
bow-windows. Early in our stay we dined with him.

The dinner table was graced with snow white linen—
a welcome change after our four weeks' old stain absorb-
ers in the ward room of the *Endurance*—and was
tastefully bedecked with a dazzling display of blue and
gold china, on which reposed a tempting and amazing
variety of sliced sausage.

After heartily regaling ourselves, the host informed us
that all the sausage was manufactured locally, the in-

gredients being whale meat and whale-fed pig. Very
excellent, too, we all thought,—until next day,—when
we observed a herd of the said whale-fed pigs emerging from a hole in the side of a highly-odorous whale,
where they had just revelled, judging by their grunts
of repletion, in a sumptuous gorge. The sight completely upset the appetites of many of the more susceptible members of the Expedition who refused all
further invitations to dine ashore. For my part, the
proof of the sausage is in the eating, and I found those
of local manufacture to be quite on a par with more
mysterious homeland products.

Diversion was added to our evenings by occasional
visits to Leith Harbour Whaling Station where a
transport had arrived from Scotland with supplies.
The celebrations aboard took the form of a novel
entertainment known as a "gramophone fling."

It was a solemn group of Scots who greeted us as
guests of honour. On one table stood an array of
bottles of their fiery national liquid, and on another
table was a gramophone that had seen better days.
As a talking machine I should say that it suffered from
a decided impediment of speech, but this heightened
the effects of the selections, which were uniformly
Scotch.

Having cleared the musical deck, as it were, by playing all the songs and monologues they possessed, and
having freely oiled the human machinery with the
national lubricant, the serious business of the evening

began. The operator put on a disc that he declared was a selection on the bagpipes, but which sounded like the Massacre of the Innocents, and to this noise two of our hosts danced a reel. Then a time-worn record of the Keel Row was produced, and reproduced, *ad lib.*, as, with energy and spirit, those hardy men of the sea performed a series of jigs and reels and hornpipes of wonderful intricacy with immense enjoyment—interspersing the dancing with weird songs and choruses. It was a great exhibition of endurance—in which we all shared in different ways; but about one in the morning, the "mountain dew" gave out, and the company broke up.

Our good friend Captain Rassmussen took us for many crazy voyages along the coast in a superannuated whaler—the *Little Carl*. Perilously thin and rusty in her plates, leaky of boiler and asthmatic in her tubes, the ancient craft danced with senile vim in rough seas which gushed through her rivet holes while steam hissed from leaky pipes and her engines clanked and knocked ominously.

The hundred miles of coast dared in the *Little Carl* presented a chain of rugged snow-clad mountains and glaciers—a wall which here and there bent into broad bays, and was occasionally broken by deep fjords wherein the sea sent softly-caressing, questing arms among black shadows. Always in the background, towering like titanic spires of glistening marble, rose the snowy splendours of the Allardyce range.

By far the most beautiful spot visited was Moraine Fjord, a narrow waterway extending some two miles between jagged-toothed mountains. The entrance is blocked by a rocky bar thickly overgrown with seaweed over which the seas roll and make even the passage of a small boat difficult, but once over the bar, a magnificent harbour opens up deep and placid—a sapphire mirror for the stately peaks and glaciers that rise sheer from the shores to great heights. Unexpectedly, terrific gusts from the interior will tear down the gorges and lash the waters white. Frequently avalanches tumbling from the heights will plunge into the bay, breaking the calm with a thunderous boom that echoes among the peaks, and sending rings of waves rippling across the tranquil waters.

During the last week of our stay at South Georgia a unique experience befell me,—or rather I fell into the experience,—which won for me the nickname of "Jonah." It happened on my way to keep a dinner engagement at Mr. Jacobsen's. The night was exceptionally black, blowing hard and snowy. The sailors had rowed me ashore and returned to the *Endurance*, and I made my solitary way along the water front by the feeble flutter of a hurricane lamp to the "flensing plan," across which I intended to take a short cut. Halfway over I found the path barred by a huge whale carcass that had been recently hauled up. I tried to get round the head, but as the tide was full and it was deeply in water, I tried the tail end. There was too

Larsen Harbour, South Georgia.

much offal that way, so I decided to climb over the obstacle. This was made possible by several small ladders which the flensers had left alongside the carcass. I reached the top safely but then the ladder began to slide and, before 1 knew what had happened, I was precipitated headlong into something yielding and horribly clammy. The lamp went out and I had no matches, so I could not see the surroundings—which was perhaps fortunate—but I realised that I had fallen literally into the bowels of a whale! The flensers had been at work dissecting the opposite side and the chasm they had dug was not visible when I climbed. The grim humour and the absurdity of my loathsome predicament was aggravating yet amusing. The more I struggled to get free, the more entangled I became and the deeper I sank. Though naturally anxious to avoid the publicity there was nothing for it but to call for assistance.

In response to repeated bellowing I heard the tread of feet and then a lamp thrust over the opening illuminated an astonished face which, peering at me, muttered a Norwegian oath. The lamp and face vanished and I heard my rescuer hurrying off. A little later and half the factory hands turned out with ropes and lamps. I was hauled out amidst boisterous merriment and an occasional cry of "Jonah." Candidly in my filthy condition I felt one! But after a hot bath, and clothed in fresh garments, I was ready to laugh at the experience which as far as I know has only once fallen to another, although on that occasion the whale was alive.

South Georgia must ever be to us who were Shackleton's men the home of many memories. Its whalers were not only ready to lend a helping hand at the outset of the Expedition, but as will be seen later, when disaster and calamity overtook us in the Far South, they came hurrying to our relief.

At Grytviken there is a little Lutheran church, and alongside, a tiny graveyard looks out over the peaceful blue of Cumberland Bay. Behind tower the mountains that Sir Ernest loved so well—the mountains that two years later he attacked and conquered in order to bring relief to his castaway comrades on Elephant Island; the mountains that stand as Nature's imperishable monuments to his memory.

In the little graveyard is a cairn of boulders piled up by the hands of Frank Wild. It marks the earthly resting place of our much loved leader who passed away aboard his ship the *Quest* on the 4th January, 1922, while making his last voyage to the Antarctic.

CHAPTER VIII

THE SEA OF CALAMITY

The ice was here, the ice was there,
  The ice was all around:
It cracked and growled, and roared and howled,
  Like noises in a swound!
COLERIDGE.

INFORMATION gathered at South Georgia from whaling captains corroborated the records of the few expeditions that had previously visited the Weddell Sea, the region of our forthcoming activities, and indicated that its waters were so congested with ice as to be almost unnavigable. Sir Ernest therefore decided to force the *Endurance* to the southernmost limit of the sea and, if a suitable anchorage could be found, to winter her there. This would avoid doubling the risks by a return voyage to pick up the land party the following year.

According to the whalers, the icefields extended as far north as the South Sandwich Islands—an indication that the season was unusually severe. If their information was correct it meant that the *Endurance* would be compelled to force a passage through more than a thousand miles of pack-ice in order to carry out the first stage in the plans of the Expedition.

Every pound of coal that the vessel could carry would be required and extensive additions would have to be made to the clothing equipment. We were fortunate in being able to procure the coal from the Grytviken station and the clothing from the stores of the various whaling companies.

On December 5th we drew away from Grytviken, to volleys of farewell cheers, blasts from factory whistles and salvos of harpoon-gun fire, which echoed and rolled among the mountains until we rounded the bluffs of Mount Dusie and headed for the open sea. Outside the weather was dull and the sea was running high but the wind blew fair. Sails were set, the order full speed ahead was rung down to the engine room, the ship's bows were turned to the south.

As we drew away from the lee of the land, the wind increased. Under steam and sail and with a heavy, following sea, our deeply laden vessel proved splendidly seaworthy, riding the combers steadily and buoyantly and shipping no water.

The scientific staff combined with the sailors in forming three watches under the charge of Sir Ernest, Frank Wild and Captain Worsley. The work ranged from sailorman's duties to stoking; and from helping the cook, to attending to the dogs. After the freedom ashore and the ample diet of whalemeat, the dogs resented their confinement and grew savage and quarrelsome. A fight between two of them—and these scuffles were frequent—was sufficient to induce in the whole pack a tumult of snapping excitement. They were chained in kennels arranged fore and aft along the port and starboard sides of the main deck, and we had to move cautiously along the narrow passages as many of the beasts snapped slyly—generally attacking just after one had passed them by.

The day following our departure from South Georgia, the first ice was sighted. A colossal berg gleaming like an island of marble rose above the indigo swells. Sapphire rollers curled in green billows over its base, and breaking, flung shimmering showers high up its white perpendicular cliffs.

During the forenoon of December 7th we made out the South Sandwich group and drew abreast of Candlemas Island at 6 P.M. A belt of pack-ice surrounded the shores which were wreathed in restless clouds. At intervals, rifts in the mists yielded glimpses of snow-clad heights and outcrops of black rock—the last rock we were destined to look upon for sixteen months. Numbers of icebergs, carved into grotesque shapes by the waves, lay to the south and west. Some were table-like masses pierced with deep blue caverns; others thrust columns and turrets and spires to the sky. In the slanting rays of the evening sun they presented a magnificent spectacle.

At 10 P.M. we received the first check,—our first actual encounter with the ice. This was disconcerting as we had hoped to find open water for another two hundred miles to the south at the least. Sails were furled and, as the pack appeared to be only a narrow belt, we proceeded under steam along the margin looking for an opening.

The swell was breaking along the edge of the ice which was crushing and grinding wildly. The conditions were much too hazardous to permit an attempt to force the ship through. The thunder of the surf and the tumult of the battling masses seemed to utter an ominous warning that the barriers of the Weddell Sea were set against us. Navigation was endangered by "growlers"—detached masses which floated surface awash—and as it was impossible to pick them out in the feeble light, the ship received many nasty blows beneath the water-line.

Towards midnight we came to a gap and headed down a narrow lane which emerged into a black pool encircled by pack in which no break was visible. The pool was snug for a time as the belt of ice calmed the sea, and we hove-to, idly swaying, waiting for the light to improve. To our consternation, however, the pool began to close and, as the entrance sealed up, the ship was in peril of being trapped. We did not doubt that the massive hull would withstand the buffeting but we dared not risk the vulnerable propeller and helm.

The barrier appeared weakest towards the north-east and the *Endurance* was put against it. It was exciting and anxious navigation as the ship lurched and rolled amidst the commotion. Under the onslaught against her sides and the collisions at her bows, she quaked and trembled: the propeller received many heavy jars, but the ship proved staunch in this preliminary tussle, which opened its long struggle in the Weddell Sea. After five hours' cautious steaming we won through and emerged into the clear water.

For three days we skirted the sea-edge of the ice which trended away to the east and, as it then showed favourable indications of thinning, the ship's bows were swung to the south and the conquest of the Weddell Sea began in grim earnest.

During the ensuing five weeks, we nosed through heavily ice-laden waters, threading a careful course down narrow ways, or ramming a path, yard by yard, through stubborn icefields.

The passage became a combination of intricate navigation, subtle seamanship and engine room tactics. The ship became a floating ram. The problem was how to reach a determined point by the shortest route, without consuming coal unnecessarily in ramming the ice and without jeopardising the vessel by getting her "nipped" between the floes.

Although barely embarked upon our adventure, we had already passed into a world of peril and wonder. From the crow's nest at the peak of the mainmast the eyes surveyed a vast inhospitable waste; a stupendous and soul-perturbing scene. Yet there were days when the sun shone pleasantly warm and the atmosphere was serenely crystalline. At home we would have called them exhilarating spring days. From horizon to horizon the sea presented itself as a vast plain tessellated with dazzling irregular sheets of white ice. It resembled a colossal jig-saw puzzle cut from slabs of spotless marble varying in area from a few square yards to expanses of square miles. The sections, all a-jumble, were seamed with the endless ramifications of a maze of waterways and pools. Each waterway or "lead" was a treacherous trap, agape like the jaws of a Titan's vise ready to close and crush the intruder. Yet the sense of constant menace was mitigated by the spectacle of the constantly changing harmonies of extravagant colour with which the sun flooded the scene. Dawn would flush the icefields with every tint in the spectrum; the summer sun, midway in the heavens, would transform the vista into a study in a hundred tones of blue.

Looking towards the sun in the vessel's wake, the leads formed a mesh of waterways, chains of silver which linked together burnished lakes like jewels on the bosom of the world. Below, the eyes would seek to penetrate the intense indigo in which the ship floated and to follow the protruding ice tongues that delved like sapphire spurs into unplumbed depths. Ahead, rivers of ultramarine wound through the maze— sometimes to lead into an unruffled lake of the colour of lapis lazuli. The sky,—a cerulean dome, graded down to a delicate pearly shade round the horizon

The Wake of the Ship Through a Field of Young Ice.

osed through heavily ice-laden waters, threading a careful course down narrow
ways, or ramming a path yard by yard, through stubborn icefields."

where it blended whitely with the reflected iceglare. Yet how capricious Nature's expression is in these latitudes. Her enchanting smile could change to scowls of devilish malice. In less than an hour frowning clouds could drape the skies and the blizzard, let loose with awful wrath, set the packs in thunderous motion, thousands of square miles of ice driving north, millions of floes in the crush. Under the irresistible compression they grind themselves to fragments, rear up and override each other in savage confusion. Pity the ship caught in the devastating turmoil.

The Weddell Sea is a prodigious breeder of pack. Blizzards, though infrequent, are invariably accompanied by low temperatures, and instead of scouring away the ice, they help its formation. When the pack moves forward under the drive of the gale, immense spaces of open water are left behind. Even during the height of summer these freeze over rapidly and add further to the ice congestion. Let us observe how the ship was navigated through this treacherous labyrinth.

Viewed from aloft our vessel resembles a huge wedge. Captain Worsley is standing on the bridge, one hand on the engine room telegraph while the other manipulates a semaphore which directs the man at the wheel. The lead through which we are steaming is narrow and winding. Worsley signals the direction, the helmsman instantly responds and we swing through. The successful navigation of open leads means selecting the one which will not terminate in a cul-de-sac and from which escape can be made if the floes unexpectedly begin to close. Too often the lead narrows or is blocked by an impenetrable floe perhaps a mile across. If not more than three feet thick, the *Endurance* can split it and wedge her way through.

Our vessel is now coming to such an obstruction. Worsley selects a point of attack that promises a line of weakness—"Full speed ahead" is rung down to the engine room. The engines throb and the ship quickly gathers speed, hastening forward to the charge. Hold on in readiness for the impact. There is a mighty collision as if we have run on a reef. The ship is brought up all standing. Her massive cutaway bows rise up on the ice nearly clear of the water. Then as if dulled by the violence of the concussion, she slides slowly back, reeling from side to side. The steel-shod prow has inflicted a deep scar in the floe but it has not yielded. We must try again. We go astern and prepare for another charge. This time the ship's bows will be directed full and square into the "V." The dogs have been stirred from sleep by the violent shock and are taking a yelping interest in the proceedings. Once more we forge ahead, gaining speed and way. The helmsman watches the semaphore keenly. One wonders whether the ship will split the floe or the floe will split the ship. Anxiously we watch and wait. Again the floe receives a 500 ton thrust from our wedge-like bows. The vessel reels under the encounter—a moment of suspense—and then to our joy—a dark streak starts from the bows and marks a jagged course, far out across the floe. It is a noble sight! The engines throb and the tapering bow drives into the cleft. It parts reluctantly, but we are persevering. The floe is large and round its margin countless other floes are crowding. They begin to move under the persistent press and pack together. The crack gradually broadens. At last it yields and we pass through.

But it is not always that we are able to force a passage so readily. Sometimes the floes are too massive and all our battering is futile. Then all that can be done is to make the ship fast to a hummock and await the opening up of the floes under the influence of winds or tides.

The further south we progressed, the heavier the ice became. The great slab-like floes gave way to floating ice islets, gnarled and contorted by terrific pressure. We contemplated these surroundings with some anxiety and speculated ruefully as to what the power that could crush ice, ten feet thick, to powder, would do to our small wooden ship.

When the novelty of our surroundings and method of progression wore off, we chafed under the exasperating hold-ups and delays. The season was rapidly advancing and we had a Herculean task before us.

Christmas festivities afforded diversion and cheer— especially as we made an excellent run of 71 miles before noon. This was the highest run we had made in twenty-four hours since entering the pack. Then heavy winds closed up the leads and obstructed further advance. In honour of the day the wardroom was decorated with bunting and the tablecloths were "turned." They had undergone the process many times, but a close investigation suggested that the underside was really the cleaner. At breakfast, Lees, who was in charge of the commissariat, presented us each with a neat packet, which on opening we found to be a small grindstone—a very useful present. That Christmas dinner came chiefly from tins—mock turtle soup—whitebait—jugged hare—Christmas pudding—mince pies—dessert and crystallised fruits.

Some guests dropped in for a visit afterwards. A bevy of Adelie penguins came from a neighbouring lead and waddled over to contemplate the ship. Hussey entertained them from the poop with his banjo and sang a number of the latest London music hall "hits." The birds seemed very appreciative and occasionally expressed their feelings with croaks of "Clark! Clark!" Clark was our biologist, and it seemed amusingly apt that the penguins should seem to be calling for him. Clark—a patriotic Scot—endeavoured to entertain our little visitors with the melodies of his native highlands: but his amiable intention failed—the penguins fled in terror and plunged back into the sea. Later in the afternoon a coterie of Emperor penguins came strutting towards the ship in a file of stately dignity. When they observed us, the strange creatures formed into a group and repeatedly bowed their heads with humanlike familiarity. Later

A Pressure Ridge in Active Formation.

on we observed that they extended this politeness to one another and even to their smaller cousins the Adelies.

During the evening we celebrated with a "Sing-song" and glad noises of voice, violin, mandolin, banjo and accordions. The festivities closed with toasts: "The King," "Success to the Future," and "Sweethearts and Wives," in which last all heartily expressed the time-worn sentiment—may they never meet.

I saw New Year's Day "in," at the wheel, under cold snowy conditions. A group of enthusiasts assembled on the bridge to "ring out the old, ring in the new" on the ship's bell. All joined their hands and lustily sang "Auld Lang Syne" which a chorus of sixty dogs accompanied with piteous wails.

The New Year augured well. We established a record run, since entering the pack, of 120 miles for the 24 hours. The prospect was improving. A few such spans and our destination would be in sight.

January 10th was a notable day. We reached Coats Land, discovered by Dr. W. S. Bruce of the *Scotia* Expedition in 1904. The "land" was a barrier of sheer ice cliffs rising from the sea to a height of seventy feet and trending away to the south-west. A light breeze was blowing off shore and this had the effect of drifting the ice away from the barrier and keeping open a wide lane of "land-water."

As we proceeded down this imposing waterway we observed large numbers of seals swimming about and basking on the pack-ice to windward. Immense schools of several hundreds were attracted to the ship, and entertained us with wonderful displays, gambolling, racing, diving and sporting like shoals of porpoises. Then they turned about and headed for the north. This migration of the seals was a warning that winter was falling. They were hastening north to escape before leads, congealing, would freeze the pack into one huge unbroken field, and trap them in a prison of ice.

On January 16th we sailed along the seafront of a majestic glacier to which Sir Ernest gave the name "Caird Coast" in honour of Sir James Caird, a staunch supporter of the Expedition. Mighty walls of ice rose perpendicularly to a height of 200 feet from the sea and sloped gradually upwards to the hinterland which we estimated to be about 3,000 feet in altitude. The ice-sheet looked bleakly inhospitable and was seamed with impassable crevasses. Not a vestige of rock was visible. We passed a large bay where the ice sloped down to the water and offered a possible location for a base, but in view of the great distance to be traversed in the projected trans-continental sledging journey, the Leader decided to try to win still further south. Noon gave our position as Latitude 76° 27' South, Longitude 28° 51' West—indicating a phenomenal gain of 124 miles in the past 24 hours.

After this magnificent run we were held up by a blizzard and took shelter in the lee of a grounded iceberg. It was the beginning of our calamities. When the blow was spent and the atmosphere cleared, a disturbing sight was unfolded. The wind had not only filled the bay before us with ice but all the sea was jammed with closely pressed pack.

We succeeded in winning a few laborious miles on the 18th, but the wind, blowing hard from the north-east, drove the ice before it, filling up the bight at the head of the Weddell Sea. As far as the eye could reach in every direction no water was visible. The ship was a helpless atom, locked in, and drifting helplessly with the pack.

The rising slopes of the inland ice came clearly into view on the 22nd about twenty miles to the south. We were in a desperate predicament. The ice-packs were rapidly freezing together and we were utterly powerless to extricate the vessel. There was nothing to do but to wait patiently for a southerly wind in the hope that it might scatter the pack. Only two hours steaming through open water and we could win through to our destination.

CHAPTER IX

IN THE GRIP OF THE PACK-ICE

Out of whose womb came the ice?
And the hoary frost of Heaven, who hath gendered it?
The Waters are hid as with a Stone,
And the face of the deep is frozen.

NEXT night (January 23rd) at midnight I climbed into the crow's nest at the head of the mainmast. The midnight sun in glorious splendour threw the shadows of our ship athwart the snows. We were the only black speck in the dazzling panorama of ice that extended to the girdling horizon.

In the absence of even a breath of wind, the air was wondrously mild, and up there alone in the intense silence and vastness I realised the helplessness of our vessel and our utter insignificance. The will that gives man might to rule and dominate avails nothing here. The breeze which wafts the snowflake, the ripple which stirs the lead, the tiny crystals which in teeming billions build this gleaming ice world, are all indifferent to man's word or will. But when the passive tranquillity changes to scourging blizzard, wrathful sea, irresistibly driving ice-packs then puny man may

"For Two Days and Nights every Endeavour was Made to Cut the Ship Free but the Temperature Continued to Fall and the Ice which was Broken, Froze again, and Matters in the End were Worse than Before."

well feel overwhelmed by a sense of his abject
impotence.

We had one faint hope—that the land which even
then I could see from my lookout might be reached
in a series of forced marches across the pack. In anticipation the motor-tractor was assembled and tried out
on the ice. It proved, however, to be a failure and
quite unsuitable for such a rough surface. To be imprisoned in the ice within view of our intended goal
was a heartrending disappointment. We strained our
eyes constantly towards the land to which our hearts
yearned—sorely exasperated by its closeness and the
impossibility to reach it. A careful survey of the ice
showed that to attempt a journey in the dog sledges or
on foot would be suicidal—the surface was utterly
impassable. As the currents and winds drifted the
icebound ship to the north, and the shore grew more
and more remote, our hopes of landing that season
were abandoned. Nevertheless we were not despair-
ful and looked optimistically towards the future,
hoping that the ice might carry us speedily to the
open sea. Once free, the *Endurance* would return to
South Georgia, refit, and make another attempt. But
these hopes of freedom grew daily smaller and smaller
and it was borne in to our minds that it was as impossible to escape to the sea as it was to set foot on the
land, and that we were in a predicament that would
test ship and men to the full.

As January closed, we faced the gloomy prospect of

autumn and winter with the best philosophy we could muster.

One exciting incident broke the monotony of the first month. Whilst at lunch February 25th we were surprised by a violent shock. All hands rushed on deck to find that the floe in which we were embedded had split across and the vessel was in the line of the crack. Cheers went up at the sight, but their echoes mocked us for the ice came together again, leaving us in the same position as before. Four hundred yards ahead, however, lay a reasonably large lead of open water and Sir Ernest determined to make one more desperate effort to burst our icy shackles. All turned to and attacked the ice with picks, chisels and saws.

In my keenness to secure records of these efforts and of the ship charging the ice, I had a narrow escape from being crushed to death. Putting my camera in a waterproof case, I stood on a small floe immediately in the vessel's path. My programme was to show the vessel making her charge, then to hop aside with the camera a few seconds before the impact. It was a thrilling experience "taking movies" whilst the vessel bore down on my floe. Larger and larger she grew in the view-finder. Two seconds more and I must jump. But I didn't jump, for even as I was preparing to spring, there came a mighty bump and I was thrown into the mushy brash-ice with the ship almost on top of me. The *Endurance* had been diverted from her course by a deep-sea ice-tongue, and had split the floe I was standing on.

By the greatest of luck, neither camera nor myself was any the worse for the crash or the ducking, and the film secured was worth the experience.

For two days and nights every endeavour was made to cut the ship free; but the temperature continued to fall, and the ice, which was broken, froze again, and matters in the end were worse than before.

Although we had known our fate for some time, it was not till the end of February that it was officially admitted. We were icebound, and on the 24th all hands were formally put off ship's routine. New forms of duty were allotted to each man. In alphabetical order we took turns as night-watchmen, coming on duty from eight P.M. till eight A.M. and being responsible for the safety of the ship, the keeping up of the bogie fire and the taking of meteorological observations. The ship ceased to be a "nautical vessel" and became practically a shore station. These conditions were observed for a full eight months, October 24th being the date on which the *Endurance* again became a ship and ship's watches were resumed.

We began the transformation by first housing all the dogs on the ice—greatly to their delight—in an extended circle round the ship in igloos—or dogloos as they were called by sailors. Some tender-hearted members made straw mattresses for them which amused the dogs immensely; they did everything to them except sleep on them.

We next discharged all the stores and cargo from the

main hold and in the space thus made erected a series of cubicles along both port and starboard sides, leaving room for the mess table. The bogie for keeping up the temperature was placed near the after end. When all was complete, the new quarters were christened "The Ritz," and the occupants—two to each cabin except the centre one in which Dr. Macklin, McIlroy, Hussey and I berthed—adopted such fancy name-plates for their apartments as "The Anchorage," "Auld Reekie," "The Knuts," "The Poison Cupboard," and, our own, "The Billabong." The ward room was also turned into a double-ender and became "The Stables" tenanted by Wild, Crean, Marston and Captain Worsley. Sir Ernest occupied his original cabin aft, and if perchance the roasting bogie fell below its normal radiance—as when for example some luckless wight mistakenly dumped into it a piece of ice instead of a lump of coal—the temperature in the immediate vicinity was raised several degrees by the heat of his comments. The fitting and furnishing of the slightly less than six feet cubicles was entered into with an amusing spirit of rivalry, and the relative merits of our dens, the degree of our capacity for entertainment or annoyance, and our hospitality or close-fistedness, provided matter for unending debates through the following months. The "Ritz" was an unostentatious abode in which one might study the anatomy of the ship—no attempt being made to disguise its strong ribs and stout timbers—but it made a

The Surface of a Newly Frozen Lead was Covered with Delicate Crystal Rosette Formations Resembling Nothing so Much as a Field of White Carnations.

snug home and was more comfortable than a hut, though eventually we paid the same price as the man in the Scriptures who built his house upon sand, our abode being founded upon something even less stable.

Meantime the sailors had been at work "ashore," encircling the ship with a chain of mounds which were afterwards linked together with a wire hawser which acted as a guide for those who strayed away from the vessel in the dark of winter or the fogs and blizzards. The mounds similarly marked a track to the lead ahead and this was called the Pylon Way; later the Khyber Pass was added to the local topography.

Life on the ship and overside was varied enough with duties and exercises. We played football and hockey on the ice, while the light was good enough, to keep ourselves more or less amused and in good fettle. Occupation for the various members and for the crew was organised and whilst the scientific work was naturally limited, there was plenty to do—particularly for the photographer whose services were requisitioned in every department for making records.

This, my own particular field, was one with limitless pictorial possibilities. The ice-sheet stretching away a thousand miles to the north was ever restless, and always changing. Its ice-blocks, contorted and thrown up into every conceivable fantastic form, presented a boundless range of subjects.

The more prominent ice pinnacles and unusual formations were fittingly christened and photographed.

Several icebergs which had become temporarily stranded in the pack became alluring objectives and, later on, serious menaces. These gigantic masses drawn along by deep sea currents forged invincibly ahead, ploughing their way through the fields, and on one occasion our doom had been sealed but for a blizzard coming up, kindly for once, and driving the ice-packs before it.

The vessel itself made the connecting link between the vast, lifeless solitudes of the south and the living humanity of the north. It was a symbol to all of us; but to me it had a double interest, for, as a factor in any pictorial composition, it was invaluable, giving point and interest, perspective and comparison to many a picture. In itself, too, the ship was an object to muse over. As time went on it became more and more evident that she was doomed. I conceived the ambition of making some pictures of the *Endurance* that would *endure*, and I spent days and weeks studying her from all angles and positions. She was never twice the same. She was indeed a lady of infinite variety. Some times she looked stark and grim, with bare poles and black ropes. Then overnight, snow would fall and the gaunt masts and their cordage would be powdered with dazzling white. Again, when a pool formed amongst the ice-floes, volumes of dense frost vapours condensed on the rigging; line and spar, stowed sails, braces, anchor chains, glittered with countless tiny ice-crystals which flashed like diamonds. But perhaps never did the ship look quite so beautiful as when the bright moonlight etched her in inky silhouette, or transformed her into a vessel from fairy-land. During the winter months, when we lost the sun for ninety days and everything was encased in ice, I took a series of flashlight pictures with the temperature at seventy degrees below freezing point.

For one of these flashlights I made elaborate preparations. In twenty-five different spots I placed charges of flash-powder, and with a simple system of electrical wiring, connected the lot. When I pressed the button, the charges went up simultaneously, and the vessel, from ice-line to topmast truck, stood out in brilliant relief against the velvet blackness of the sky. But that came later.

Meanwhile the skies by daylight were ever a sublime spectacle. At times the dome of heaven was as iridescent as a lustrous shell in which the mist-veiled sun was poised like a dazzling pearl.

Then there were times when the whole sky was a rainbow, flaming with radiant mock suns and one's very heart and soul cried out in rapture: "These things are not earthly, this is heaven."

There was such a day, just before the sun went down and the long Polar night drew on, when the ice split up in gaping leads and laid bare the sea.

The extremely low temperature of the air meeting the comparatively warm sea water set up a process of condensation. Immense clouds of dark vapours rolled skyward from the water as if from a boiling lake. These mists solidified into crystals which fell in shimmering showers from the clear blue sky—a rain of jewels. The sun shone through the glinting fall in great rainbow circles which spanned the sky. The crystal showers carpeted the pack-ice and ship until she looked like a tinselled beauty set on a field of diamonds! Walking on this crystal carpet in a scintillating world —a million crystals flashing at every step—I found the lead just beginning to freeze over, and in a few hours' time the ice was two inches thick. The vapour, now no longer able to escape from the water, was manifesting itself in another process. The thin ice was still very mushy and the cold atmosphere smiting it, produced a local surface condensation which assumed the form of miniature crystal rosettes. These rapidly grew in size until the entire surface of the lead was covered with the most exquisite and delicate formations, which resembled nothing so much as a vast field of white carnations. With the growing thickness of the ice the action ceased. As the sun went down, sending a last flush across the pack, this wonderful white field of ice-flowers was flooded with a thousand rosy tints.

It was not only the contemplation of the vastness, painted by the sun with scarlet, purple and gold, the dawn flushed with pink, magenta and lilac, the stars which like celestial lamps lit the infinite spaces and glittered from crystalline skies, that enraptured us.

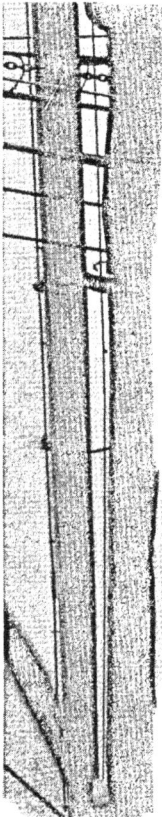

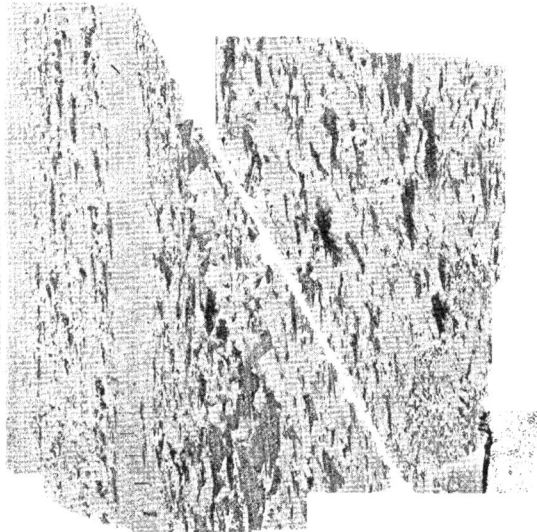

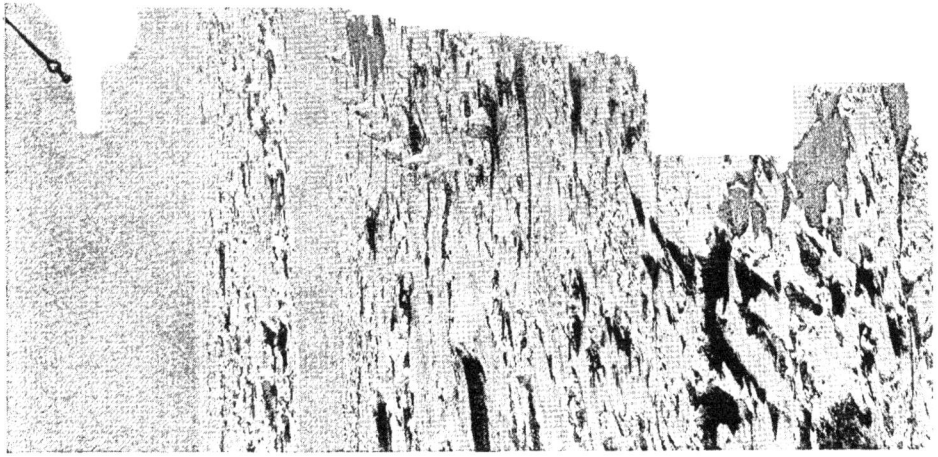

Occasionally the ice split up in gaping leads and laid bare the sea. Immense clouds of dark vapour rolled sky-

There was as much glory and wonderment to be discerned in the smallest things about us,—even the most minute crystal. Things the unaided eye could not see became worlds beneath the microscope; worlds conceived with that perfection and love with which the Almighty Sculptor has fashioned the Universe.

Our nights—and they grew longer and longer— were frequently enlivened with home-made entertainment. The gramophone proved a god-send at first— and many an hour we lay in our bunks listening to its music. Memories of other days were awakened by familiar tunes; speculations, too, as to when we would hear them again. Curiously enough, the "talking machine" became the object of one of those superstitions to which men fall victim under unusual conditions.

After a time it was noticed that no sooner did the music begin than the ice-pressure commenced, and the vessel began to quiver and creak. The fact was that the pressures recurred at regular intervals, but nothing would convince certain members of the party that the music did not conjure up the elements and originate the pressure. The belief became so strong that eventually the gramophone was placed under a ban. When the ship broke up, the instrument, by some freak, was forced up to the top of a pile of wreckage, and there it was left when we took to the ice-floe, not a soul putting forth a hand to salvage it. But our music was not all of the "canned" variety. As early as March 7th my diary records that:

During the evening a singing competition took place: the prize being unanimously awarded to Sir Ernest. His voice is quaint, vacillating uncertainly between sharps and flats in a unique manner. Wordie, now ex-champion, renders an old favourite, "The Gambolier," in a voice resembling the shrill tone caused by drawing a rasp smartly across a sheet of galvanised iron. Clark chants, to much applause, "My Nut Brown Maiden," in a nasal falsetto, and I render "Waltzing Matilda," in the melting dulcet tones one often hears from a "swaggie" when crooning at sunset and "punching" his frugal damper. It is astounding the musical talent we do *not* possess!

An excellent projection lantern had been brought along and illustrated talks on such topics as the Mawson Expedition and travel in sunny lands. Then about the end of May I noted in my journal that a form of mid-winter madness seized all members, a craze for clean-shaven heads setting in, and great amusement being caused by members decorating their bald pates with various devices. It was suggested that a bright advertising man might have made a fortune letting the "vacant spaces."

Birthdays were of course celebrated in proper fashion but our most ambitious entertainment occurred on June 22nd in celebration of Mid-Winter Day. A "close holiday" was observed. After an excellent breakfast and lunch of reserved dainties, we partook of a "feast" dinner after which all retired to their cubicles to array in stage dress. I erected a stage with acetylene footlights, and decorated it with bunting. Sir Ernest opened the evening with a satiric harangue which was

ectre Ship Looming Stark and White Against the Darkness of the Polar Night."

The night-watchman returns after making an inspection of the ice in the neighbourhood of the ship.

admirably responded to by the Rev. Dr. Bubblinglove (Lees). An overture, "Discord Fantasia" in four flats by the "Billabong" band worked the audience up to concert pitch, the B. B. then opportunely retiring to their retreat. There were many humorous sketches and make-ups, interspersed with merry banter. Rickinsen made an admirable flapper, and McIlroy a very gay grisette, highly perfumed and bewigged with oakum and teased out rope yarn. Greenstreet, the dashing "knut," was a great success. James's humorous brogue dissertation on the calorie was loudly applauded. Marston as a country farmer was superb. The programme which comprised some thirty items, with an interval, concluded with "God Save the King" and "Auld Lang Syne." Afterwards we partook of a midnight supper.

It may be added that at that time we had only two hours of very poor twilight each day, in which stars of the fifth magnitude were visible; and that our ship was embedded in a frozen sea that stretched away nine hundred miles to the north, before reaching the open ocean, and that below us the waters were 2000 feet deep.

Individual pastimes, too, took various forms. Our library was fairly extensive and reading varied. Vast and purely imaginary sums were won and lost at dice and cards.

The daily round and the nightly task were summarised in the diary thus:

My turn to night watch.   The duties of the night watch are to keep the Ritz bogie glowing, The Stables roasting, and the Boss, who is right aft, at an equable temperature. The latter is a difficult job as the Boss's room is but a small cabin.   The temperature within is either ninety degrees or well below freezing according to the wind, which greatly influences the bogie draught.   Sir Ernest's temper oscillates inversely with the room temperature.   The nightwatchman also arouses friends, and they sit around the bogie fire, discoursing in subdued whispers, and partaking of the watchman's bounty, to wit, sardines on toast—a great favourite—grilled biscuit and cocoa or tea.   Frequently, a special "perk," reserved for the occasion, is produced, and the visitors, termed "ghosts," are appreciative.   All hands are called at 8.30 A.M.

2nd July.—A typical day.   Rise at 8.30 A.M. (generally 8.50 A.M.).   Breakfast at 9 A.M. sharp, else woe betide! Sir Ernest's humour in the morning before breakfast is very erratic.   Morning: exercise the dogs and "dinkass" about generally.   Lunch 1 P.M.   Afternoon, no work till afternoon tea 3.30 P.M. till 4 P.M.   Then nothing to do until 6 P.M.   Then turn in at own desire after an arduous day endeavouring to make time pass.

The weather during the six months we had been encumbered by the floes was on the whole quite reasonable; compared with the climate of Adelie Land it was heavenly; though blizzards were not unknown. The temperatures ran as low as seventy degrees below freezing point and those of us whose occupation necessitated dabbling in water found our fingers splitting and our hands nipped with frost-bite.   But within the shelter of our stout vessel, with a perfect lighting system, a well-stoked bogie and a generously served

Hurley (left) and Hussey (right) Engage in a Friendly Game of Chess.

Icebergs were a constant menace. These gigantic masses, drawn along by deep sea currents, forged ahead, ploughing their way through ice fields.

galley, little we recked of driving snow and shrieking gale. The uncomfortable work of attending to the dogs during blizzard times and the job of cutting ice for drinking purposes and of removing the accumulations from the ship's sides and propeller only heightened by contrast our appreciation of the comforts of our station.

Yet during the whole of this period, we were conscious of all sorts of peril. Sometimes as we lay snug in our bunks, the wind, roaring across the hummocked spaces and shrieking through our top hamper, would set the vessel trembling from stem to stern till we wondered if the masts would be torn out like gale-uprooted trees. Sometimes a towering berg would be seen ploughing a drunken passage through the ice as if bent on crushing the intruding ship; and always, away to the south and east, could be heard the infernal growl and groan of the pressure-tortured ice. We were, however, at this time alert rather than anxious, assuring ourselves, perhaps bluffing ourselves, if the truth were confessed, that the time would come when the ice would open naturally and our staunch little craft would fight her way clear of the pack.

CHAPTER X

SLEDGE DOG PALS

To Shakespeare, the leader of my team and the King of the pack.

HOW dreary the frozen captivity of our life but for the dogs. They were born, bred and trained in the Hudson Bay territory. When we first made their acquaintance on board the *Endurance*, they were fierce, sullen and shy, and appeared but little removed from wolves. Our complement when we reached the Weddell Sea was fifty-four. In addition, six were "added to the strength" after we had been frozen in some months. Four pups belonging to Sally became great favourites, not only with their foster father, Tom Crean, but with the entire company, who watched their development through frolicsome puppyhood to sturdy doghood, with all the interest usually bestowed upon an addition to the human family. Sue, of Macklin's team, was not so successful in her maternal adventure, for of a litter of eleven pups, only two opened their eyes upon a white and troublesome world.

The dogs being housed on deck, in individual kennels, stood the outward voyage remarkably well,

"Shakespeare." The Leader of my Team and the Most Sagacious Animal of the Pack.

though naturally they lost condition, and as soon as the *Endurance* became immovably bedded in the ice they were transferred to the floe alongside.

When seal meat became plentiful they quickly recovered their frolicsome spirits and eagerness for work. The average weight of our sledge dogs was 85 pounds— the smallest scaled 70 and our heaviest, a powerful brute named Jasper, went to 132 pounds. Shakespeare, who was four years old, weighed 115 pounds.

At first the dogs were to us, just dogs, a mere heterogeneous pack. Certain members of the Expedition were responsible for their feeding and others for their care. But later, Sir Ernest adopted the wise plan of dividing them into five teams and apportioning them, by lot, to the five members of the party who were to accompany him on his proposed trans-continental journey. It was expected that this would take about 120 days, consequently each driver was instructed to train his team for a march of that duration.

The feelings of proprietorship and the competition thus set up, were speedily reflected in the improved condition of the dogs. I was singularly fortunate in drawing what was probably the best team and had certainly the best team leader. Rival teamsters asserted that I started with an unfair advantage in once having served a brief apprenticeship to a bullock driver in the back blocks of Australia, while few of them had driven even a golf ball! Nevertheless I maintain that though language is important, leadership is paramount; and so I pay tribute to Shakespeare, the finest sledge dog that ever wore a leader's harness. He was irreverently called "Tatcho" because his tail had been shorn of all hair by his brother Bob in an historic fight. In the North he had been called "Light," possibly on account of his wonderful learning. Others had called him "The Holy Hound" because no matter what dog devilry was afoot, he was the leader; yet, when it came to an investigation of the trouble, no saint ever presented a more innocent face, no dog ever wagged a more virtuous tail. But when his energies were applied to breaking the trail, in sledge harness, he showed a sagacity that was uncanny, and as a companion he was better than some humans. All in all, his wisdom and knowledge of men justified his new name; he was the Shakespeare among dogs.

The erection of "dogloos" gave us considerable amusement. At first they were strictly utilitarian, but later when we were able to secure flat slabs of newly-formed ice from a neighbouring lead, the teamsters were as keen to outdo each other in the building of dog kennels as in the improvement and training of the tenants. The slabs of thin ice could be readily chipped into any desired shape and cemented together by pouring seawater over the joinings. Snow mixed into a mush with seawater also made an effective cement and, in order to secure the dog chains, it was only necessary to cut a shallow hole in the ice, insert the end of the chain and pour in a little water. In a few moments the chain was frozen in and held so strongly that the combined efforts of a whole team could not wrench it free.

Crystal villages quickly sprang up round the ship and the facilities afforded by the endless supply of building material and the ease with which it could be assembled afforded much diversion. Architectural design was limited only by the imagination of the builders. The crystal homes were provided with wooden floors and door frames,—windows were unnecessary for a faint blue light filtered through the walls. "Sailor" was the tenant of a model church, which boasted an icy spire and portico. He, like many another sailor, preferred to curl up outside its precincts.

It was in fact only when the weather was specially bad that the ice kennels were used as sleeping quarters. Only then would the occupiers retire within them to sleep peacefully while the wind howled and the snow piled up and up above them. Some of them, by scratching away the snow, maintained little peep holes through the doorway either for fresh air or to watch for the "hoosh." They also regarded their houses as useful sanctuaries when the stings of conscience troubled them and they had a foreboding that retribution would be exacted by the driver's whip.

Our teams were generally made up of a leader and eight dogs clipped to the main hauling trace in pairs, each dog having its own particular harness. The training and handling of a dog team is a fine art. The wise driver first gets to know his dogs and teaches them to know him, and to recognise his mastery. Then he learns to use his words of command with decision, and his long-lashed whip with precision. He practises hour by hour with the whip until with unerring accuracy, he can flick a coin from the ground at the length of his twenty-foot lash. Dog-team driving then becomes as instinctive as motor-driving; but the man who gives confusing commands or makes mistakes with his whip, has a sorry time. One of our party was an exponent of the "rule-by-kindness" theory, but it was proved beyond a doubt that the only way to handle these dogs is by enforcing rigorous but fair and just discipline, under which the animals will thrive and work perfectly. Weakness, unkindness, and above all injustice, will destroy efficiency. A good dog will see that the one in front of him keeps up to his work, snapping at his heels if he shows signs of "slacking." Every dog is capable of hauling about 115 pounds when in good fettle.

The only dog in my team who was a consistent slacker was Sailor. He was a powerful, cunning creature who performed all the actions of a hard worker, but exerted only just sufficient energy to keep the trace taut. While on the move he would peep furtively over his shoulder watching his master and the whip. At the swing of its thong, Sailor would halt instantly, so that the lash would expend its flick in the

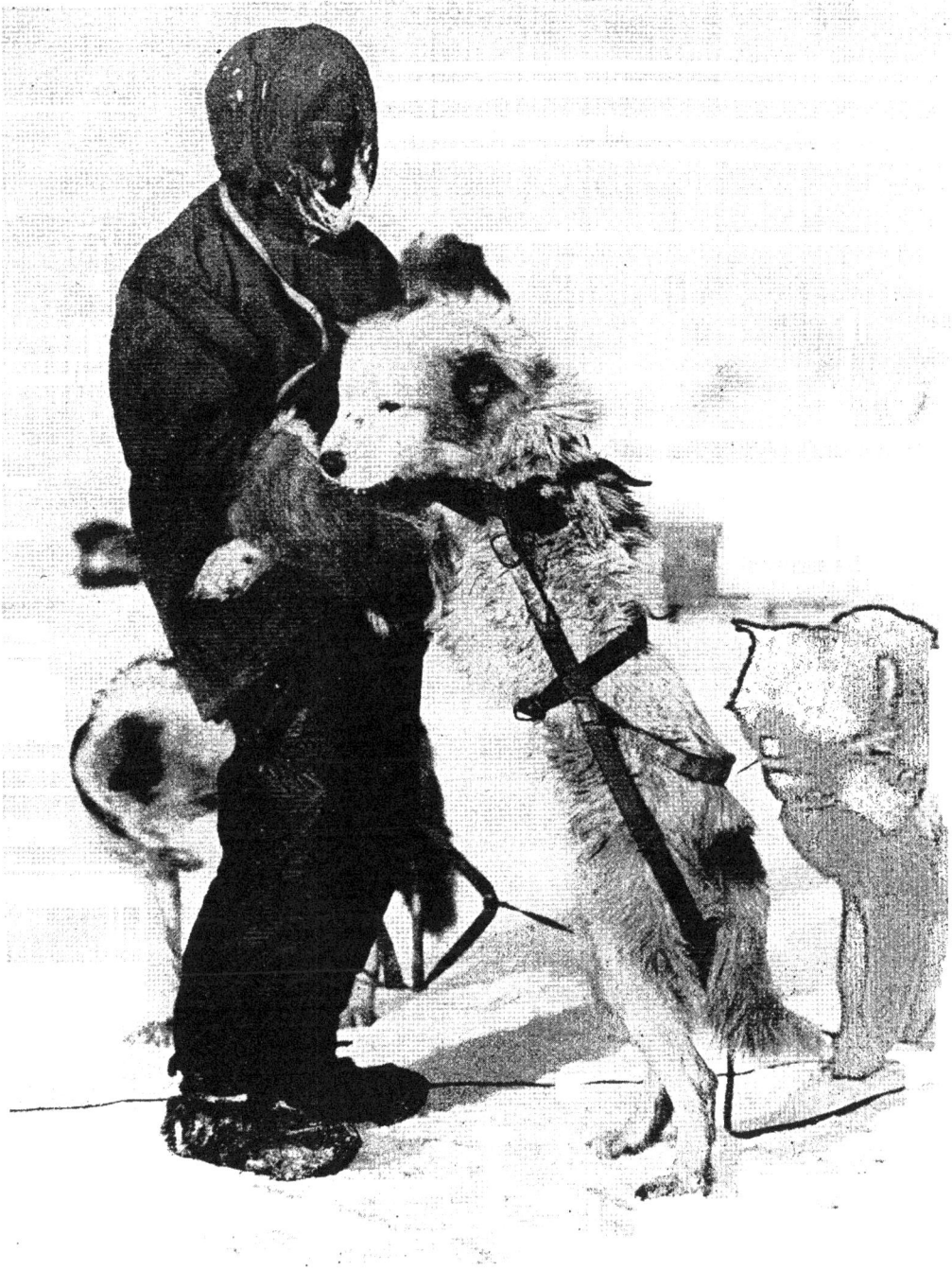

Wild was a great favourite with the dogs and he is here seen with one of his "pal
both harnessed up ready for the trail.

ummer" was an Ardent Worker, with
Tail that never Ceased Wagging.

"Colonel," one of Mawson's Dogs
and Presented to him by
Amundsen.

aint." The Most Virtuous Dog of
the Pack.

"Lupoid." So Named because of his
Wolfish Appearance.

air—just where Sailor ought to have been—but was not!

We followed the established method of driving. Dogs, when clipped to the trace, are trained to sit absolutely still on their haunches. At the word "Ready" they leap to attention. At the order "Mush" they give a quick jerk, to break the runners free of the ice, and then move off at a steady gait, each dog putting his back into the work. In turning the team, the order "Ha!" swings them to the right; "Gee!" turns them to the left, and the universal "Woah" brings them up standing. During the winter months, when there was no sun, and the whole world was grey and trackless, when an ice hummock was not distinguishable from a hole, it was impossible for a human being to keep a direct course without a compass; but an intelligent leader—such a dog as old Shakespeare—once put on a set course, would pilot his team unerringly, swinging round hummocks in detours to avoid rough ice, without losing a point of direction.

Astonishing, too, was the complete understanding and sympathy that grew up between dog and man. Time and again during some moment of acute danger —especially after the wreck of our vessel, when decisions and immediate compliance became matters of life and death—the dogs responded to orders with an alacrity they had never displayed before. I am confident they apprehended the danger in our desperate circumstances and exactly as each member of the

Expedition instantly obeyed the judgment and decision of his leader, so also did these sagacious creatures eagerly respond to the command of their master.

I found it possible to dominate my leader by telepathy, if I may use the term. Times out of number I found my team wheeling and obeying an unspoken order. Times out of number my old leader would slacken pace and look round inquiringly. What instinct was it that indicated that danger lay ahead? It was not evident to my human intelligence until we drew closer and I observed a rift in the sea ice and the dark waters of the sea, bared ready to engulf us.

My dog team greatly widened my field of operations. With a comrade on my sledge I would scout the pack-ice far and wide in quest of subjects for the camera. These trips were not without a certain risk, for frequently the ice would open up between us and the ship, and then we would be compelled to await a closing up, or to ferry ourselves across on a loose floe. But the dogs' sagacity was by no means infallible.

One day after a solo drive with my team I was returning to the ship, lying back on the sledge, deeply engrossed in studying an atmospheric phenomenon, the dogs scampering back over the beaten trail, when suddenly I felt myself falling, and before I had time to collect my thoughts I was floundering in icy waters. The cold immersion quickly brought me to my senses, and I realised what had happened. The ice had broken away into a lead right across the track, and the team had all gone in with the sledge on their heels. On either side, the fractured ice walls rose perpendicularly from the water, which looked like an inky river running east and west twenty yards wide. The dogs swam for the opposite bank, towing the sledge, to which I clung for dear life, after them. My life, and the team's, was saved by a large waterproof box which I had attached to my sledge for carrying the photographic instruments. On reaching the opposite side, I guided the sledge close against the ice-face. It had just sufficient buoyancy to bear my weight, and standing precariously on the top I managed to clamber to safety. Securing an emergency line to a hummock, I hauled out the first three dogs. Then they pulled the rest of the team onto the floe. On regaining safety they all turned on the leader and attacked him revengefully for having led them into the lead and I had to rush to Shakespeare's rescue and stun half the team with the whip handle or he would have been torn to pieces.

The Antarctic explorer has one foe in the water that he fears—the dread killer-whale. With its cruel double row of teeth and its wicked eye, it looks like an exaggerated shark, only more horrific. The killer— or the orca—is a constant menace to the seal, and the traveller over the ice has always to be on guard.

When we set out on our dog journeys, this danger always lurked beneath the ice. Once I was out with one of the sailors, and we were crossing a wide lead that had just frozen over. We had not gone half a hundred yards when we heard whales blowing close by. Quickly I wheeled the dogs on the thin and treacherous ice, and, swinging as sharply as possible, made a dash for safety. No need to shout "Mush! Mush!" and swing the lash. The whip of terror had already cracked over their heads, and they flew before it. The whales behind—there were three of them—broke through the thin ice like tissue paper, and, I fancy, were so staggered by the strange sight that met their eyes, that for a moment they hesitated—and we were not lost. Had they gone ahead and attacked us in front, our chances of escape would have been slim indeed; but fortunately we reached the solid ice and made for a big hummock. The killers charged the floe, and poked their heads over the edge. Never in my life have I looked upon more evil and loathsome creatures. Yet, being now in comparative safety, the one thought that came to me was: "What chances one misses when he ventures out without a camera—or a gun."

The sledge dog is a most accommodating animal in his diet. If pressed by hunger he will cheerfully consume his brother in harness and if hard pushed will make a meal off the harness itself. Fortunately the dogs of the *Endurance* were never reduced to such desperate straits for early in January we began to make a store of seal meat and secured enough to last through winter till the seals reappeared in spring. Variety of food being essential to dogs and men alike, a routine of diet was arranged, each dog receiving on one day a pound of seal meat and half a pound of blubber, the next, a pound and a half of dog biscuits and the third a pound of pemmican which, being designed for sledging rations, is very concentrated. This routine was altered to suit the circumstances and the condition of the dogs. Nourishing "hooshes" were regularly given and, when available, bones for gnawing. Once the cook, when the dogs were kennelled aboard, unfortunately put some salt beef brine into the "hoosh" by mistake. The result drove the dogs nearly mad with thirst and kept the drivers busy all day melting ice to quench it.

There were few bad-tempered dogs in the teams and fights were comparatively rare; but when exercise was limited through bad weather or broken surfaces they grew very difficult to manage. Occasionally they became highly excited, sometimes temporarily uncontrollable. The sight of stray seals or penguins would start them barking frantically, and the appearance of killer whales blowing in the leads would excite them to a frenzy. Wild's team, catching sight of a penguin, after a long absence of bird life from the floe, could not resist the temptation. A quiver ran down the line. Training vanished at the call of primal instinct. With one accord they dashed for the luckless bird and in an instant were tearing it to pieces regardless of shouted commands and the flaying lash that the driver laid on the snarling mass of hair, feathers, trace, rope and tangled harness. On another occasion three of the teams commenced a fierce fight that required all the energy of the three drivers to quell.

But perhaps the most glorious medley occurred when the *Endurance* was squeezed out of the water by the closing of a lead and rolled heavily to port. The dogs were at this time housed on the vessel and those on the starboard side were shot down the sloping deck into the port kennels. Instantly there was pandemonium and a free fight, marked by much noise but little damage.

About mid June when the teams were at their best a Canine Derby was arranged. The racing track was the Pylon Way, the starting line 200 yards away and the winning post by the ship. All hands were given a day off to see the race and all entered thoroughly into the spirit of the meeting. Bets were freely laid in the currency of the Antarctic—chocolate and cigarettes— and some of the sailors dressed themselves up as book-makers, Wild's team having, in racing parlance, a shade the best of the odds. It was a weird and curi-ous event run in the short dim twilight of the Antarc-tic winter. The teams had all been trained over the course and seemed to enter into the fun of the thing. Sir Ernest, who was the judge, also started the com-petitors by flashing on the electric light that stood at the head of the Khyber Pass. The teams were sent off to the accompaniment of encouraging cheers from the backers and shouts from the drivers. Judg-

efore calamity overtook the ship the dogs were kennelled on board again.   They
are here seen being taken down the gangway for daily exercise.

ing by the barking of the dogs, they seemed to realise what was expected of them. Wild's team won, covering the distance in two minutes, sixteen seconds. Shakespeare led in his team-mates ten seconds later and Macklin's lot, with Bony Peter in the lead, was third. Next day I challenged the favourites to another spin "with passenger up" and won on a protest, Sir Ernest, who was Wild's passenger, having been ignominiously pitched off the sledge en route.

Towards the end of July a three-days' blizzard, accompanied by a heavy fall of snow, raged day and night. No one was allowed to leave the ship, except to attend to the dogs. When the wind dropped the aspect of the entire landscape was changed. A huge dump of snow had collected on the port side, depressing the floe and completely covering the kennels. All hands were engaged with shovels. But all the dogs emerged none the worse for their experience. In fact, they were unusually active. My own sledge was loaded with five cases of benzine, each weighing one hundred pounds, yet when I sprang on top, bringing the load up to 681 pounds, they started off as if pulling an empty sledge, and I had great difficulty to keep them in hand.

A few days later heavy ice pressure was observed S.W. of the ship. Sounds like the breaking of surf could be heard and during the day the decks were cleared and chains secured so that the dogs might be brought aboard at any moment. A constant lookout was maintained throughout the day and an hourly watch kept during the night. A crack started from the lead ahead and ran to within thirty yards of the ship. A bare four hundred yards away on the port bow the ice became very active, crunching and rafting. Huge fragments, many tons in weight, were forced up and balanced on the top of pressure ridges fifteen feet high. Then on the morning of August 1st the floe began to move in our vicinity. The dogs were hurriedly brought aboard and gangways raised just in the nick of time, for shortly afterwards a pressure ridge was thrown up close to our starboard quarter. The edges of the floes came together with such force that huge blocks of ice were thrown up and the dogs' crystal palaces were crushed to powder. Next day wooden kennels were constructed on the deck and thenceforward the dogs were kept on board.

They were still taken overside for necessary exercise, however, a track of some three hundred yards in length being made round the ship. Neither the dogs nor the drivers relished this restricted exercising ground and it was varied by adventurous excursions into the hummock field. A keen watch was kept from the crow's nest for ice workings, and recall signals were hoisted whenever danger threatened.

During one of these outings I was forced to make my team cross a working pressure ridge. They became terrified and bolted; both driver and passenger were tossed off the sledge but the team continued and stampeded madly for the ship. We raced them for two miles but they arrived first and when we came up they regarded me most uneasily. Guilt, if not penitence, was written large across the faces of all except the ever-resourceful Shakespeare, who wore the injured air of one who had been dragged into trouble by his harness. However, so conscious were they of coming retribution that when I attempted to drive them out again, they became panicky, and taking control, carried me round and round the ship, crossing patches of thin ice that kept on opening under our weight. When I did at last get the crazy animals in hand I dealt with them one at a time, after which they became normal obedient dogs.

Let me record as a conclusion to this chapter on the dogs a typical drive. August was ushered in and the black darkness of winter skies, dread and dead, was beginning to liven and brighten, for the sun was hurrying south. It was gloriously calm when Macklin and I harnessed up old Shakespeare and clipped my team into the sledge. Crisp was the air and very keen, for the temperature lurked at 70 degrees below freezing point; but oh! the glamour of that ride! The exhilaration of being alone on the drifting pack-ice, privileged humans at the bottom of the World.

A dawn of rose and gold lay over the Northern sky. Mists from an open lead rose writhing and turgid as with the flame of a prairie blaze. The Northern sky flared, brilliant and radiant, but over the South the wings of night were still spread. The full moon was fast rising over the jagged South, painting an alluring silver path across the glinting ice. Into this silvery way I swung my team, allowing the old leader to meander and pick his own track through the maze of hummocks. As we drove to the moonlit South, the Northern face of the pack which fronted us glowed with reflected pink from the bursting dawn. Turning and looking back we saw the South side illumined by the bright moonlight which converted fantastic ice ridges and fangs into ghostly shapes. The silence was profound; we were in a dead and frozen world. Then the short day ended. Dawn in the North waned to sunset; Northern stars added their jewellery to the skies. We wheeled about in our tracks and the team sped merrily homeward to the jingle of Shakespeare's bell. We were soon back to the ship whose hull, ropes and shrouds, heavily coated with crystals of rime, stood in gaunt detail, etched sharply against the dark sky and glistening in the moonlight—a spectre ship. We tore ourselves from a phantom world to reality. We unharnessed the dogs, kennelled and fed them—and then went down noisily to the warmth of the "Ritz," where the others sat around the bogie fire, carolling merrily to the strains of Hussey's banjo.

CHAPTER XI

THE DEATH OF THE SHIP

Nor dim, nor red,
Like God's own head,
The glorious sun uprist.

COLERIDGE.

ON July 26th, the first time for 79 days, the sun peeped above the horizon and, after winking at us for nearly a minute, set in glorious majesty, blazoning the Northern sky with crimson and gold. It was a sign that all had been eagerly awaiting and we gathered on deck and lustily cheered "Old Jamaica" on his reappearance.

Condensation crystals were falling from a cloudless sky, and the golden flood of the sun's beams converted them into showers of scintillating gold. This sparkling rain fell far and wide over icefields, transmuting them into an aureate world. At last dawn was breaking, the long polar night had ended. The dawn was also a signal that the siege of the *Endurance* was about to begin in earnest.

The dogs were brought aboard on August 1st, and on that day the ice surface, seen from the masthead, appeared as a chaos of hummocks, ridges, needles and broken blocks, piled up in wildest confusion.

The north-east drift had been accelerated—doubtless on account of the vast "sail area" presented to the wind by the surfaces of millions of ice hummocks—and the ocean depth increased rapidly from 2712 feet to 6876 feet. That the pack was breaking up and leads opening everywhere, was evident from the clouds of condensation vapours that rose in all directions, some resembling bursts of smoke from a grass fire, others looking like smoke trails from a slowly puffing locomotive.

The nights became times of great anxiety for the ship now lay in the heart of an icy battlefield. We would be awakened by most fearsome noises of grinding ice and creaking timbers. The floor buckled under the strain and the tongues of boards in wooden partitions between the cubicles would spring from the grooves with sharp reports. For ten weeks the ship was in continual danger, but it was not until early October that its position became desperate. On October 14th the ice was in convulsion ahead of the ship, and a splitting crash suddenly caused all hands to rush up on deck to find that a crack had opened from the lead ahead and had passed along our starboard side to another crack that had opened aft. The ship was free for the first time in nine months. At midnight she drifted from her cradle and fell astern, leaving her form moulded in the splintered floe. The

"On October 14th the ice was in convulsion ahead of the ship, and a splitting suddenly caused all hands to rush up on deck to find that a crack had opened fro lead ahead and passed along our starboard side to another crack that had opened

spanker was hoisted and we actually sailed one hundred yards.

We were now in a narrow lead, double the width of the ship's beam but blocked immediately ahead. Our position caused gravest anxiety as the floes came gradually together. With silent irresistible force, they nipped the ship in their terrific jaws. She creaked, shivered and protested in agony, but tighter and more relentless was the grip, until just when we expected to see her sides stave in, she slowly began to rise above the ice.

At this critical juncture the pressure fortunately ceased—as suddenly as if an arresting hand had been placed upon the controlling lever of some gigantic machine. We were balanced on the top of a pressure ridge and in imminent peril of toppling over on our beam ends. For several hours we remained thus poised precariously, then the floes drew gradually apart and we resumed a normal position.

The ice remained quiet throughout that night, but late the following afternoon it was seen to be again in motion. Watching from the deck the grinding of the floes against our sides, one could not but feel apprehensive. Every timber was straining to breaking point. The decks gaped; doors refused to open or shut; floor coverings buckled; and the iron floor plates in the engine room bulged and sprang from their seatings. The ship groaned, whined and quivered like a tortured creature in agony. Shortly after five P.M. she began to rise from the ice much after the manner of a pip squeezed between a giant's fingers. In the short space of seven seconds we were ejected from the floes and thrown over to port at a wicked angle. On deck great was the chaos—dogs, kennels, sledges, and emergency gear were thrown into tangled snapping confusion. Below deck men were pitched from their bunks, the cook's range upset, and all unsecured gear went the same way as the deck cargo. Laths were nailed to the deck to give foothold and order was laboriously restored.

Despite our predicament, dinner in the ward-room that evening was an occasion of great hilarity. We all sat on the floor with our feet jammed against the laths to prevent sliding, while the steward performed miracles of balancing passing round the plates of soup. Unthinkingly somebody would put down an empty plate or vessel on the floor and away it would career to port. We were all fervently thankful when the pressure was relieved at nine P.M. and we once more swung back to an even keel. During the last week of October the climax was reached in another act of our Antarctic drama. We had at this time twenty hours of daylight and the weather, though calm, was piercingly cold. I quote from my diary:

October 24th.—The floes which have been in motion during the afternoon, were assailing the ship on the starboard quarter with great energy. At 6 P.M. all hands go down on to the floe with picks, shovels and chisels, and cut trenches to try and relieve the strain, but we are miserably impotent. As fast as the ice can be hacked away new masses are hurled forward. At 7 P.M. an oncoming floe impinges on the helm, forcing it hard over to port and wrenching the rudder post. The ship's sternpost is seriously damaged, and the hidden ends of the planking started. Soundings in the well announce the gloomy tidings that we are rapidly making water. The pumps are manned, but it is a great task keeping them going as the water continually freezes and clogs the valve. The carpenter sets to work on a coffer dam in the shaft tunnel in the hope of sealing off the damaged stern of the vessel. Watches keep the pumps going vigorously. Their clickety clack resounds throughout the night above the ominous creaking of timbers. The position is serious.

October 25th.—Went down into the engine room this morning to see the progress made by Chips on the coffer dam. The water is level with the engine room floor but is still being held in check and we still hope to bring our staunch craft through. Outside, the configuration of the ice has undergone another complete change, most of the pools in our vicinity have been converted into pressure ridges, while there is an extensive lake half a mile away. Heavy pressure ridges menace us on starboard quarter and astern. The ship is in a highly dangerous situation with a heavy list to starboard. If the ridge advances it is obvious that the assailing ice will impinge above the sheer of the bilge and, as the ship is beset on every side with great masses of shattered ice, she will be unable to rise above the pressure. However, all is quiet for the present.

October 26th.—Fine clear day. The ice in a state of turmoil all the morning subjected the ship to terrific strains. I was assisting Chips on the coffer dam down in the shaft tunnel when the pressure set in and the creaking and groaning of timbers mingled with the pounding and scrunching against the ship's sides produced a hideous deafening din and warned us to make for safety. As there was a likelihood of the ship's sides crushing in and trapping us in the tunnel we hastened up on deck. All were actively engaged clearing the lowering gear of the boats and stacking the emergency stores in case of compulsory disembarkment which now seems inevitable.

The dogs, instinctively conscious of the imminent peril, set up distressed wails of uneasiness and fear. Sir Ernest stands on the poop, surveying the movements of the ice, and giving an occasional peremptory order. Sledges and all gear are being rapidly accumulated on deck, without confusion as though it were ordinary routine duty. At 6 P.M. the pressure develops terrific energy; apparently our vicinity is the focus, as the ice, a short distance off, remains motionless. The ship shrieks and quivers, windows splinter, while the deck timbers gape and twist. The brunt of the pressure assails our starboard quarter and the damaged sternpost. The ship is forced ahead by a series of pulsating jerks, and with such force that the bows are driven wedgewise into the solid floe ahead. This frightful strain bends the entire hull some ten inches along its length. At 7 P.M. the order is given to lower the boats. They are hauled some distance away from the *Endurance* and out of the zone of immediate danger. At 8.15 P.M. there is a welcome cessation in the ice movement, and all go on board to take their turns at the pumps and secure what rest they can.

October 27th.—Chips expects to complete the coffer dam to-night and great hopes are still entertained that he will be able to. All, including Sir Ernest, continue turns with the pumps which are able to keep pace with the inflowing water. We have just finished lunch and the ice mill is in motion again. Closer and closer the pressure wave approaches. Immense slabs are rafted, balance a moment, then topple down and are over-ridden by a chaos of crunched fragments. Irresistibly this stupendous power marches onward, grinding through the five feet ice floe surrounding

Sir Ernest stands on the poop surveying the movements of the ice.

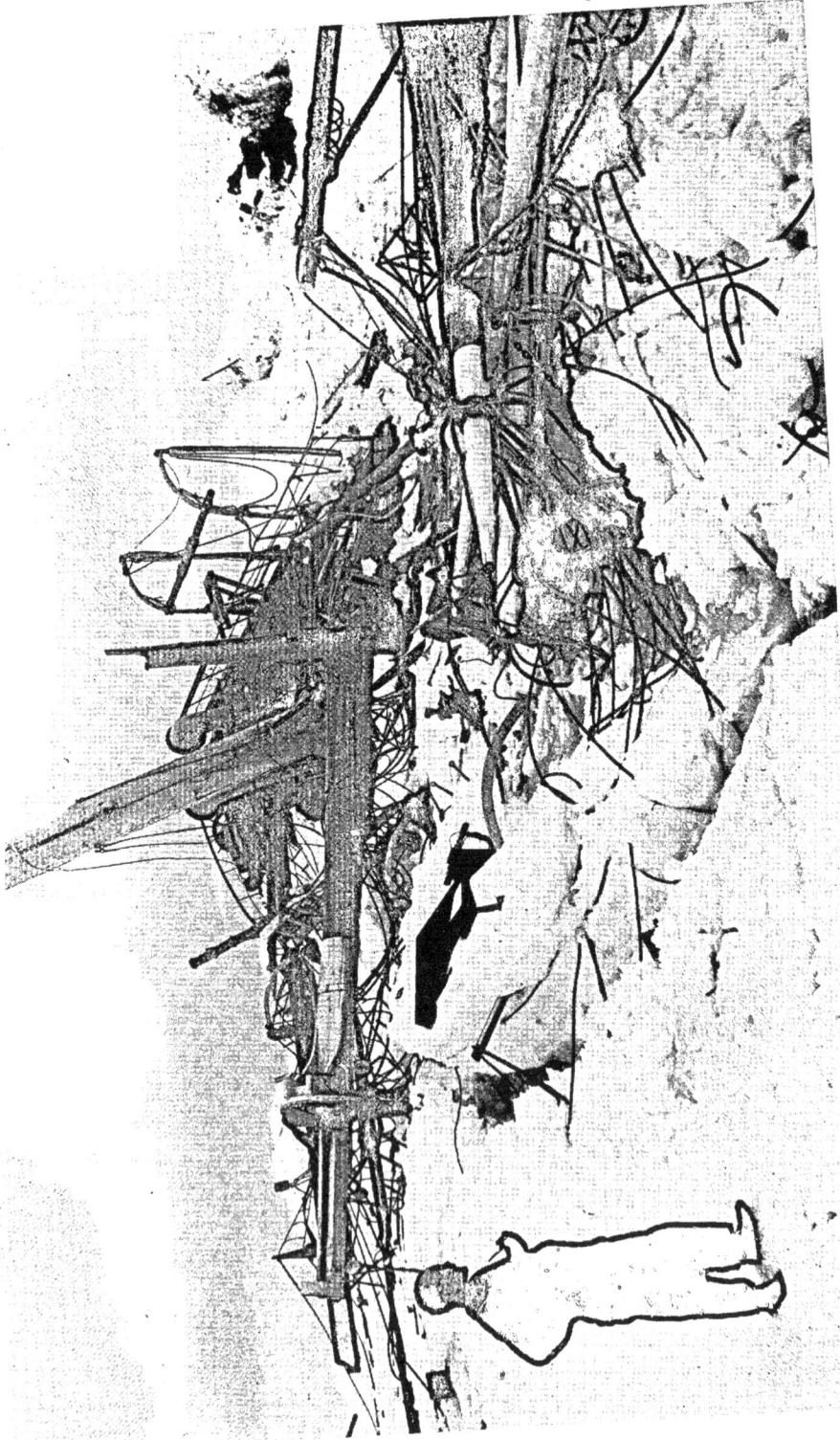

The ship was dead. Her proud timbers were rent apart and scattered in savage confusion.

us. Now it is within a few yards of the vessel. We are the embodiment of helpless futility and can only look impotently on. I am quickly down on the moving ice with the cinema, expecting every minute to see the sides, which are springing and buckling, stave in. The line of pressure now assaults the ship and she is heaved to the crest of the ridge like a toy. Immense fragments are forced under the counter and wrench away the sternpost. Sir Ernest and Captain Worsley are surveying the ship's position from the floe when the carpenter announces that the water is gaining rapidly on the pumps. All hands are ordered to stand by to discharge equipment and stores on to the ice. The pumps work faster and faster and someone is actually singing a chanty to their beat. The dogs are rapidly passed out down a canvas chute and secured on the floe, followed by cases of concentrated sledging rations, sledges and equipment. The ship is doomed.

By 8 P.M. all essential gear is "floed," and though the destruction of the ship continues, smoke may be observed issuing from the galley chimney—the cook is preparing supper. All hands assemble in the ward room to partake of the last meal aboard the good old ship. The meal is taken in silent gravity, whilst the crushing is in progress and an ominous sound of splintering timbers arises from below. We have grown indifferent to dangers for we have lived amongst them so long, and our sadness is for the familiar surroundings from which we are being expelled. The clock is ticking away on the wall as we take our final leave of the cosy ward room, that has for over twelve months been connected with pleasant associations and fraternal happiness. Before leaving, I went below into the old winter quarters, the Ritz, and found the waters swirling in and already a foot above the floor, the ribs disrupting and tongues of ice driving through the sides. Our ship has put up a valiant fight and done honour to her noble name, *Endurance.*

Sir Ernest hoists the blue ensign on the mizzen gaff to three lusty cheers and is last to leave. All equipment and boats are moved some three hundred yards as the floes are in active commotion in the vicinity of the ship. During the dim hours of midnight, the calm frigid atmosphere is resonant with the grinding of the pressure ice, and the hideous noises coming from the dying vessel. By some curious happening, the electric emergency light becomes automatically switched on and for an hour more an intermittent making and breaking of the circuit seems to transmit a final sad signal of farewell.

CHAPTER XII

ADRIFT ON THE SEA ICE

—to reside
In thrilling regions of thick-ribbed ice;
To be imprisoned in the viewless winds,
And blown with restless violence round about
The pendent world!

SHAKESPEARE.

SO ended our twelve months' sojourn on the *Endurance*, so began our five months' drift on the precarious sea ice.

During the 281 days in which the *Endurance* had been beset, we had drifted on a zigzag course approximately 1,500 miles—an average of about five miles a day. Actually we were 570 miles north-west of the position where our vessel had first been imprisoned and could no longer say:

Man made me and my will
Is to my maker still.

Our first night on the ice was bitterly cold. We were harassed by the working ice which split up beneath the tents or rafted into hummocks and pressure waves. Sir Ernest was ever on watch and, as I took refuge in one of the tents from the stabbing wind, the last sight I had was of a sombre figure pacing slowly up and down in the dark. I could not fail to admire the calm poise that disguised his anxiety, as he pondered on the next move. What was the best thing to do? How should he shape his tactics in the next round of the fight with Death, with the lives of 28 men as the stakes? I realised the loneliness and penalty of leadership.

Early next morning, before the others were astir, Wild and I rejoined him and together we went aboard the *Endurance*. Poor old ship, what a battered wreck she was! All the cabins along the starboard side had closed up like the bellows of a folding camera. The alleyways were under water and blocked with debris and ice, while the wardroom was crammed to the ceiling with ice blocks and splinters. Riding on the top of all among wrenched timbers and twisted steel were two objects that had survived without a scratch, the gramophone and a glazed picture! On the lower deck a veritable "hummocking" of timbers had taken place, the entire upper deck had been sheared off and fell away to starboard so that we could step from it on to the floe. Fore and aft resembled a switchback. The jibboom had snapped off, the fo'c's'le was overridden with ice, the foremast splintered at the crosstrees, the main shattered six feet above the deck, while the mizzen, with the Blue Ensign still floating at the gaff, remained staunch. The refrigerating chamber, which

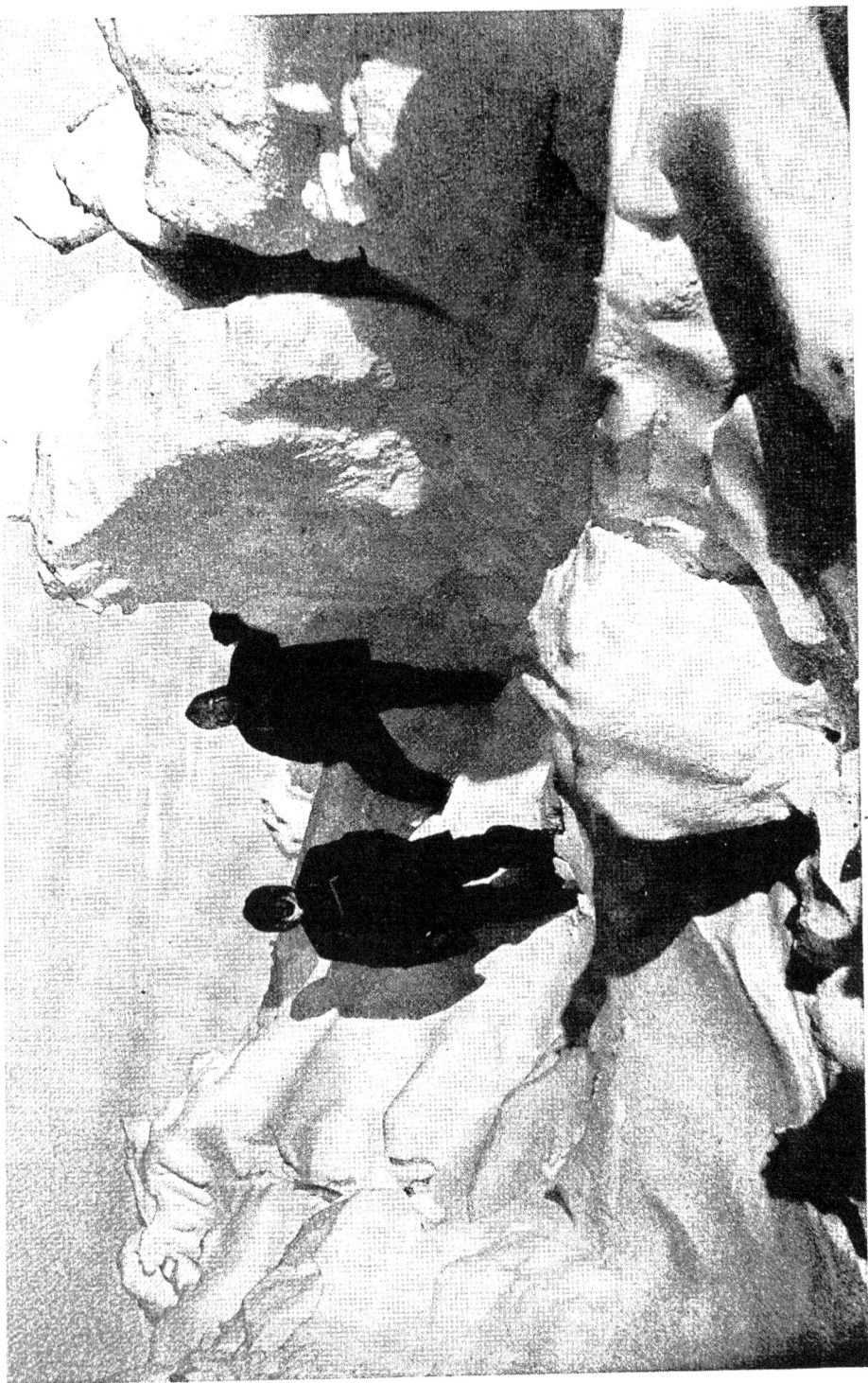

Sir Ernest Shackleton and Frank Wild scouting for a path to the land through the hummocks.

once served as my darkroom, was a wreck of timbers filled with mushy ice. Somewhere in the icy waters lay submerged the hermetically-sealed cases containing my films and negatives. I had been warned not to remove them from the ship owing to the desperate struggle which now lay before us in a march to the land—a march on which food alone could be carried.

With her stern cocked high in the air, it would have been difficult to recognise the *Endurance*, the acme of man's ingenuity in shipcraft, and his challenge to the might of the polar seas. It was evident that the wreck would sink as soon as the pressure relaxed and the piercing tongues of ice acting as supports were withdrawn. We returned with several tins of benzine, kindled a fire and roused the camp.

For the past two months, most of us had realised that the vessel was doomed. The inactivity aboard had become a dreary monotony, and though the outcast life into which the destruction of the ship now exiled us was desperate enough, we looked forward to the future optimistically. The last weeks had been filled with anxiety and uncertainty and we felt relieved when Fate proclaimed the verdict, cruel though it seemed.

Sir Ernest decided that an attempt must be made to reach Paulette Island, 350 miles to the N. N. West. There was a small hut, and a cache of food left in 1902 by the Swedish Expedition under Otto Nordenskjold. Before setting out each man was provided with his share of the salvaged clothing, into which he changed.

It was so evident that we could win through only by the barest margin that every superfluous ounce was seen to be a handicap and everything beyond the barest necessaries was abandoned. I observed Sir Ernest take a handful of sovereigns from his pockets and toss them down a crack in the ice. He lifted from the dump, that represented the trimmings of civilisation, a pocket volume of Browning. "I throw away trash and am rewarded with golden inspirations," he said. Little indeed did he think at the time what a source of consolation and inspiration that volume was to be, not only to himself, but also to his tentmates.

Before setting out Sir Ernest addressed the party, thanking them for their loyalty towards him during the trying conditions of the past and asking them to continue their faith in him during the severe trials that threatened the future. His simple words, nobly spoken, touched the heart and put every man on his mettle. It was a sad scene. The leader with his men around him; the discarded gear strewn about on the snow; the sledges lashed, and whining dogs harnessed ready for the march; the cheerless sky; and in the background the grim outlines of the crushed ship surrounded with ice and debris.

We started for Paulette Island full of hope and vigour, for the general health of the party had been good, and the dogs were in fine condition. They seemed to realise the straits we were in and behaved magnificently, working as I had never seen them work before.

My team generally took the lead, as Shakespeare—good old fellow—was unrivalled for picking out a track. The orders issued for the march were as follows:

A pathfinding party of three will start at 7 A.M. with a light sledge, and demolish hummocks, bridge cracks, and smooth out the track. This party has a couple of hours lead on the main body. Then follow seven sledges, each drawn by seven dogs and with an average load of 100 pounds per dog. Five teams to return and bring up the balance of the gear loaded on five sledges. The remaining two teams, Wild's and Hurley's, will link together and bring up the light boat. The balance of the party, eighteen members, will manhaul the large boat—the *James Caird*.

The arrangement dispensed with the disheartening relaying by the men, this work falling to the lot of the dogs which, even with the double haulage, were working at about half their capable efficiency. However, almost from the start the going was so hard that we had to go over the ground three times to bring up the loads. Then the weather grew so thick that we were forced to camp for hours at a time. The surface was terrible, deep in soft snows through which we trudged, and treacherous with pitfalls into which we fell. On the third day we toiled like Titans, and advanced a single mile! On the fourth it was a little better. There were deep holes to be negotiated and sharp ice-blades to avoid. A patch of rotten ice would give way, and let us into the sea. Water leads and hummocks barred the way.

At the end of the fourth day Sir Ernest called a halt,

and announced his intention of abandoning the attempt, and establishing a permanent camp on a piece of old floe-ice. The sledges were beginning to break under the rough going, and the boats were showing signs of damage. The other members consulted wished to push on and try to win through, but the leader was firm. It was one of those crises in an expedition when the true leader proves himself; and Shackleton stood the test. On his decision hung the lives of the party, and his judgment was, that the icefields which barred the way to Paulette Island were impassable.

The positive plan of escape having definitely failed after heroic efforts, we settled down to the only alternative, a negative policy—a policy of watchful waiting. Our hope now was that the ice-pack would drift northward to the open sea, when the boats would be launched and an endeavour made to reach one of the whaling stations at the South Shetland Island, 450 miles away. It was a slender enough thread of hope for twenty-eight men to hang upon; yet like a golden strand it held us up during five wretched months. We knew generally that the prevailing winds were from the south, and that the tides were setting in a northerly direction. Moreover, we were aware that even while we had been confined to the ship the whole vast field had been in motion; for every day our position had been determined by the theodolite, and we knew it to within a few hundred yards. In brief, we were on a gigantic raft of ice, which, in due course, must inevitably go to pieces, and our problem was to travel as far as it would carry us, and then get clear of the disintegrating material without loss of life or stores, and without damage to our final resource, the boats.

The first duty was to form a more or less permanent camp, and the second was to furnish and provision it. The point at which further progress on our march to the land was blocked, seemed to offer a favourable site, and there one section was set to work while another, under Wild, sledged back to the ship for salvage.

Ocean Camp, for so we called it, was situated about four miles from the *Endurance*. Here the boats were drawn up, tents to accommodate the party were pitched, and the sailors erected a canvas hut twenty-three by eleven feet for galley and shelter which was christened the Billabong.

In the smallest tent, the leader, James, Hudson and myself took up our crowded residence, while those who had formed close friendships aboard the vessel were likewise clubbed together.

Meantime, the dog-teams and their drivers were busily employed, and without exception relished the activity. We proceeded to salve the wreck systematically, and to transfer from the "dump camp" beside her all the gear that might prove useful. This adventure—owing to the fact that the *Endurance* merely hung suspended in two thousand and sixty fathoms of ocean by the great tongues of ice that were thrust through her ribs—was liberally spiced with danger. Having removed the overhanging spars and cleared away many tons of ice and snow, Wild and his men had rigged up a reciprocating drill—made from a large ice-chisel lashed to a spar—and cut a hole in the deck just above our old living quarters. As soon as the planking was removed, there was an outrush of walnuts, onions, and small buoyant articles. By diligent probing round with boathooks, case after case was directed to the opening, from which they emerged buoyantly to the surface.   If one of the fishers brought to light a case of high food-value, a great cheer arose. I arrived on the scene just in time to see a keg of soda carbonate greeted with groans. The party worked at high pressure all day, taking advantage of the tranquil state of the ice, and by evening, practically all the cases were retrieved. All the flour was saved, as well as a large quantity of the sugar—the two commodities we counted most essential. The teams were busy transporting the ice-covered cases, timbers and salvaged sundries to the camp all day, each team averaging five trips loaded to full capacity.

Next day, after the salving of the stores was completed, unknown to the leader, I went down to the wreck with one of the sailors to make a determined effort to rescue my films and negatives. We hacked our way through the splintered timbers and after vainly fishing in the ice-laden waters with boathooks, I made up my mind to dive in after them. It was mighty cold work groping about in the mushy ice in the semi-darkness of the ship's bowels, but I was re-warded in the end and passed out the three precious tins. While seaman How was massaging me vigor-ously to restore my blood's circulation, the vessel began to shake and groan ominously. We sprang for our lives and leaped onto the ice—almost into the arms of the astonished leader who wanted to know—

"What the hell we were up to."

However Sir Ernest at once accepted the position with his usual good humour and I fancy was glad of the salvage. A large sum of money had been advanced against the motion picture rights to help to finance the Expedition and these were the assets.

I might mention in this connection that when it came to a question of selecting only such negatives as might be taken with us, so as to keep down weight as much as possible, I had a painful hour. Sir Ernest and I went over the plates together, and as a negative was rejected, I would smash it on the ice to obviate all temptation to change my mind. Finally, the choice was made, and the films and plates that I considered indispensable were stowed away in one of the boats, having first been placed in double tins hermetically sealed. About 400 plates were jettisoned and 120 retained. Later I had to preserve them almost with my life; for a time came when we had to choose between heaving them overboard or throwing away our surplus food—and the food went over! All my photographic gear was compulsorily abandoned, except one small pocket camera and three spools of unexposed film. I wonder if three spools of film ever went through more exacting experiences before they were developed.

While on the subject of salvage I might add that I recovered the volumes of the Encyclopædia from the chief's cabin, and a good deal of my own personal library, as well as several packs of cards. Many a day we had cause to bless the fact. What tedious hours were whiled away in reading; what wonderful and purely imaginary fortunes changed hands at poker patience!

One of the last objects hauled from the wreck was the steel ash-chute from which I constructed a blubber-fed cooking range, cutting pot-holes through the quarter-inch mild steel with a tiny chisel. Sundry oil drums and empty cans completed the contraption which added materially to the cook's comfort, and our well-being.

Thus, well-sheltered and amply-provisioned, we settled down to what was surely one of the most extraordinary cruises in the history of deep-sea navigation. Around us spread as far as the eyes could reach, fields of snow, which not even the most fertile imagination could conceive to be the frozen bosom of the sea. We ourselves could scarcely realise that we were dwelling on a colossal raft, with a few feet of ice separating us from twelve thousand feet of ocean. Our motive power was the mighty forces of Nature, which we could neither regulate nor control, and our Pilot was the Originator and Director of these forces.

On November 8 we paid the final official visit to the remnant of the *Endurance*. From the shattered poop we fired a detonator to salute the ensign that still fluttered over the heap of fragmentary timbers and twisted rails. And so we left her. It was not until a fortnight later, however, that the derelict escaped from further tortures and dived to her last resting place. It was evening and we were all in our sleeping bags when Sir Ernest called from the lookout, "She's going, boys." We hastened out of the tents and climbed to the lookout and vantage points. Sure enough, a mile and a half away the poor old ship was in her final death throes. The stern rose vertically in the air. Then she dived quickly below the ice. A little later the ice-floes came together and threw up a high pressure ridge—a monument to her. Her name *Endurance* was a fitting motto to inscribe upon our banners as we moved forward into the unknown future.

The disappearance of the ship cast a temporary gloom over the camp. Although battered beyond recognition she still stood as a symbol of civilisation and a link with the outside world. Now that she had gone, a feeling of intense isolation and loneliness fell over us. But it passed and later at meal time all were as cheerful and bright as ever and Sir Ernest was bantering the cook over the thinness and smallness of the bannocks. The cook with ready wit replied "that the disappearance of the ship had given Lees the storeman such qualms and doleful visions of the party perishing through starvation that he had only issued him half a ration of flour for the bannocks." "Oh! Well, issue double the number of bannocks and get more flour from Lees," responded Sir Ernest.

From this date till the close of the year, our camp in happy contentment—come fair, come foul—reflected good leadership and fine comradeship. We had good health and ample food; which was further supplemented with stray seals and penguins.

In six weeks we drifted one hundred and twenty miles. During the last week of the year we struck camp and made another desperate effort to reach the land. This attempt also had to be abandoned. The surface was a chaos of hummocks, ridges, fissures and hidden treacheries which made progress absolutely impossible. A new camp was then established—Patience Camp. It was some ten miles west of Ocean Camp, and was in a stronger strategic position in relation to Paulette Island, which now bore N.W. 189 miles.

We hailed the New Year with a cheer. Leads and pools on every side gave satisfactory indications that the ice would break up and afford us an early chance of launching the boats. But during a fortnight of abominable weather, the floes closed up again, and the drift and adverse winds forced us back upon our tracks a distance of seven miles.

Then came a very sorrowful incident. For some little while it had been felt that the time had arrived when the ranks of our dogs must be thinned out. It was a painful thought but owing to the increasingly broken nature of the surface, their use was becoming more and more limited and in addition they were becoming a grievous tax on our larder, as the supply of seals diminished. On January 14th I made a laborious scouting trip for seals—the going over the broken and cracked ice was very difficult—and reached Pinnacle Berg. From its summit I closely examined the floes for miles round with 12 magnification prisms, but there was not a sign of a flipper at any point of the compass. This report finally settled the fate of the dogs and during the afternoon four teams—those of Wild, Crean, Marston and McIlroy—were shot. They were 35 magnificent sledgers and they had done us good service, but it had to come sooner or later and since they consumed an entire seal a day, enough to last the whole party for three days, the decision was un-avoidable. My team and Macklin's were under sen-tence, but execution was suspended upon my sugges-tion that we should first make an attempt to reach Ocean Camp—to retrieve what was left of the farin-aceous food and odd stores.

Macklin and I spent the afternoon cutting a road-way from the camp to an adjacent large floe to give us an unencumbered start to Ocean Camp. At 6.30 A.M. we set out and after two miles of desultory going came across an extremely difficult area of leads and pressure ridges. We had to bridge the leads with ice-blocks and cut a way through the ridges. After some four hours of solid pick and shovel work another mile was covered. The surface then became disheartening, the dogs sinking deep to their bellies in soft snow and having to paddle their way. At every few steps we sank in to the thighs. Finally the two teams were linked together while I went ahead on skis and broke trail. This answered much better, but travelling was still so heavy that frequent spells had to be allowed the dogs. We arrived at Ocean Camp at 4.30 P.M. It had taken us ten hours to cover the ten miles. A good brew of coffee and a meal of tinned cauliflower and Irish stew, which we selected from the stores that we had been obliged to abandon when we left this spot, cheered us up immensely. We then set about collecting our load.

Ocean Camp presented a forlorn appearance and resembled a deserted Alaskan mining village ransacked by bandits. The abandoned gear was half buried in snow, and pools of water had formed everywhere. The Billabong itself was surrounded by a lake three feet deep. We gave the dogs a full ration of pemmican, and after a couple of hours' rest, made a much easier run back in spite of the heavy load, having the advantage of the track we had broken down. We returned to camp after a six hours' run—having added an additional 900 pounds to the larder, nearly an extra month's supply of concentrated rations.

Sunday was an easy day in camp and Macklin and I were not sorry to make it a day of rest. Wild shot my team during the afternoon—a sad but imperative necessity. I said goodbye to my faithful old leader Shakespeare with an aching pang in my heart. It seemed like murdering in cold blood a trusty pal—alas! there was no alternative. Food was running short and the end was inevitable as the dogs could never be taken in the boats.

A fortnight later it was decided to try and bring in the third boat, the *Stancombe Wills*, which had remained abandoned all this time at Ocean Camp. Observations showed that the distance between our old Ocean Camp and our new "Patience Camp," owing to the shuffling of the icefloes, had decreased from ten miles to six. As it was still light all night, Crean and I with the dogs left camp at one A.M. path-finding, and a party of sixteen men followed our trail, covering the distance in a couple of hours as against the ten which we had taken on our first trip. The venture was entirely successful. On the return journey Crean, James, McIlroy and I went ahead as "trail breakers"—demolishing ridges, breaking down hummocks and bridging gaps in the ice—and the others dragged the boat on runners. The dog team hauled a load of stores and sundries. Sir Ernest, with one of his brilliant inspirations, sledged out to meet us a mile from camp with two cans of steaming tea, and with lusty voices, grateful, if husky from fatigue, we all cheered and sang "He's a jolly good fellow." Nothing in the whole of the world's "wet" resources could compare with that jorum of hot tea. Nothing stimulates and heartens a toiling body like tea. Like the famous Doctor Johnson we all could have consumed 27 cups. Renewed and refreshed we made light of that last mile and in less than an hour the boat lay on the floe at Patience Camp. How she served us in a pinch will be told later. A few days afterwards Ocean Camp was observed to be several miles farther away; the ice had opened out and an attempt to reach it with the last dog team was frustrated. We never had the opportunity of visiting it again. The boat had been salvaged just in the nick of time.

Our meals were now cooked on a portable "bogie" which I improvised from two oil drums and sundry scraps of metal. This small range would consume anything combustible but roared away like a miniature furnace when fed with seal blubber or penguin skins. Green, our capable cook aboard the *Endurance*, continued his duties undaunted. A "galley," or more correctly speaking, a wind screen, had been rigged up, by pushing four oars into the snow and straining round them an old sail. Green's never-ending activities among the flying blubber soots gave him the appearance of a merry chimney sweep who had not washed for many months. He did his cooking thoroughly—too well at times—and if chided about the leathery toughness or cinder-like crispness of a seal steak, had a ready fund of wit which always completely exonerated him and laid the blame on the seal.

Each man took his turn to act as mess "Peggy" for his tent. His duties for the day were, to go to the "galley," collect the steaks in the hoosh pot and return with them to his hungry tentmates. The "Peggy" then proceeded to sort out the steaks into portions as equal as possible and "whosed" them. One of the occupants turned his back, so that he might not see the steaks, and the "Peggy," skewering a portion, would demand "whose?" The questioned one then pronounced the name of one of his tentmates, and so the steaks were "whacked out." This method entirely dispensed with any suggestion of favouritism or unfairness.

Table furniture was of the simplest. Our tent possessed a sheath knife which was common property. Each man had, in addition to a tin lid which served as a plate, a spoon, either a souvenir from the *Endurance*, or one carved from a piece of wreckage. To lose a spoon or a knife was a calamity. By this time we had begun to fear a shortage of food and rations had to be strictly economized. It was therefore customary to dally as long as possible over meals so that their meagreness might not be so apparent, and mental satisfaction at least be stimulated.

With a sigh the last morsel was sedulously scraped from the tin lid, spoons licked and put by into the indispensable pocket on the chest of the jersey. "Peggy" then took the "hoosh" pot outside and scoured it with snow. Occasionally meals were modified with a ration of dog pemmican. This was canned by the makers in one pound tins and the "Peggy" for the next day took the tin into his sleeping bag overnight to thaw it out. For breakfast the square of pemmican was cut into four equal cubes and "whosed." A beverage was concocted from powdered dry milk and hot water, its redeeming quality being its warmth. This potion mixed with the dog pemmican in proper proportion and vigorously stirred, produced a doubtful mixture not unlike haggis.

Meal times, too, especially after evening dinner, when pipes were lighted, were the times of conversation.

Weather!—a commonplace topic in the cities of civilisation, meant life to us. Weather was the paramount tent topic. Wind was the propelling and guiding influence that held our freedom in its breath. If the breeze was fair and there had been sunshine, talk was gay and hopes ran high. Adverse weather, false winds and set-back drifts were received with silent gravity. "What is the wind's direction?" was the never-ending query in the camp. Every puff or caprice was given as much attention as if it were a delicate mechanism to be cajoled. Temperatures, blizzards, inconveniences, worried us not, so long as the wind was with us.

Every four hours, Hussey, the meteorologist and the bringer of tidings of gladness or consternation, reported at our tent and gave Sir Ernest the weather forecast. Worsley with his sextant and James with the theodolite had a competition at noon each day to determine the latitude and compute the distance the sea ice had drifted during the twenty-four hours.

Their report was anxiously awaited by all. If exceptionally favourable, our scanty ration would be increased; if we had been set back, the gloom was doubled by shrinking economy.

Second in importance as a subject of conversation, came "grub." But if there had been a dearth of seals hunger pinched and conversation waned. Much speculation ensued over the compilation of prospective menus though all were agreed that their desires were for good and plenty, rather than a procession of "tantalising" flavours, devoid of substance, even if they could be served on silver salvers. For such repasts as we craved the descriptive designation of "Gorgie" was coined.

At rarer intervals there were poetic outpourings; and though we loved to hear snatches from Tennyson, Service, Keats and Browning, strangely assorted companions in that wilderness, I recall an amusing incident which indicated forcibly the real trend of our thoughts.

Sir Ernest, reciting Browning's "Rabbi Ben Ezra," came to the well-known lines:

And all the world's course thumb
And finger fail to plumb.

He was interrupted by a muffled voice from a sleeping-bag with the feeling interjection of "Couldn't we do with plum duffs now!"

And what a grand tentmate Sir Ernest was. A close friendship had sprung up between us and always when things were blackest he rose to his best. He was the very soul of encouragement, though in those days he seemed to have grown old. I could read in the furrowed lines behind his smile, that his mind was never at rest, but was always working to devise plans for our safety or to anticipate the unexpected. He was completely unselfish and wondrously tolerant—never thinking of himself and, in spite of his constant anxiety, had regard for our most trivial wants.

It is in these circumstances, stripped of the veneers of civilisation, that one sees the real man. Living in such intimate contact, under conditions of ever-present peril, one senses his fellow's thoughts, ay, scans his very soul. And I must say that whatever dangers or hardships I may have experienced, were generously paid by having had this man's confidence and comradeship.

And we talked—of what did we not talk!

In spite of his heavy burdens Sir Ernest retained all that wholesome boyishness of spirit that had endeared him to all. When elated by a favourable drift or brighter prospect he would discourse enthusiastically on such subjects as the recovery of the treasure of Alexis, or of King John's Train. Then he would lead

imaginary expeditions to the Indies and South Sea Isles in quest of buried treasure and pearls. He would even give us the exact latitude and longitude where they lie buried! Often indeed in imagination I wandered with him in some glorious adventure, excited by the lust of the treasure hunt, not for the sake of the booty but for the sheer joy in winning it.

Sir Ernest's memory was inexhaustible. He had a ready phrase or a quotation for everything. A born poet, through all his oppressions he could see glory and beauty in the stern forces which had reduced us to destitution and against which he was fighting.

Sometimes conversation glided into strange channels, such as the development of commerce on the Yenesei, the arts and crafts of Ancient Egypt, comparisons of the social life of London, New York and Paris, etc. Then we had debates on such varied subjects as the birth rate, the liquor question, the mysteries of lighthouse optics, ship construction, the elusive unknown quantity "X," and so forth, and disputations were referred to the arbitration of the *Encyclopædia Britannica*. But by far the most popular of tent topics were talks of other lands and unknown places. I told of travels in the East Indies and wanderings in hidden Australia, and delighted to hear in return of the tinkling temple bells of Burma, and about the homeland, from the heaths of bonnie Scotland, to London with its "stream of liquid history"—the Thames. After evening "hoosh" had set the blood coursing and the body aglow with tingling warmth, we would lie in our sleeping-bags and meditate. We longed to indulge in the lassitude of the hot room and feel the exquisite sensation of donning the latest cut clothes. Our pockets (or where they would have been had we any) burned with desire to patronise the refinements of civilisation and its gaieties. Darkness quickly came in the tents, when winter drew nigh, and with the final prayer of "Blow, good breezes, blow," we turned over in our bags to dream of safety, home, dances and dinners, that would afford food for the conversation of the morrow.

Each day during the afternoon, Sir Ernest and I made it a regular practice to play six games of poker patience and at the end of ten weeks our aggregate scores were within a few points of each other. I had become the possessor of an imaginary shaving glass, several top hats, walking canes enough to equip a regiment, sets of sleeve links and a library of books. Moreover, I had dined at his expense at Claridge's and occupied a box at the Opera. Sir Ernest had become the owner of scores of fine linen handkerchiefs, silk umbrellas, a mirror; a coveted collector's copy of *Paradise Regained;* and had been my guest at dinner at the Savoy and visited at my expense most of the theatres in London!

During our life at Patience Camp it fell largely to my lot, as being expert on skis, to be the hunter of the party and keep the larder and fuel stocks supplied.

Seal hunting can hardly be classed among the nobler sports, but when twenty-eight men are depending upon the chase for fresh meat, firing and lighting, there is a keenness about the hunt that no mere sport can equal. Shod with a pair of reliable skis the hunter would sally forth to look for game and if none was visible a visit would be paid to one of the bergs—Flat Berg or Pinnacle Berg—and from that vantage point the icefield would be minutely raked through a pair of powerful glasses. In the distance a dark slug-like object would be seen basking beside a hummock or lying on the edge of a lead. Perhaps two or more would offer and, choosing the one most accessible to camp, the hunter would lope off and, taking care to approach without being seen, come up with his quarry. Sometimes, indeed, no precautions were necessary, for the Weddell seal, though a superb swimmer, the embodiment of sinuous grace in the water, is, when on the ice, very slow-moving and easily killed. The ski makes a handy weapon, and pursuing the orthodox method, the hunter stuns his victim with a shrewd blow on the blunt nose and cuts its throat with a sweep of the knife. It is brutal and a messy business, but it is one of dire necessity.

Hunting on the solid floe presented no danger, but when scouting amongst loosening pack one must needs be both alert and cautious. Skis were then indispensable for cracks four and five feet wide had to be crossed. The negotiation of them and of the brash ice developed in us a cat-like delicacy of tread.

Penguin stalking is much the same. But while neither seal nor penguin put up any defence, the element of risk is supplied by the killer whales which are apt to poke their ugly heads through the thin ice with a snort that immediately imparts to the hunter a marvellous turn of speed and a keen desire to get back to a solid floe. Frequently during these excursions I had many narrow escapes. Occasionally the ice would open up into a wide lead and I would ferry across the water on a small floe using my skis for paddles. I speedily abandoned the habit of taking these short cuts, as one day a school of seven killer whales began blowing in the lead around me and gave me the scare of my life.

Occasionally I came on large convoys of penguins too numerous to cope with single-handed. Then I would heliograph to the camp with a small pocket mirror and all hands would turn out armed with clubs to the necessary slaughter. One day we added 300 penguins to our depleted larder. The birds were evidently migrating from the southern rookeries to the northern pack limits. The skins were reserved for fuel, the legs for "hoosh," breasts for steaks, and livers and hearts for delicacies. A seal was consumed by the party with restrained appetites in five days—just as long as his blubber lasted to cook him. Twenty penguins cooked by the fuel of their own skins was a fair daily average. The floe, had, by pressure, formed ice ridges and hummocks. These by a process of exfiltration had discharged the brine of their original sea water and what remained—fresh water ice—was the source of our supply of drinking water. Through all our experiences on the floe, game never entirely failed us. At times, we were compelled to go on short rations, but when we were hard pressed, something had a curious and providential knack of turning up.

Just at the end of March, for example, when a severe shortage was felt, a huge sea leopard was secured and in its stomach were found some fifty fish in excellent condition. These were eaten with much gusto. Immediately afterwards a second leopard, eleven feet long, was enticed from a lead by several of our men who hopped about on its icy shore like penguins! A crabeater seal actually blundered into our camp the same night in the dark!

All through these times we kept anxious watch on the weather. It was not the wind's roar and buffet that worried us; but its absence. There was one special period of exasperation. For a tantalising month we zigzagged a score of times to and fro across the Antarctic Circle. It really seemed as if the spirit of Antarctica held us in durance and refused to permit us to cross its border line, the 67th parallel. At last, a blizzard sent us to our tents for several days, while the wind roared constantly from the south-west. When the murk cleared enough for an observation, we awaited the verdict of the navigating officers (Worsley and James) with anxiety. It was not merely favourable;

it was amazing—Latitude 65.43. We had been posi-
tively "bowling along." Through four days we had
averaged nearly twenty miles per day! A total northerly drift of seventy-four miles was the record we established! The spell was broken! The sun came out, and
the camp assumed the appearance of a laundry.
Clothes, sleeping-bags, gear, sundries of all kinds,
swung on lines hung in the warm sunshine, and as the
soggy condition of the past few days gave place to dry
comfort, spirits rose, and visions of the open seas
framed themselves in our minds.

But the caprice of Antarctic weather again exhib-
ited itself and we were blown back three miles by
adverse winds.

The disappointment, awful monotony, inactivity,
and the return of wretched weather now made life
well-nigh unbearable. To add to our plight food was
scarce and we were everlastingly hungry. The biting
cold of the blizzards pierced through our threadbare
garments and deluged us with wet snow. When calms
fell and the temperature rose, conditions were scarcely
better, for the warmth of our bodies thawed the soft
snow beneath our sleeping-bags into puddles and
everything became soaked. When the temperature
fell again our clothes and sleeping-bags froze as stiff as
boards.

We seemed to be in an icy maze. When the floes
opened up, a dense wet fog rose from the water and
obscured everything fifty yards away. Then when

the south wind came and cleared it away, and we looked eagerly for a chance to launch the boats, the temperature fell rapidly and the open water froze over again.

On March 17th Paulette Island lay abreast 60 miles to the west, but the surface which had barred us previously by its insurmountable hummocks and ridges was now infinitely worse through decay. We turned our hopes to the Danger Islands, mere pinnacles of rock 35 miles distant, said to be inaccessible, but still a possible refuge to castaways in our predicament.

On April 2nd Wild shot the remaining dog team. The carcasses were dressed for food but we found the meat extremely tough as the poor creatures had been on very scant rations for some time. We had dearly hoped that the ice would have carried us close to the land and we could have saved their lives. But the culminating struggle lay close before us and it would be quite impossible to take them on such a voyage as we would soon be forced to undertake.

Sir Ernest, who was on watch, on the night of the 22nd March called me early the next morning to corroborate his view that a point lifting its bulk through the fog was land. It was one of the Danger Islands, and, later in the day, we sighted a range of misty peaks on Joinville Land. Forty miles only separated us from it, but the forty miles were over impassable icefields, and might as well have been forty thousand! A single day at the oars would have taken us there—but our boats might as well have been bicycles!

Nevertheless, our eyes had seen that which confirmed our faith. That point of land looming through the mist was evidence that there was still something solid in the Universe. It was a peak of actuality in the landscape of uncertainty. It was the seal upon the knowledge of our scientists; the assurance that we were not to spend the rest of our lives in nightmare wanderings inscribed like a gigantic fever-chart upon the map of this desolation.

However, the precise landing-place which was to be our stepping-stone to the world of men was still, and, for many a day to come, was to remain a matter of conjecture. We knew for certain that forty miles to the west lay Joinville Land and the Danger Islands. One hundred miles to the north were Elephant and Clarence Islands, King George Island lay a little farther north-west; which was it to be? A sweep of twenty-eight miles in a single day pointed to Clarence Island as our possible destination; then a strong north-west drift turned our thoughts to Elephant Island; but again a current carried us so strongly westward that Elephant Island was placed beyond the range of our hopes, and King George Island—best of all, on account of its accessibility to the whaling station at Deception Island—seemed to lie directly in our path.

The first unmistakable intimation that we were approaching ice-free waters was the opening and closing of an insignificant crack around the margin of the

The castaways adrift on the sea ice. Sir Ernest Shackleton and Frank Wild are standing together at the left of the picture.

floe. Although only just perceptible, it indicated that the swell from the open ocean was working through and that the ice was swaying under its influence.

The news caused a sensation in camp and, throughout the day, we loitered by the working crack—noting with intense satisfaction that the action was gradually increasing. It was a gladsome sight—a welcome presage that our long tedious drift on the floes was at last drawing to a close.

Visions of the wide ocean, rolling deep, blue and free, filled our minds and we eagerly discussed the respective merits of various refuge points to which we might sail. Elephant Island sounded enticing; the name suggested the haunts of the succulent sea-elephant. Prince George Island, eighty miles farther west, was equally attractive; sea-elephants would doubtless be found there as well, and Sir Ernest informed us that the Admiralty Sailing Directions mentioned a cave. We were indeed fortunate. Sea-elephant for food and a cave for shelter! What more could any man desire! We unanimously agreed, however, that Deception Island, still further west, was preferable, as the whalers made it a headquarters during the summer months. In its favour, there were huts, a depot of stores, and a small church. The stores would enable us to survive the winter months, and if necessity compelled, we could build a seaworthy vessel from the timbers of the church! The carpenter drew designs in the snow, and pictured to us a sturdy craft built from beams and pews. His dream ship looked wondrously alluring with her swelling sails of threadbare tent fabric bearing us over seas of fancy to freedom. How simple and easy it all appeared!

But as day followed day and the Atlantic surges drew closer and the ponderous ice-floes drew apart, only to crash together thunderously and splinter, we ceased all comparisons and came to the conclusion that any bit of rock capable of affording refuge would be a glorious haven after all our tribulations.

The long life on the floe had lulled us into a sense of false security. We scarcely thought of the icy plain on which we were camped for what it was—a treacherous layer covering the surface of an ocean two miles deep. Now that the white floor began to shatter and disintegrate beneath our feet, feelings of helplessness and utter dereliction crept insidiously over us.

We had cherished hopes that the floes might have carried us close to land, or at least have opened up into navigable leads that would have enabled us to reach the shore without facing the open sea. This was now impossible, as the currents had carried us beyond the northernmost limit of the mainland.

How often we had buoyed our hopes on empty objectives and unrealised fancies. How often had miraged shapes stirred us to excitement that was followed by depression when the "dream islets" melted away into deceiving clouds or resolved themselves into icebergs as we drifted closer to them. It was natural, therefore, that Captain Worsley and I should gaze doubtingly over the pack-ice to the swaying horizon and to a nebulous contour to which Sir Ernest was pointing under the impression that it was land. Even as we strained our eyes, anxious to confirm yet sceptical, the sea haze cleared a little and we made out black patches of rock! The peak, which was about sixty miles distant, could be no other than Clarence Island. It lay directly in the path of our drift and if the current and winds continued fair, in a few days we would be walking on solid rock. What a sensation! It was sixteen months since we had seen rock and walked on it at South Georgia. Oh! blessed memory!

Late in the afternoon a group of low peaks loomed up to the north-west which our charts indicated to be Elephant Island.

Elephant and Clarence Islands were the last outposts of Antarctica. Between them the sea rolled as through a broad portal and, if we failed to land on one of them, we must be swept through into the tempestuous spaces of the open ocean. We were indeed the forlorn playthings of colossal forces.

The daily spectacle of the disruption of the ice-packs on which we were living so precariously was appalling and terrifying. The swells of the ocean now came surging through the icefields from the north, in great undulations from horizon to horizon. The floes bent under the heave, yet no open water was visible. When exceptionally violent swells reached the centre of the floes, they splintered like sheets of glass, and then, as the fragments drew apart, the inky waters showed through. A few moments later, the fractured pieces would batter and grind into one another adjusting their new shapes to the oncoming waves.

As we continued the northerly drift the floe on which we were encamped shared the fate of its neighbours. Yet there was no water in which to launch the boats. We shuddered at the thought that the ice might split into fragments too small to carry the camp, and yet remain in a compact grinding mass without opening up.

Whatever might be in store for us, one thing was certain; it would call for the last ounce of our strength, and in order that our emaciated bodies might be more capable of enduring the coming conflict, extra seal-steaks were issued while everything was held ready for a hurried effort.

Guards patrolled the camp day and night to give warning at the first sight of danger. Rest was not for us. The battering impact of the floes and the dread of the ice splitting beneath our tents and letting us drop through into the sea was ever with us. We sat up in our sleeping-bags fully dressed, shivering through the laggard nights waiting for the dawn. Haggard faces and dulled eyes told painfully a story of fatigue and anxiety.

In these times of bitter adversity, Sir Ernest's leadership was a supreme encouragement. He too felt as we felt, but never a word nor sign betrayed him. He sank his own distress. Although burdened with the knowledge that the lives of twenty-eight men depended on his judgment, he still had an eye to each man's smallest wants, and words of hope and cheer to inspire his followers.

There were times, however, when his overwrought mind cried out against the nerve-rack and excessive responsibility. There were nights when startled by a cry or groan I would rouse him from a troubled sleep. Sitting up in his sleeping-bag, Sir Ernest would then relate some horrible dream of the boats being crushed between floes, the camp being engulfed, or other such nightmare. Plans would then be discussed to avoid these calamities, for these dreams he regarded as warnings.

It was to his unrelaxing vigilance and planning that we owed our lives. I will never forget those cold, hideous nights in our tent and those discussions of the problems of the future, with the floes hammering sinister warnings a few paces away.

It was now April 8th. The Antarctic Winter had already set in and the nights were rapidly lengthening. Shortly after 6 P.M. the watchman raised the alarm that the floe was splitting. We hurried from the tents in the gloom and observed a dark jagged line gradually broadening through the centre of the camp. It passed directly under the *James Caird* and separated the other two boats from us. In a few minutes we rushed the boats across to the section where the tents stood. Our camp was reduced to an overcrowded rocking triangle and it was evident that we must take the first opportunity to escape no matter how desperate the chances might be. During the night a strong breeze sprang up from the south and under its influence the pack began to scatter.

On the 9th April, we found that the previous night's wind had loosened the ice but it was impossible to launch the boats as the leads were opening and closing so rapidly that should we attempt to navigate them, we would be crushed like egg-shells.

Changes took place so rapidly that a clearing that appeared to offer an excellent opening at one moment, was a grinding ice-mill a few minutes later. In our awful dilemma we all turned our eyes to the leader who was standing surveying this baffling maze. Action was imperative at the first opportunity. After a hurried breakfast, tents were struck and all made ready to launch the boats. Crews were allotted. The leader, Frank Wild and eleven men, of whom I was one, manned the *James Caird*—the largest yet frailest boat. Captain Worsley with nine others formed the crew of the *Dudley Docker*, and Tom Crean had charge of the *Stancombe Wills* with the remainder.

These preparations proved to be opportune, for, as we stood by, the ice parted beneath our feet. Hastily, we hauled the boats and gear to temporary safety on the larger piece, which was barely big enough to accommodate everything. The crack had ripped in an uncanny fashion through the old camping site which the leader and myself had vacated but an hour previously. We stood on the brink of the widening fissure and watched the depression where we had slept for four months drift away amidst the churning ice. How insecure it had been. The warmth of our bodies had thawed the ice, until we had been sleeping, happily unconscious of the fact, barely a foot above the surface of the sea!

The first desperate chance came just after lunch. At one o'clock a treacherous lead opened up through the heaving ice. Sir Ernest gave the order "launch boats." We slid them over the jagged edge of the floe into the inky waters. The gear and supplies were hurriedly stowed and, for dear life, we rowed through the devious channel and entered a vast lake of gently heaving deep blue waters in which floated a solitary mammoth berg. At last we were Free! Free!! No more idle captives with capricious winds and tides for gaolers but free to shape our destinies by our own wills and strength. Our adventures during one hundred and fifty-nine days on the floe had come to an end. How thoroughly the happenings of the next six days were to eclipse them and indeed all the experiences of the preceding sixteen months!

CHAPTER XIII

THE ESCAPE IN THE BOATS

. . . the tempest screamed,
Comfort and warmth and ease no longer seemed
Things that a man could know: soul, body, brain,
Knew nothing but the wind, the cold, the pain.

MASEFIELD.

THE *James Caird* took the lead, and as we bent to our oars we sang joyfully—bound for Elephant Island at last!

But we sang too soon!

We had covered but a few miles when we observed the eastern horizon of pack-ice in violent agitation and rapidly bearing towards us. The noise of the oncoming jostling sounded like the inrush of a tidal bore up a river. We stopped rowing for a brief moment and observed that the whole surface of the sea was covered by a mass of churning ice and foam which was driving towards us in a broad crescent in the grip of a furious tide rip. The horns were converging and it seemed as though we must be trapped in a rapidly closing pool. Sir Ernest shouted to the boats to make for the lee of the mammoth berg. Tossing, plunging and grinding the fearsome menace swept after us with hellish speed and though we pulled with all our might we could not draw away. The ice-laden surge was only one hundred yards behind and tongues of ice were flicking out ahead of it. One of these reached to within a few yards of the *Stancombe Wills* which was bringing up the rear end; disaster was only averted by the greatest exertion of her crew and Crean's skilful piloting.

After fifteen minutes' race for life, the phenomenon ceased as quickly as it had begun. All became quiet save for the groaning and creaking of the floes as they fretted in the rising and falling swell. The waters were now badly littered, and night coming on apace, the leader decided to rest his weary men on an enticing floe. The cook with his small stove and assistant were first put "ashore" and, by the time the boats were discharged, hauled up, and tents pitched, "hoosh" was ready. The full ration set our cold bodies aglow and with the cheerful prospect of a night's rest, laughter and song came from the tents.

We had lived so long in this vortex of peril as to become almost indifferent to hazards and dangers. Little did we reck that our camp was pitched on a brittle ice raft scarcely more than fifty paces across, adrift on an unplumbed sea. Nor did we heed the schools of killer whales patrolling the neighbouring waters in search of prey. Guards were set—each man taking an hour's watch—we snuggled down into our sleeping-bags and were soon rocked to sleep by the swaying floe. But the promise of a night's rest was dishonoured. Shortly after 11 P.M. a loud cracking caused us to hasten from our sleeping-bags and examine the floe for a fracture. A minute investigation by the light of the hurricane lamps displayed no other sign than a subsidence of the surface snow layer. Once more we turned in and had just dozed off when another report turned us out again.

There was no false alarm this time—the watchman was yelling that the floe was splitting. The crack passed beneath the tent occupied by the sailors, and so quickly did it draw apart that before the men could escape one fell through into the sea. By marvellous good fortune the leader was near, and, rushing to the breach, flung himself down by the brink and hauled seaman Holness, who was drowning in his sleeping-bag, from the water. An alarm was raised that a second man was missing, but before a search could be made the fractured floes came together again with terrific impact. The *James Caird* which had been separated from the body of the camp was hurried across the rift which was opening again and so rapidly did it widen, that Sir Ernest who was waiting on the far side till the boat reached safety was unable to leap across.

A few minutes later he drifted away and was swallowed up in the darkness and falling snow. We heard a voice calling for one of the boats, but Wild had already anticipated the order and manned the *Stancombe Wills*.

Owing to the darkness and congestion of ice it was with great difficulty that the leader was rescued. The "roll" was called and with deep relief all hands were accounted for. A roaring blubber fire was kindled and, as the floe was rocking badly in the increasing swell and might fracture again, the tents were struck. We huddled close to the fire and spent the rest of the night praying that our camp would remain intact and longing for the dawn. It came at 6 A.M. and the sight revealed was disturbing as the sea was closely packed with ice. A good hot hoosh and a cup of hot milk banished to some extent our fatigue and we stood-by waiting for an opportunity to get under way. At 8 A.M. a lead opened and the boats were launched and loaded. The previous day's experience showed that the boats were too deep in the water, so we left behind some cases of dried vegetables, a number of picks and shovels and sundry oddments which we considered could be done without. A strong east wind was blowing and gradually increased to a moderate gale. At noon we won through to what appeared to be the open sea. Heavy rollers were running outside and breaking on the margin of the pack-ice and the deeply laden boats began to labour badly. Sprays continually broke over them, freezing as they fell. Everything became sheathed in ice and our soaked garments froze as stiff as mail and cracked as we moved.

It was too hazardous to face the dangerous sea and we were reluctantly compelled to run back to the shelter of the pack where the sea was broken down by the weight of ice. We continued sailing westward until late afternoon, when we entered an extensive calm pool in which drifted a massive friendly floe—an excellent camping place. Soaked to the skin, weary through lack of sleep and utterly worn out, we were thankful for any place on which we might lie down and snatch a few hours' rest. Guards were set to watch over the safety of the camp and we managed to get more sleep than we had known for a fortnight.

The dawn broke foggy, cheerless and sinister. A piercing wind was blowing from the north-west bringing sleet that froze in a glassy veneer. While we were making ready to get under way fields of pack came rapidly driving down from the north. There was no choice. Our floe appeared capable of withstanding a buffeting and Sir Ernest decided to remain and await events.

Driven on by the swift tides and heavy swell the ice swirled round our floe bearing it along, rolling and rocking alarmingly. In less than an hour the bosom of the sea was obscured by a seething expanse of crushing pack-ice. Climbing to the top of a reeling knoll, we gazed spellbound on a terrifying spectacle. Furious warfare was raging on one of Nature's age-old battlefields. We had reached the northern limit of the ice-pack where the endless streams of ice cast adrift from the Polar Continent were being lashed back remorselessly by temperate seas. Here the conclusion of a cycle in Nature's equilibrium was taking place. The ice-packs, pounded up and eroded by wave action, were returning to their primal element. Around us churned the mill of the world. Gnarled old ice-floes, weather-worn bergs, fragmentary stumps and decayed ice-masses, crowded together in one heaving, rolling grind. To the girdling horizon stretched this tempest-ridden and battling confusion. It was sublime— irresistible—terrible. Our rocking floe was suffering the fate of its neighbours. We experienced a series of sickening impacts as its ramparts were torn asunder. What helpless atoms we felt—mere human flotsam— caught in a maelstrom of unlimited power and separated from eternity only by a thin partition of crumbling ice.

We stood by the boats, ready should our frail raft shatter. A large section of it sheared from its margin and a broad icefoot formed over which the surf swirled and on which masses stranded. It would be difficult to launch the boats over this lunging ice reef. Sir Ernest and Wild stood on the peak of our foundering berg, patiently watching and waiting for a chance.

There was a cry—"She's splitting." We manned the boats, waited, but nothing happened—it was only the surface snow subsiding. Our floe was wallowing like a sinking ship before the last plunge—the end seemed near.

The leader called that a lead was approaching, that

we were to stand by to launch the boats. On the horizon we noticed a dark line cleaving through the tortured ice—a narrow open lead—would it never hasten? A flock of seabirds came and circled over us like messengers of freedom—a few seals drifted past sleeping peacefully and safely on rocking floes: but we men in spite of our superior intelligence were in peril yet, powerless; how anomalous it seemed. Slowly, stealthily, with exasperating deliberation, the lead crept closer. At last it reached our floe. Sir Ernest stood by the rising and falling icefoot, directing the launching which was extremely hazardous. When the floe rolled favourably, the order was given "launch boats." The *James Caird* barely swung free and the uprising ice caught her bow and she was nearly swamped. We flung stores and gear aboard, leapt in and rowed desperately. The three boats in procession headed along the lead to the west and soon entered large stretches of water, sufficiently open to allow the sails to be hoisted. Light snow and biting winds numbed us to the bone, but our spirits were cheered by the excellent progress.

Wild was at our helm and Sir Ernest stood up in the stern keeping a watchful eye on the two boats following in our wake and occasionally shouting words of direction. As night drew on we ranged up alongside a floe that promised shelter and made fast. The cook was put ashore just long enough to prepare "hoosh." We had had enough of the floes and preferred to remain in the boats until daylight. In the dark we were compelled to cast off, as streams of ice threatened to hole the boats. It was a stern night—snow and sleet fell; killer whales skirmished round and we were in constant apprehension lest they might rise to "blow" beneath the boats or capsize them with their massive dorsal fins. We had seen the killers charge and upset heavy masses of ice on which luckless seals basked and we had little doubt that these voracious monsters would appreciate a variation in their diet if a boat overturned.

Dawn rose on a pitiful scene. Haggard, drawn faces, with beards encrusted with ice, peered out from garments shrouded with snow. The boats were drifting idly on a stagnant mushy sea. Before getting under way we set about looking for a piece of ice large enough on which to land the cook to prepare breakfast. Such a piece was difficult to find without running into the body of the pack and it was amusing to note the keen interest that was displayed in finding a friendly ice island. At last we drew up alongside one. Cook —excellent fellow—though stiff with cold soon had a hot "hoosh" ready, and we were heartened for what the immediate future might bring.

The day proved to be clear, and radiant with sunshine. Sails were set and the purl of a silver bow wave sang merrily in our ears as we moved over the deep blue.

For the first time for months we admired the callous

beauty of the pack-ice, eroded by the waves into count-less fanciful forms. Penguins rode on crystal gon-dolas and countless seals basked on marble-white slabs which swayed gently in the swell. Beyond the margin of the pack, rolled the seas, deep furrowed and white crested.

Since embarking on April 9th, thick weather had obscured all view of land, nor had there been an oppor-tunity of determining our position by sun observations. All the time we had been sailing west, but as we knew little about the set of the currents, our precise loca-tion was a matter of conjecture. We imagined, how-ever, it must be highly favourable as far as Elephant Island was concerned. With keen speculation we awaited noon, when Captain Worsley would check up our "dead-reckoning" by a "sun shot." As the time approached we watched Worsley stand up in the *Dudley Docker*, put his arm around the mast to steady himself, for the boat was rolling badly, and manipu-late his sextant. We then rowed the *James Caird* alongside the *Dudley Docker* and the leader jumped into it. After the observations were worked out he returned aboard the *James Caird* and held a whis-pered discussion with Wild. The outcome was that our destination was changed from Elephant Island to Hope Bay—roughly 80 miles to the south-west—on the Antarctic Mainland. Fearing the reaction it might have had on the party at the time, we were not made aware of Worsley's calculations, though Sir Ernest informed us our progress was not as favourable as our optimism had anticipated.

In fact we were actually thirty miles east of the position where the boats had been launched three days previously. Though sailing west during the day the currents had carried the ice-floes on which we had rested during the night swiftly to the east. Not only had we lost all the distance sailed but the drift had actually gained thirty miles on our efforts! This was heartbreaking.

Throughout the day we continued until dusk made navigation dangerous and then set about finding a suitable floe behind which to shelter for the night. The ice was so broken and tossed by the surge that it was unapproachable. At last in the darkness we succeeded in making the boats fast to a large floe, tethering one behind the other. The swell prevented the cook being put "ashore," so hoosh had to be prepared by the aid of Primus stoves. This was a lengthy business as the boats were rolling violently and sprays occasionally broke over them extinguishing the stoves.

It seemed as if evil forces were arrayed to torment us. No sooner was one peril overcome than another arose in its place. Streams of ice fragments, borne along by surface currents or driven by the winds, were attracted to the lee side of our floe and this became a new annoyance. For several hours we staved off the ice with boathooks and paddles and then, shortly after midnight, the wind suddenly chopped round and began to drive the boats back broadside on to the ice spurs of the floe. There was no time to cast off, so reluctantly we had to cut our valuable mooring line and back away to save the boats from being holed.

So that we might not drift apart, the boats remained tethered to one another and all night long we lay hove to in the freezing sea. We huddled together, clasped in each other's arms, so that we might glean a little warmth from our bodies and consolation from our whispered hopes. Where our bodies touched, the warmth thawed frozen garments and, when we moved, the icy wind stabbed through. Would the dawn never come—would the sun never rise again? Night seemed an eternity. Where our wet clothes chafed, sea boils swelled up and throbbed intolerably in the piercing cold. It seemed that the limit of human endurance must soon be reached.

Dawn came at last. We were denied the cheer of a hot breakfast as everything was iced up and the sea was running high. But that did not matter—there were other compensations. No restraint was placed on the amount of cold ration we might eat, the sun was rising, and the wind had changed fair for Elephant Island. We had much to be thankful for.

As the pack-ice had closed up to the south in the direction of Hope Bay, the boats were headed for Elephant Island again. It now lay 100 miles to the north. Sails were hoisted and with a strong fair breeze our three small vessels sped forward to the land of hope.

The pack was rapidly thinning out and it appeared as if we were nearing its northernmost limit. Shortly after noon we passed through a narrow belt of ice and unexpectedly emerged into the open ocean.

Had we not been driven by desperation we would not have dared in three such puny boats the heavy seas that were running. It was amazing that our spent and weatherbeaten bodies responded so heroically to the occasion and I doubt if any creature but man could have survived the excesses of exposure, fatigue, hunger, and lack of rest to which we had been subjected. It was the will that made it possible—the will that enabled us to rise above suffering and to dominate and drive our jaded bodies.

Again, I cannot speak too highly of our leader. The piloting of the party through the perilous adventures from the time the ship was beset, up to our escape from the ice—without loss of life—was a far greater achievement than would have been the realisation of the original plans of the Expedition. If ever environment was likely to breed pessimism, ill-feeling and revolt, it was that which surrounded us during the monotonous months on the floe. Scientists and sailors of widely diverse natures, training and outlook—cooped together in tiny tents—hungry, cold, with tempers exasperated by Nature's despotism, betrayed neither enmity nor discontent. All this I attribute to the leader whose magnetic personality inspired cheerfulness, hope and encouragement.

The three small boats and their weatherbeaten refugees had proved themselves in the conflict with the ice—now they were to measure their worth with the sea. The ocean seemed an old friend and though our vessels were mere cockleshells, their pilots were skilled mariners, and He who had directed the floe through its tortuous wanderings was surely still with us. In an indefinable way we felt that our escape was no matter of mere chance. Always when on the brink of doom an outlet of escape had saved us in some miraculous way.

So our hearts swelled with exaltation as our crazy boats bounded over the glinting seas, while the white crested sapphire combers chased us, passed us, and led on.

During the afternoon, an icy wind worked up the seas, sails were reefed and spray dashing on board froze and caked boats and men with ice. The salt water saturated our garments and provoked split skin and sea boils to fresh miseries. But this was not all, many added seasickness to their afflictions.

Even under these conditions we were still capable of seeing the humorous side of things. One of the party who had consistently skimped and saved tidbits from his frugal rations and kept them reserved in a bag against the day of starvation of which he lived in constant dread, became violently seasick, and was unable to eat even a crumb of the liberal rations that were issued and on which the more fortunate gorged themselves. It brought smiles to cracked lips, for we felt our doubting companion was doing just penance for his lack of faith.

Most of us were badly frostbitten and it was notable that the old campaigners, Shackleton, Wild, Crean and myself, though not seriously affected by most conditions were not immune to frostbite. My hands became badly frozen through the continual wearing of wet mits. The leader noticing my endeavours to restore circulation took off his warm gloves and handed them to me. "Take these until your hands are right," he said. As he was suffering himself I refused. But he was determined that I should have them. "All right," he replied, "if you don't take them I'll throw them into the sea." It was a kindly action—characteristic of the man.

We had burst so unexpectedly into the open sea that we had not taken any ice aboard for drinking purposes nor had we any drinking water. In order to alleviate our burning thirsts, we had eaten raw seal meat cut into squares, but this had unfortunately been drenched with salt spray, and only aggravated our condition. One wondered what additional anguish and suffering the body was capable of feeling and the mind of withstanding.

Night fell and, though we wished to continue and take advantage of the fair wind, our leader decided to heave to. This was a wise policy, for it would have been impossible to keep the boats together in the darkness.

Sails were lowered, a sea anchor was hastily made by lashing together the oars and the boats were tethered to it one behind the other. Owing to the cross seas and currents the boats would not keep head on to the seas and kept continually bringing up and bumping together. The temperature fell below zero and as our vessels tossed and plunged the sprays broke over them and quickly froze. The added weight of the accumulating ice caused the boats to wallow and we spent the night chipping the ice away, staving off the boats and trying to keep ourselves from freezing. They were hideous hours and the flame of hope all but died in many a heart. Indeed many of the party were crazed by their agonies. It was a night of terror, horror and despair.

Sharp indeed are the contrasts in these latitudes. With the dawn came an abatement of the sea and a glimpse of land! It was a sublime revelation. I am convinced that nothing less could have brought the party from its state of death-like apathy back to life again.

A grey fog had hung over the sea, screening all distant prospect. Then the sun burst through pink vapours. Like an enchanted curtain the mists rolled skyward and revealed a sun-gilt mountain—like a colossal pyramid of gold rising from the purple seas. It was Clarence Island! Magical had been its appearance— magical the reaction on us. Our moribund party flickered into life again. A little later we observed on

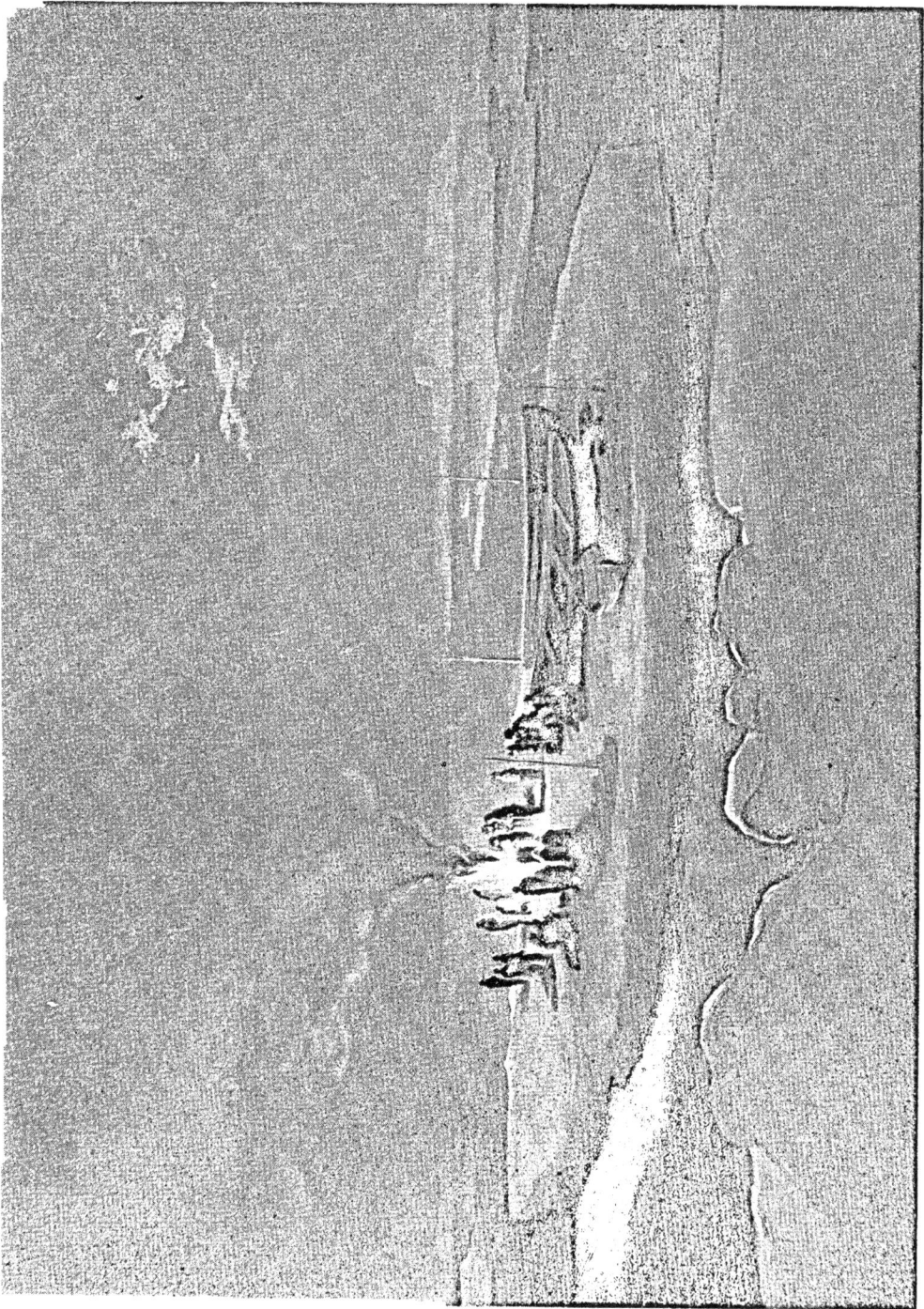

our port bow—some thirty miles away—seven domed peaks, the ice-clad summits of Elephant Island.

The tethering lines were cast off and our sea-anchor of bundled oars, which had grown to the thickness of tree trunks through accumulated ice, was chipped clean and taken on board. Sails were hoisted with difficulty as the ropes and pulleys were fouled with ice and the sheets were frozen stiff like metal plates. With a fair breeze the three boats headed for Elephant Island.

Breakfast rations were served but, we found it only possible to nibble at them, as our cracked lips bled painfully and our parched throats and swollen tongues would not permit us to swallow. The sun mounted in the sky and beat down on thirst-maddened men, but somehow we seemed indestructible in spirit and body. At last the land lay within our grasp—the land that we had been patiently longing to reach for sixteen long months. We could stand a few hours more suffering. A few hours and we would be walking on good solid rock.

At noon the breeze died down and we took to the oars. How we laboured! How anxiously we watched the land gradually draw closer and the snowy peaks grow clearer.

"I can see rock!" cried one. And "Look! the crevasses are now showing up!" said another. We strained our eyes towards the goal, measuring the distance by details gradually revealed as we drew closer.

At three o'clock we were within eight miles. Wild picked out a little bay sheltered by white peaks, with rocks standing out boldly from the iceclad shores. It was to us a sunlit homely prospect. We rowed with joyful eagerness—tonight we would be camped on solid rock. Oh! heavenly prospect!

The minutes grew into hours. The sea was calm, the water was rippling from our bows, but somehow in spite of our efforts, we were drawing no closer. Then the terrible truth burst upon us—we were caught in an adverse current. It was only just possible to hold our own against it. Curdling despair crept into us and all the agonies that hope had dulled throbbed with fresh acuteness. We could not row much longer. The reserve energy which the near realisation of freedom had called up was almost spent. It was cruel, uncharitable, relentless. There was not a man whose soul did not cry out in anguish to the Controller of the winds and tides, not to forsake us.

Through the dreary suffering months we had quelled our heartaches by the consolation that the future would one day reward our hopes. That time, the panacea for all tribulations, would solve the problem of our destinies as our hearts desired. Barrier after barrier had raised itself and had been surmounted, but now on the very threshold of salvation it seemed we must fail. Only a miracle could save us—the wind; a favourable wind that would swell our sails and tear us from the merciless suck of the tide. Our plight before

had never been so desperate as now.   Most of the party were at the last gasp, crazed and dazed, and could **row** no more.

Night shut down black and pitiless.   The open ocean lay to the right—the tide was hurrying us into its greedy spaces.   Down fluttered the snow, coming from the south-east in whirling flurries.   It fell in a soft shroud over forms huddled down in the boats, listless and careless of death.   An occasional moan came from the men.   We were helpless.

Then a great black cloud filled the sky and the wind came.   It came from the south, first gently—it seemed a sigh.   Then the waters rippled under its caress.   More passionately it came till the sea swept up in rolling waves—waves rolling to the shore.   The miracle had happened.   It was not chance—our prayers had been heard.

Shackleton called to the men in the boats to hoist sails.   Those aboard the *Stancombe Wills* were too far spent so we took them in tow.   On through the dark, towards our goal, now swallowed up in the blackness, plunging through a void of waters swelling up in the gale.   Those that were able trimmed the boat as she heeled to the wind's press—the others lay corpselike.

The noise of tumbling crests was all round and the spume flung forward by the wind raked the boats.

Wild had not left the helm for forty-eight hours, and was now frozen so that his arms and hands would not function.   He was relieved by "Chips" the carpenter, but he too, overcome by exhaustion, swooned at his post. Instantly the boat turned broadside to the seas, a huge wave leaped aboard, drenched everything and we were nearly swamped. Wild carried on again. In the darkness and agonising cold the worn-out party fought the storm, chipping away the accumulations of frozen spray and frantically bailing the boats to keep them afloat. Every billow brought a spasm of misery. Each black gulf, viewed from the crest of a spuming comber, yawned to swallow us.

Scourged by the winds, mocked by the storm, we wondered if ever the night would end—or if ever there had been such a night.

With the *Stancombe Wills* in tow, we were making bad weather. It seemed from moment to moment that we should have to part the line and leave her to her fate. Sir Ernest, in the stern, strained his eyes into the darkness, watching that black object tossing in the dark torment and shouting at intervals words of cheer and inquiry. "She's gone!" one would say as a hoary billow reared its crest between us. Then against the white spume a dark shape would appear, and through the tumult would come, faint but cheering, Tom Crean's reassuring hail, "All well, Sir!"

So we lived through each wave and the night. In the darkness we lost sight of our third boat, the *Dudley Docker*.

Anxiously we peered through the mists and snow whirls towards the land. As we drew closer, the

watery moon broke fitfully through the storm-wracked sky, and shone on nebulous contours of peaks and phantom-like glaciers. The land seemed like a spectral fantasy conceived by our distressed minds. Our overwrought nerves were steadied somewhat when we heard the growl of surf on the reefs. It must be real! We stood off till the dawn which came at last to reveal leaden clouds, great grey seas, and—the land!

Land! Land! Mountains and glaciers peeping through the mists—and blessed rock! We made into the lee and rowed over the heaving surges that swirled at the base of mighty cliffs. Our boats were dwarfed to puny specks by the magnitude of mountain and sea. A thousand feet above, the rising sun was tipping with gold the summits of Elephant Island. Everywhere the land was burdened with ice. Snow piled in masses on mountain crests, ice festooned the rocky terraces and filled the defiles with convulsed glaciers.

And—the perpendicular mountain walls rose sheer, relentlessly, from the sea. We had reached land but, to our dismay, to set foot upon it appeared to be impossible.

CHAPTER XIV

LAND! LAND! LAND!

WE made the lee of the land and rowed along the coast over inky reflections of beetling black mountain walls searching anxiously for a breach or ledge that might afford refuge, but could find nothing that promised even a foothold.

Ahead, an avalanche had tumbled into the sea, and littered the water with ice-blocks. From its margin we eagerly hacked fragments and hauled them aboard to quench our excruciating thirst. It was the land's first blessing and seemed likely to be its last.

Black despair again gripped our hearts—until we reached Cape Valentine, the north-east extremity of the island, and observed a small channel-way running up to a possible landing place. It seemed our last hope.

The *Wills* rowed in through the surf and reported favourably. It was a mere foothold, yet it offered a temporary shelter. Her party landed and then those of us who were able began disembarking the stores and helpless men from the *James Caird*. While this was in progress, our third boat hove in sight. She had been blown into an adjacent bay during the night, where she weathered the gale with great difficulty. Her party and stores were landed, the boats hauled up, and a camp made. We were a pitiful sight; the greater number terribly frostbitten and half delirious. Some staggered aimlessly about and flung themselves down on the beach, hugging the very rocks and trickling the pebbles through their hands as though they were nuggets of gold. It is hard to describe the joy we felt, walking on land, feeling and looking upon solid rocks after having lived through the terrible experiences of the past sixteen months. To feel land under our feet —land that would not split and disintegrate!

And then to fall asleep; to rest unperturbed; to turn over and hearken to the music of the surf; the swirl of the ice-blocks; the croak of the penguins; to dream with hope of the future; to experience the unspeakable joy of awakening in the morning to find we were still on something solid, something that had not drifted miles in the night. It was the realisation of all our hopes. It was Heaven. Nothing else mattered. A terrible chapter in our lives had ended; we scarcely cared what was to open the next.

In the morning we made an investigation of the refuge to which the Hand which had led us through peril and tempest had guided us. It was a wild place. Behind us rose sheer cliffs of rock over 1,000 feet high. At their base stretched the narrow strip of shingly beach on which we were camped, strewn with ice-blocks, and swept by the stormy billows of the wild Antarctic Ocean. High on the cliffs was a dark line which indicated the encroachment of storm-flung seas and further along the beach lay piles of rocks that had tumbled from aloft. It was perfectly obvious that the place would be untenable in bad weather, and at any moment we might be buried by rock avalanche. Sir Ernest despatched Wild and several sailors in the *Dudley Docker* in quest of a new home. Early in the afternoon they returned, having located a promising site nine miles to the west on the north coast. The tides and weather being in our favour the party embarked, after having first lightened our cargo by making a depot of a quantity of stores in a cave above the sea's reach.

Treacherous is the weather in these latitudes. On this little trip we ran into a gale when rounding Cape Valentine. The south-west wind shrieked down from the mountains, smiting the sea white. Hour after hour we toiled at the oars. Sometimes the tempest drove us back; then, while it seemed to pant for breath, we gained. We all knew only too well our fate should we be driven out into the wild west sea. Emaciated and worn out as we were, the paralysing thought that icy death was still stalking us took possession of our minds. But the example of our leader and Wild made men of us again, and we shook off our dread and fought our way through the storm inch by inch to the lee of the land. Painfully we rowed along, while the hurricane

raged on the pinnacles a thousand feet up. The scurrying rivulets of snow that rushed down the sheer faces
of the cliffs were caught up in eddies, and whirled out
over the sea; there the tempest smote, and the tortured waters leapt to meet them. But with the evening came an abatement and we reached our new
haven.

Camps were pitched, a hot meal made, and the low-
burning flame of life was fanned again. Once more,
with gratitude for the stability of the good old earth
we lay down and stretched ourselves in the dreamless
slumber of the utterly fatigued. But alas! we were
not to rest for long. The wind fiends of the place
attacked again with diabolical malice. The blizzard
fury hurled gravel and ice splinters at us and ripped
the tents to shreds. Only the tent occupied by Sir
Ernest, James and myself escaped, as we tumbled out
and dismantled it before the blizzard reached its full
might. In the seething dark we crept beneath the
flapping folds, once more to seek sleep. Was there
ever a place so pitiless and inhospitable.

At four o'clock we were again awakened by a new
alarm. This time the rising tide was creeping upon us
and the waves were washing our canvas covering.
Turning out we moved higher up the beach. It was
atrociously cold, with a dense drift and not a square
inch of shelter. Making a feeble rampart of cases we
lit the bogie, laid our tent on the ground, and, weight-
ing the skirting with stones, crawled beneath and en-

dured the conditions with what stoicism we could muster. The monotony was broken by shouts, and looking out from beneath the canvas we saw the occupants of what was "No. 5" tent emerging from a pile of snow and trying to make a shelter by overturning one of the boats. At the same time we observed that the ringed penguins inhabiting the rookery near the camp, having had enough of the weather, were congregating on the beach. They migrated during the morning. Lucky, lucky birds! The homeless party from "No. 5" succeeded in overturning the *Dudley Docker* and converting it into a safe and comparatively comfortable shelter.

A wretched day was followed by a miserable night and another day of atrocious weather, the air being thick with wet and drifting snow. But during the evening the wind dropped and we were treated to a magnificent moonlight night, that silvered sea and glacier with mystic charm, the frowning coast line standing out in dark silhouette against a starry sky. But morning ushered in a day of incessant, heavy, wet snowfalls which, however, could not make us wetter for we were already soaked to the skin.

Those first few days on Elephant Island were Hell, and it appeared at first as though many who had endured so far, would be unable to survive further persecution and exposure. Our new refuge was named Cape Wild—at once an apt description and a tribute to a great-hearted comrade. It was a spit of rock thrust out into the sea—with a sheer icecliff on the land side and a cluster of huge boulders just off its tip. The island coast curved towards it on one side, and formed the bay into which we had run and found our landing place.

Food had been reduced to vanishing point, and the party had no protection against the weather. What was to be done? To remain meant death from slow starvation or exposure. The situation was desperate, but again our leader rose supreme. He consulted with Wild, and decided that some of us must attempt to reach South Georgia, and bring relief to the others. He determined to make the endeavour himself, taking with him five who were skilled sailors. The remainder of the party, twenty-two men, would be left at Elephant Island under the charge of Frank Wild. The decision was characteristic of the man, and undertaken in the grand spirit which had distinguished his leadership.

"Chippy," the indispensable carpenter, now started to deck over the *Caird* with odd fragments of wood and scraps of canvas in preparation for the proposed voyage, which now became our all-absorbing interest. Personnel, equipment, chances, and the journey's duration, were topics of keen discussion. During a let-up in the weather, penguins were slaughtered and skinned for their meat, whilst a fat Weddell seal that waddled ashore also found its way to our larder. This solved temporarily the food problem.

We re-rigged our tent and all hands turned to in the erection of a wind shelter for the cook's galley. Green, our indomitable cook, showed signs of a breakdown, so I was appointed chef and found ample occupation in serving meals at 8 A.M., 1 P.M. and 4.30 P.M., and quickly assumed a piebald appearance as the blubber soot and snowdrift formed a mottled mixture over me. Weather conditions being still wretched, we retired daily at five o'clock to our saturated sleeping-bags to steam and fug for fourteen long hours. The tent walls, becoming thickly covered with condensation rime, showered us with every gust. Nevertheless, the invalids were recovering, frostbites were healing, and the general spirits of the party were rising with the prospect of the relief expedition—forlorn hope though it might be.

All apparel and equipment were in deplorable condition owing to continued despicable weather and nothing would have been hailed more gladly than a sunny day.

On Easter Monday, April 24th, the weather let up. A moderate sea was running, but Sir Ernest deemed it inadvisable to delay his departure any longer.

At any hour the pack-ice from which we had escaped might drift northward, engirdle the island and make navigation impossible. With a rousing cheer we slid the *James Caird* down the gravelly beach and launched her through the surf. Disaster was narrowly averted

at the outset as the unballasted boat capsized, and McNeish and Vincent who were on the deck were precipitated into the sea. Relieved of the top weight the *James Caird* righted, but was caught in the heavy undertow and carried towards the reefs. By a resolute effort those aboard managed to row her out to safety beyond the breakers.

The *Stancombe Wills* carried out the ballast—bags made from blankets filled with sand—and the concentrated rations which had been reserved for the voyage. By mid-day the little vessel was loaded. It was a desperate venture, yet her crew, already spent, faced this terrible voyage with the hearts of British seamen. They who ventured their lives to succour their comrades were Shackleton, Worsley, Crean, McCarthy, McNeish and Vincent. We shook hands and sent them off with a cheer.

We stood on the beach watching the tiny sail grow smaller and smaller until it diminished to a minute speck. How lonely it looked. Then it disappeared from sight.

Before our gallant comrades lay a voyage of 750 miles across the most tempestuous ocean in the world; yet we never doubted the issue, for the Providence which had already guided and delivered us would surely never forsake us in this hour of our direst need.

Our hope was that they would reach South Georgia in fourteen days, charter a steam-trawler from one of the whaling stations, and return to us within a month.

How opportunely Shackleton's departure was timed, may be gathered from the fact that the next morning a shift of wind filled the bay with pack-ice, blocking all access to the sea for many weeks. Regarding his escape as a favourable omen we shut our eyes to the hazards, and fixed our minds on the hope. Great is the tonic effect of hope—and great was our need of its stimulus as the weeks passed. Here we were, a party of twenty-two, maintaining a precarious foothold on an exposed ledge of barren rock, in the world's wildest ocean. Our leader had departed, taking with him the pick of the seamen. Of our party, one was a helpless cripple, a dozen were more or less disabled with frostbite, and some were, for the moment, crazed by their privations. Our refuge was like the scrimped courtyard of a prison—a narrow strip of beach 200 paces long by 30 yards wide. Before us, the sea which pounded our shores in angry tumult, would at night be frozen into icy silence, only to break up again under tidal influence with a noise like the churning of some monstrous mill. Behind us, the island peaks rose 3000 feet into the air, and down their riven valleys, across their creeping glaciers, the wind devils raced and shrieked, lashed us with hail, and smothered us with snowdrift.

Inhospitable, desolate and hemmed in with glaciers, our refuge was as uninviting as it well could be.

Still, we were grateful. It was better than the ice-floes. Here before us lay our hope—the great open rolling ocean, that washed the shores of tropic and pole, the highway to lands of human beings, our homeland—and freedom.

CHAPTER XV

Our Hut is double-storied, with bedrooms twenty-two,
A library and a drawing-room, although indeed 'tis true
We haven't any bathroom, at which perhaps you'll smile;
But we found it warmer not to wash in our Hut on Elephant Isle.

TOPICAL SONG.

MAROONED—we devoted ourselves to making our lot as tenable as possible. We estimated optimistically that the *James Caird*, under the guidance of Providence, might reach South Georgia in fourteen days and that another two weeks at the outside should see the rescue party at hand.

It had been decided, after examining every square yard of the beach for possible shelter, that the only hope was to excavate a cave in the dead end of an adjacent glacier, and to this task we applied ourselves with a will.

Meantime, as all gear was thoroughly wet and no drying was possible, we had to turn into wet sleeping-bags, and after wringing out our soaked garments, take them into the bags with us so that they might not freeze stiff by the morning. We suffered no ill effects from this practice, and attributed this immunity to

254

the fact that we were absorbing considerable quantities of blubber which thoroughly waterproofed us! A good seal "hoosh" with plenty of blubber just before turning in, induced a steamy heat and we slept soundly although pools of water were thawed from the ice beneath our sleeping-bags!

It may seem incredible that human beings could live in such circumstances. What is perhaps more remarkable is that our men, many of whom were at Death's door when we landed, were making rapid recovery in this, surely the weirdest and most unfavourable convalescent home that can be imagined. The fact was that the period in which we had become inured to these conditions had been a lengthy one. We had been gradually broken-in to Antarctic rigours by our life aboard the ship. The *Endurance* was a nightly refuge in which we could repair the physical ravages of our daily outside exposures. Thus prepared, we were able to face the strenuous life on the floes, which might well have ended disastrously for untrained men. On the drifting ice we increased our powers of resistance to cold and accustomed our bodies to assimilate the blubber, and seal and penguin meat upon which we had largely subsisted. Had we not been thus toughened during those five weary months we certainly could not have faced the appalling boat journey. No men, shipwrecked and suddenly confronted with such a voyage amid the ice, could have withstood its hardships—they must have perished. The human body's adaptability is marvellous. We had grown almost as fit to endure the climate as the very seals themselves.

Four days' hard work on the ice grotto in which we proposed to camp saw the end of our hopes for a "home." It was soon evident that thaw water would be troublesome. When the temperature rose, streams welled up through the floor, drippings from the roof fell as from a fountain and rivulets gushed and gurgled from the walls. From our labours in excavation we reaped nothing but exercise.

Then Wild hit upon the happy scheme of converting the two remaining boats into a hut. All hands were engaged in erecting low shelter walls of stones on which the two boats were overturned and laid side by side. The sails and tent floorcloths were next stretched over the boats to form a roof. These were secured with lashings and thin laths of wood which were split from food cases; the extracted nails were used to tack them on. The sides were walled round with fabric from torn tents, and a tent doorway was sewn in on the side sheltered from the prevailing storms. The floor —which by the way was an old-established penguin rookery—was covered with gravel from the beach, and this extemporised structure afforded a shelter superior to anything we had known for many long months. The work occupied us many days, for we had to improvise with sundry scraps and remnants, but finally the "house" was voted weatherproof and James and I, who in the meantime had occupied the only tent that the wind had left intact, took up our quarters. I marked the occasion in my journal thus:

James and self take up residence in the boat shelter, which we have christened *The Snuggery*. Night of terrific winds threatening to dislodge our new refuge. The wind is a succession of hurricane gusts that sweep down the glacier immediately S. S. W. of us. Each gust heralds its approach by a low rumbling which increases to a thunderous uproar. Snow, stones and gravel are whirled before it and any gear left unweighted to heavy stones flies seaward. The shelter is decidedly comfortable compared with tents and will ameliorate our existence considerably. The size of ground space enclosed is 18 feet by 12 feet and the height of our ceiling is only four feet nine inches above the ground. The small blubber bogie radiates a pleasant warmth, does the cooking, and so fills the place with soot and smoke that our eyes run painfully and our lungs nigh choke. Still it is a step in the direction of making life more endurable under such fiendish conditions. The entire party of twenty-two sleep in this small space snugly packed like smoked sardines. Crude improvised stretchers are arranged between the boat thwarts, six sleeping in each boat, the remainder "dossing" on the floor.

Light, or rather a faint glimmer, is shed over all this through two tiny windows—one, a tiny pane eight inches across made from the glass cover of a chronometer, and the other, from a small square of celluloid that at one time covered a home photograph. Further feeble flicker is provided by a couple of blubber lamps, made from discarded food tins with wicks of stranded clothing. They smoke and reek to such effect, that after awhile the atmosphere is so dense that they choke their efficiency and us too.

When draughts drive the bogie fumes back down the chimney, it is impossible to see more than a yard or so, and the place croaks with coughs and compliments.   Then one escapes out into the blizzard with a fervent—Thank God!

With meticulous precision Wild doles out the rations, which comprise all portions of seals and penguins except hair and feathers.   We are just as hungry after meals as before; strictest economy has to be observed, and the climate produces prodigious appetites.   Seals and penguins are exceptionally accommodating creatures to the Polar castaway.   Not only do they provide him with food, but their blubbery skins furnish sufficient fuel to cook all edible parts.   Salt for cooking purposes speedily became exhausted, but we have discovered that fifty per cent of salt seawater added to a stew or soup supplies an excellent substitute without ill effects.

As time went on, it became evident that the blizzards which had assailed us at the outset were a chronic condition.   In fact had it not been for occasional brief lulls, the climate was nearly as evil as that experienced in Adelie Land.   In Adelie Land, however, we had a warm comfortable hut and no dearth of foodstuffs. Now we were existing in a miserable hovel and had to exercise the most stringent economy for the spectre of starvation ever haunted us in our desolation.

Except for a few odd cases of "palate ticklers," which exasperated more than fed us, we were entirely dependent on the creatures that came to us from the sea.   Many times when the ice-packs sheathed the ocean for long periods, we were on the verge of starvation, but just as desperate crises approached, blizzards invariably dispersed the ice-packs and penguins and seals came from the open water!   It seemed indeed as

rank Worsley, captain of the "Endurance." He piloted the small boat, the "James
rd," across 750 miles of tempestuous ocean from Elephant Island to South Georgia

g the "James Caird" on the relief voyage to South Georgia. The boat was but a frail cockle-shell with an improvised deck made ents of canvas and packing case lids. The successful crossing of 750 miles of tempestuous icy sub-Antarctic Ocean is one of the if we were in the safekeeping of the Almighty. Not once did this happen but five times!

When we were inclined to become apprehensive, Wild inspired us anew. "Surely," he said, "the Almighty who has already led us through great ordeals and hazards, has never guided us to this haven of refuge to let us die miserably of hunger."

As the wisdom of Wild's words was fulfilled, doubt left us and a great faith took its place. Strangely, only sufficient penguins and seals came ashore to satisfy our wants—until towards the end of our tenancy there was never a surfeit.

Though the tempests smote us sorely and kept us for days beneath the boats, there were brief spells which atoned for all this savage cruelty and I wrote the following effusion during such a respite to describe the outlook from the summit of the pinnacle where we were wont to climb each day to scan the bare sea line for sight of a sail.

The weather is delightful, bright warm sunshine and dead calm. Cape Wild is a narrow neck of rock jutting out from the mainland at the base of a magnificent spire-shaped peak, where it is only sixty yards wide, is practically flat and about nine feet above high tides. The ocean end rises to a precipitous rocky bluff about 120 feet in height which is guarded oceanwise by a rocky islet that presents a flat jagged face 300 feet in height which we call the Gnomon. To the east the coast stretches in glorious vistas of perpendicular peaks terminating at the exquisitely castellated Cornwallis Island, heavily capped with glaciers that hang like frozen cataracts over the sea. Looking west there is a

gorgeous blue glacier down which from the interior roar
S.W. blizzards and from which frequent avalanches debouch.
Distant view is obscured by a noble rocky headland though
one has glimpses of some islets known as the Seal Rocks.
From my elevated lookout, seaward, there is a view beautiful beyond imagination, yet unwelcome, for it is over an
ocean obscured by ice-pack—a vast unpenetrable field,
driving rapidly from east to west.   On the eastern side of
the spit there is at low tide a fine gravelly beach on which
we secure seals and penguins.   In fact it appears that Cape
Wild is a penguin rookery during the breeding season.

For a fortnight after the departure of Shackleton
and his companions, the days, filled with endeavours
to make a habitable camp on this wind-blasted ledge,
passed without any sense of dragging.   Our minds
dwelt constantly on the stout little craft which we pictured winging its way across the waste of waters like
the dove, to carry the news and bring rescue to us on
our Ararat.   We believed the *James Caird* to be sufficiently seaworthy in such capable hands to win through
even such seas as we knew she must encounter, but
as the south-east winds brought up increasing masses
of ice, and our bay was frequently packed with floes
that reached away to the horizon, we began to realise that only a vessel built for navigation in the ice
could possibly reach us, and then only if she came
before capricious Autumn gave place to grim Winter.
We passed the day which marked the minimum time
in which we calculated the *Caird* might have reached
the whaling grounds, and then as day succeeded day,

and no sign appeared on the horizon we resigned ourselves to the inevitable. We must winter on this
bleak, storm-hounded spot and await the coming of
a vessel in the early spring. Life was still bearable.
Hardships endured had inured us to weather conditions; dangers survived had bred in us a measure of
philosophy. We settled down to make the best of it.
And this was the camp routine as recorded in my
blubber-stained and soot-begrimed journal.

It is just daylight at seven A.M. when the cook is called.
His duties of preparing the breakfast of penguin steaks take
till 8.45 A.M. when those who have not already risen and gone
for a constitutional are awakened by a raucous cry from
Wild of "Lash up and stow." "Clearing decks" is effected
by rolling up all gear and stowing it in the "thwart"
bunks overhead. The boxes which have served for the
cook's bunk are then arranged in an eccentric circle around
the bogie, previously set going by the messman, and all
take their appointed places thereon. So that all may have
their share of bogie warmth, the circle moves one seat
round each meal. With the welcome cry of "Hoosh-O!"
the "peggy" from each mess—there are four—takes his pot
to the galley where Wild officiates in the "whacking out."
The steaks are divided into individual portions as accu-
rately as possible and "whosed." After breakfast there is a
break of fifteen minutes for "smoke-o'" and Wild allots
various occupations. These are neither arduous nor
strenuous and are essential as exercise. "Hoosh-O!" is
again called at 12.30 and is a light meal, generally a palate
tickler such as paddies, fried biscuit, thin soup, hoosh or the
greatly appreciated yet seldom served nut-food. After-
noons are spent in nominal occupations—mending, snaring
birds, skinning penguins, etc. The evening hoosh is served

at 4.30. One can always be sure what it is going to be. Seal hoosh, although not admired for its flavour, is esteemed on account of its quantity. Extra blubber lamps are lit in the centre of the seated circle, lighting up grimy faces with their smoky flare. It is a weird sight—the light thrown up by the lamps illuminates smoke-grimed faces like stage footlights, and is reflected in sparkling eyes and the glint on the aluminum mugs. The stream of flickering light thrown out from the open bogie door makes weird dancing shadows on the inside of the boats, suggesting a council of brigands in a huge chimney or the corner of a coal mine, holding revelry after an escapade. I can imagine the look of surprise and bewilderment with which any visitor would regard this grizzly-bearded and unkempt assemblage could he be suddenly thrown among us. Bewilderment would speedily become aversion; for our blubbery emanations and the odours from twenty-two crowded and seven-month-unwashed men coupled with the blue tobacco smoke "fug," must be productive of an atmosphere distinctly unsavoury.

Conversation after evening hoosh generally wanders back to the civilised world, to places, feasts and theatres; to what we intend doing—chiefly eating. Holidays such as we outline will be spent in ever-sultry climes, our dreams are of wanderings in equatorial lands and tropical isles. Travel in unexplored New Guinea is a favourite subject and we all vow that if ever we escape from the frozen captivity we will forthwith embark upon an expedition to thaw out amid steaming swamps and jungles.[1]

After "smoke-o" the decks are again cleared by stowing the box seats to form the cook's bunk, the tenants of the attic bunks swing into their places of repose with monkey-like agility and the ground floor is spread with sleeping-bags, into which the owners wriggle like gigantic slugs.

[1] This expedition in after years actually matured and is chronicled in my volume *Pearls and Savages*, published by G. P. Putnam's Sons.

Hussey generally treats us to a half hour's banjo serenade in which our choristers join their voices. Then we sleep. The dim rays from the blubber light which is kept burning continuously to save matches, sheds a feeble glow over objects resembling mummies. Loud snores from our reindeer sleeping-bags mingle with the roar of the blizzard.

It was not astonishing that the unchanging diet of penguin and seal meat should produce a curious physical and psychological reaction. We slept for fifteen hours at a stretch. We dreamed dreams of wondrous banquets and fantastic dishes that vanished with tantalising regularity just as we were about to devour them. Physically we grew fat and blubbery but the least exertion produced a muscular weariness that tired us. The most annoying manifestation, however, was the production of an epidemic—of snoring. It was almost impossible to hear one's own snores above those of the others. Nevertheless there was one who easily outdid all and earned the title of "The Snorer."

His consistent efforts outrivalled those of a wandering minstrel with a trombone. He survived all efforts —and they were many and varied—at suppression. Wild laid a cord through eyelets past each man's bunk and attached one end to the snorer's foot. When anyone was awakened he hauled on the rope with the result that up went the leg and down went the snores. But at the end of a week the snorer grew accustomed to these interruptions and took no notice of the leg pulling. Topical verse relates how peace and quiet were eventually restored:

'Twas on a dark and stormy night,
Much snow lay on the ground.
Stealthily from my sleeping-bag—
Casting furtive looks around,
I groped towards the snorer;
His snores I vowed to wreck.
I took the cord from off his leg
And placed it round his neck.

And how we talked food! A doughnut would provide a topic for an hour's discussion; a five-course dinner would keep us arguing for an evening. The most popular book in the world for us was Marston's *Penny Cookery Book*. With watering mouths and straining ears we devoured every word of it. It was fortunate, indeed, that we had not to suffer the physical after-effects of the mental "gorgies" to which its pages helped us. Our minds in fact were obsessed with food. This strange phase was due not to starvation which sharpens the wits and quickens the mental faculties but to the monotony of our blubbery diet. For amusement I jotted down a few scraps of typical conversation and the very page from which I now transcribe it is black with sooty seal grease:

Snatches of conversation while in sleeping-bag:

Wild: Do you like doughnuts?
McIlroy: Rather!
Wild: D——d easily made too. I like them cold with a little jam.
McIlroy: Not bad but how about a huge rum omelette?
Wild: Bally fine (with a deep sigh).

Overhead two of the sailors are discussing some extra-ordinary mixture of hash, apple sauce, beer and cheese. Marston is holding debate with the cook as to whether all puddings should have bread crumbs as their base. Further down the room someone eulogises Scotch shortbread. Several of the sailors are talking of "spotted dog," "Sea-pie" and Lockhart's, with great feeling. Then someone reminiscently murmurs the praises of our Nut-food sledging ration, upon which conversation becomes general.

Another entry in the diary runs:

Autumn's days are shortlived; for the sun, after describing his short arc of four hours in the heavens, goes to rest in the ocean in a blaze of golden glory. The landscape assumes once more a flame-red tinge and then, like the dying embers of a fire, takes on the cold ashen tint of evening. The stars rush out and fill the sky with silver spangles, the waters lazily lap the shingly beach. Then, from out the "snug-gery" come the strains of Hussey's banjo and a well-remembered tune.

> Soft o'er the fountain
> Lingering falls the silver moon,
> Soft o'er the fountain
> Breaks the day too soon.

What a wild setting to a sweet song. For the moment I am home again in dear old Sydney, when I am suddenly brought to bearings by the glacier debouching an avalanche into the bay. The echoes roll and reverberate amongst the hills, followed by the wave wash, then all falls silent. We turn into our bags, perchance to dream of home and familiar faces, and so our tiny world sleeps with this wild slumber of nature.

The month closed with winter hard upon us. The spit and gravel beach were hidden beneath a deep layer of ice and the reefs and outlying rocks wore ice caps of frozen sea spray. The frozen breath of the South poured its blizzard drifts seawards and lashed the ocean into flying spume and spindrift. It streamed like a river down the glacier slopes, roaring over our home, serenading us with an incessant shriek as its sweeping eddies played amongst the rocks. Terrific gusts flapped the thin canvas walls and so shook the boat superstructure as to keep us in a constant state of anxiety. Nor dare we leave the shelter of the boats for fear of being cut with flying panes of "Window ice." This phenomenon is produced during a calm, when the sleet and rain freeze over the ground in a thin glassy layer. The furious winds smash up this icy veneer, which is about half an inch thick, and whirl it in flying panes up to a foot square in area. Our shelter was subjected to a continual bombardment as of crashing glass which continued until the window ice had all been swept seaward. Nevertheless our position might have been infinitely worse. Especially comfortable did I feel when I remembered the fearsome blizzards of Adelie Land with their 30° below zero temperatures, endured in a sledging tent. And as the month ended I made an entry in my diary expressing thankfulness that we had at last arrived at a condition of filthiness in which it was impossible to become any dirtier. Inability to wash was our greatest hardship.

June opened with a threatened shortage of fuel.

Six hundred and six penguins had been captured in the six weeks since we landed; but while we had cold storaged the carcasses, we had used up the skins for the stove. Fortunately I was able to construct a damper from an oil drum that saved 50 per cent of the heat from escaping up the chimney—though we were all nearly choked and smoke-blinded when making the experimental fitting. Then, in keeping with our usual good fortune, over a hundred birds came ashore on two successive nights, while I surprised a huge bull seal—the equivalent in food value of 80 penguins.

The event of the month was the celebration of Midwinter Day (June 22). The shortest day was further abbreviated by a dense fog but we marked it with feasting and we honoured the longest night with song.

The sea-elephant which I captured, when cut open, was found to contain some thirty recently swallowed fish. This unexpected gift provided us with a fish and entrée course, snared sea gulls, the poultry, but the *pièce de resistance* was a pudding composed of twelve mouldy nut-food bars, twenty mouldy biscuits, and four mouldy sledging rations boiled together. In an extra strong potion of Trumilk we toasted "The King," "The Sun's Return," "The Boss, and Crew of the *James Caird*," and "Sweethearts and Wives" with no lack of genuine sentiment.

A single seabird remained over after the feast and Wild decided to allow our begrimed pack of cards to determine its ownership. The cut went round the circle until it narrowed down to James and myself.

By the smoking flicker of the blubber lamps the bearded sooty faces drew closer as cut followed cut without decision. Wild shuffled the pack, but the even cutting remained unchanged. The cards seemed under a spell. At last on the thirteenth cut I won; only to find the bird an extremely tough proposition in more ways than one.

I wonder if a popular concert was ever conducted under more peculiar conditions than that Midwinter Revel of ours! Take a glimpse through the chronometer glass that had recently been fitted into the wall of our hut, and through the murk of blubber lamps and bogie stove, note the audience—which has, perforce, retired to its sleeping-bags; for the concert hall is but four feet nine inches high, and for an assemblage of twenty-two provides merely lying-down accommodation.

At the far end, Wild, Dr. McIlroy, James the physicist, and the writer are ranged on the ground. Being nearest the stove I am alternately roasted by day and covered with frost rime showers by night. In the foreground are five recumbent forms—Dr. Macklin, Kerr, Wordie, Hudson and Blackborrow—the last two being invalids. The middle distance is occupied by cases which do duty as the cook's bed, boxes of fuel, and a solitary mummy, which is Lees in his reindeer sleeping-bag. Above this is our attic or second

storey. In it reside, and now recline, some ten un-kempt and careless lodgers. From every available point hang blubbery garments that would reek to Heaven save for the fact that in the reeking business competition is so keen that their comparatively faint aroma is unnoticed. In the daytime we crawl through these hanging smells like a brood of incubated chicks in a "foster mother"; in the height of a concert they are pulled down and stacked, to allow the music to percolate more readily through the thickened atmos-phere.

The programme of that midwinter concert may not have been high art, but Covent Garden has held no more appreciative audience. How could it, when every member was also a performer! Of the thirty-odd items fully half were topical songs, stories, and recitations, on which the brains of members had worked overtime for days, and no body of undergrad-uates ever relished their own wit more keenly, or roared their topical choruses with greater fervour.

"The Village Blacksmith" was translated into "The Snuggery Cook." Whatever may be the merits of the song "Solomon Levi" as a chronicle or biography, it has nothing on the substituted words "Franky Wild-o!" in point of literal truth, for as the last verse beautifully expressed it:

O Franky Wild-O! tra-la-la-la-la-la!
Mister Franky Wild-O! tra-la-la-la-la-la;
My name is Franky Wild-O; my hut's on Elephant Isle,

The wall's without a single brick, the roof's without a tile;
But nevertheless, I must confess, by many and many a
    mile
It's the most palatial dwelling-place you'll find on Elephant
    Isle.

As might be expected food formed a fertile subject for topical wit, and the following ballad was soulfully rendered by James to the lilting melody "Egypt my Cleopatra":

Upon an Isle whose icy shores are washed by stormy seas,
There dwells beneath two upturned boats in comfort and in
    ease,
A grimy crew of twenty-two who've drifted many a mile,
And oft at night within each bag a face beams with a smile.

Chorus

It is dreaming of choice sweetmeats and rare confections,
Drowsy reflections of rich plum cake,
It is tucking into almond icing and duffs enticing,
Which mortal baker could scarcely bake!

Hussey, brightening the atmosphere with his witty rallies and sparkling repartee, leading the songs with his clear notes, and giving body to the choruses with his banjo, was the life and soul of the party, and with "the common tunes . . . that make you laugh and blow your nose." Yes! he "tore our very heart-strings out with those."

Constant danger and privation had infused into us a philosophy of toleration and unselfishness, and enabled us to see the other man's point of view as well as our own. We learned too how to find fulness and contentment in a life which had stripped us of all the distinctions, baubles and trappings of civilisation and brought us all to a common level. Necessity compelled us to support life in the most primitive fashion conceivable and to share with one another, not only material things, but the sorrows that ache and the joys that transcend. Only one fight occurred, between one of the sailors and myself. It was over a trifling incident and took place in a blizzard when all the others were inside, so no one knew about it. We were both of hot headed Irish temperament, and after going at it with characteristic fervour, the fire died down as suddenly as it flared; we flung the brands of discord to the winds, shook hands, and cemented a great friendship.

It was during this month of June, that Drs. McIlroy and Macklin transformed our snuggery into an operating theatre and amputated the frost-bitten toes of our youngest member, Blackborrow, who had been suffering severely and was a chronic cripple. Wild and I acted as hospital orderlies and maintained the temperature of the "theatre" at 50°, by stoking-up the bogie fire with penguin skins. In the dense smoke, by the feeble glimmer of blubber lamps, Macklin administered the chloroform and McIlroy performed the operation which saved Blackborrow's leg if not indeed his life.

It is worth noting that the general health of our party

was good throughout, and scurvy, the bugbear of Polar expeditions, did not manifest itself. On the *Endurance* we had sufficiently varied foods, and on Elephant Island our ample diet of fresh fats doubtless acted as an anti-scorbutic. Our palates so adapted themselves to our bodily needs that raw blubber, stripped and cut into thin slices, was eaten with relish, and half a cup of penguin oil could be quaffed like a draught of mellow vintage.

July was a particularly obnoxious month. The variable temperatures of early Spring frayed our tempers and added to our discomforts. Warmer days were marked by increased humidity in which we felt the cold more than in the actual winter. We now experienced occasional rain, and the stronger rays of the sun thawed the snow that had heaped round our hut. Our floor, a mosaic of pebbles laid in penguin guano, became slushy and malodorous. I woke one night from a dream of falling through a crevice into the sea and found my hand in water, which was inches deep and rising. There was nothing to do but to turn out all the "Ground Floor" hands, dig a sump-hole and bale out some 60 gallons of evil-smelling liquid—a performance that had to be repeated before morning came, and three times day and night onwards.

The odour of this liquid was worse, if possible, than the mingled perfumes—distinctly not of Araby— which accompanied various experiments in tobacco substitutes. The last pipeful of genuine leaf was smoked by Wild on August 23rd; but long before this we had been stifled with fumes of penguin feathers, rope yarn, dried meat and other pipe-fuel, with which the confirmed smokers had endeavoured to satisfy their cravings. One evening I was awakened from a doze by the familiar smell of an Australian bush fire. Rubbing my eyes I beheld McLeod, one of the sailors, contentedly puffing out volumes of heavy smoke. The day before he had borrowed all the pipes and boiled them in a tin to extract the nicotine juice. McLeod then discovered that, by steeping the grass lining of his padded footwear in the concoction and drying it before the fire, an aromatic "tobacco" of exceptional flavour resulted!

The unusual "perfume" awakened everyone, and in a twinkling one and all were busy slitting open their boots to remove the padding and a few moments later clouds of this new incense were ascending—not to heaven, alas! but into the upper regions of our hut, to fall again in ever-thickening volume. That we had worn those padded boots continuously for seven long months was but an unconsidered trifle. Then I discovered that cigarettes could be made with the India paper of the only remaining volume of the *Encyclopædia Britannica* and pages containing articles of inhuman interest went up in smoke.

With Spring firmly established, August found us daily looking out with growing eagerness for the expected relief. Wild was ever a comforter. Each morning he encouraged us with "Lash up and stow, boys, the boss is coming today!" Four times a day we would climb, separately or in groups, to the summit of Lookout Bluff, on which our flagstaff had been erected, and scan the horizon for some sign.

Our supplies of concentrated food had long since disappeared, but as the beach became once more ice-free we gathered limpets from the rock and dulse from the pools, and these made a welcome change in the monotonous diet; but what we were most grateful for was that the return of seals and sea-elephants rendered the ceaseless slaughter of penguins no longer necessary, for we had developed a great love for these beautiful creatures.

But we were still surrounded by dangers. The glacier, that extended from one side of the Spit around the head of West Bay, suddenly became active under the influence of rising temperatures and became a menace. Thousands of tons of ice constantly calved from its seafront, and falling into the bay, displaced great seas that rolled ice-laden towards us like tidal waves, sweeping over the lower areas of the flat. On two occasions huge ice-laden surfs surged across the entire Spit into the bay on the opposite side and encroached to within a few paces of our home. In a few moments the Spit had undergone a complete transformation and was from then on heavily littered with stranded ice-blocks.

The deep roaring of avalanches crashing into the

bay, the tumult of jostling and splintering ice, and the reverberating echoes among the mountains, gave us many sleepless nights. We never knew what might happen next in this hostile place where all Nature was at war.

Sometimes the ocean, save for stray bergs, would open and become almost clear of ice; but more often the prospect was most depressing, with no water visible even from the highest point, and the foreshore, owing to prevailing low tides, became littered with stranded floes. Always—always—the horizon was desolatingly empty of sail or smoke-plume. The Spit itself was covered with wet and sloppy snow and walking was restricted to a tramping track of a bare 80 yards.

These were our circumstances until well past the middle of August. Almost without hope, we had begun to discuss the despatch of a party to Deception Harbour in one of the other boats.

On August 30th, the one hundred and thirty-seventh day of our maroonment, Marston and I were scanning the northern horizon, when I drew his attention to a long curious-shaped berg: "Been watching the infernal thing for a couple of months," was his terse reply. Nevertheless, we continued to gaze at it, when, miracle of miracles! a vessel came in sight from under its lee. We immediately raised a cry, which was greeted from the interior—where the others were at lunch—with scoffing shouts of derision and mocking choruses. When at last we made them realise the truth of the joyful news, there was an astonishing display of energy. They came crawling through the roof, and breaking through the walls, frantic with joy. Wild gave orders to kindle the beacon, and soon a goodly pile of penguin skins and seal blubber was sending a dense oily smoke signal across the sky. It was a worthy occasion on which to expend one of my three remaining spaces of film, and I am glad to say that, despite everything it had been through, it recorded faithfully that truly historic scene.

Suspense was over. The vessel, which proved to be the Chilian trawler *Yelcho*, hove to and a boat was dropped for the shore. Ringing cheers greeted its approach. Those on board returned our salvos. Cheer followed cheer, the mountains cheered back, the sun even burst momentarily through the clouds. It was not only the sight of relief that warmed our hearts, for as the little boat drew near, we recognised our long-lost and heroic comrades, Shackleton, Crean, and Worsley! But there was no time to be lost in greetings, rejoicings and salutations; they could come later when we were safe on board. Our relentless gaolers the icefields were hurrying to close the portals. Scurrying clouds were drifting over the mountains and obscuring the sun; the wind began to pipe, bleak and gusty. A blizzard was coming; there was not a moment to lose. Our few scientific specimens and records were gathered, the boxes of negatives and cinemato-

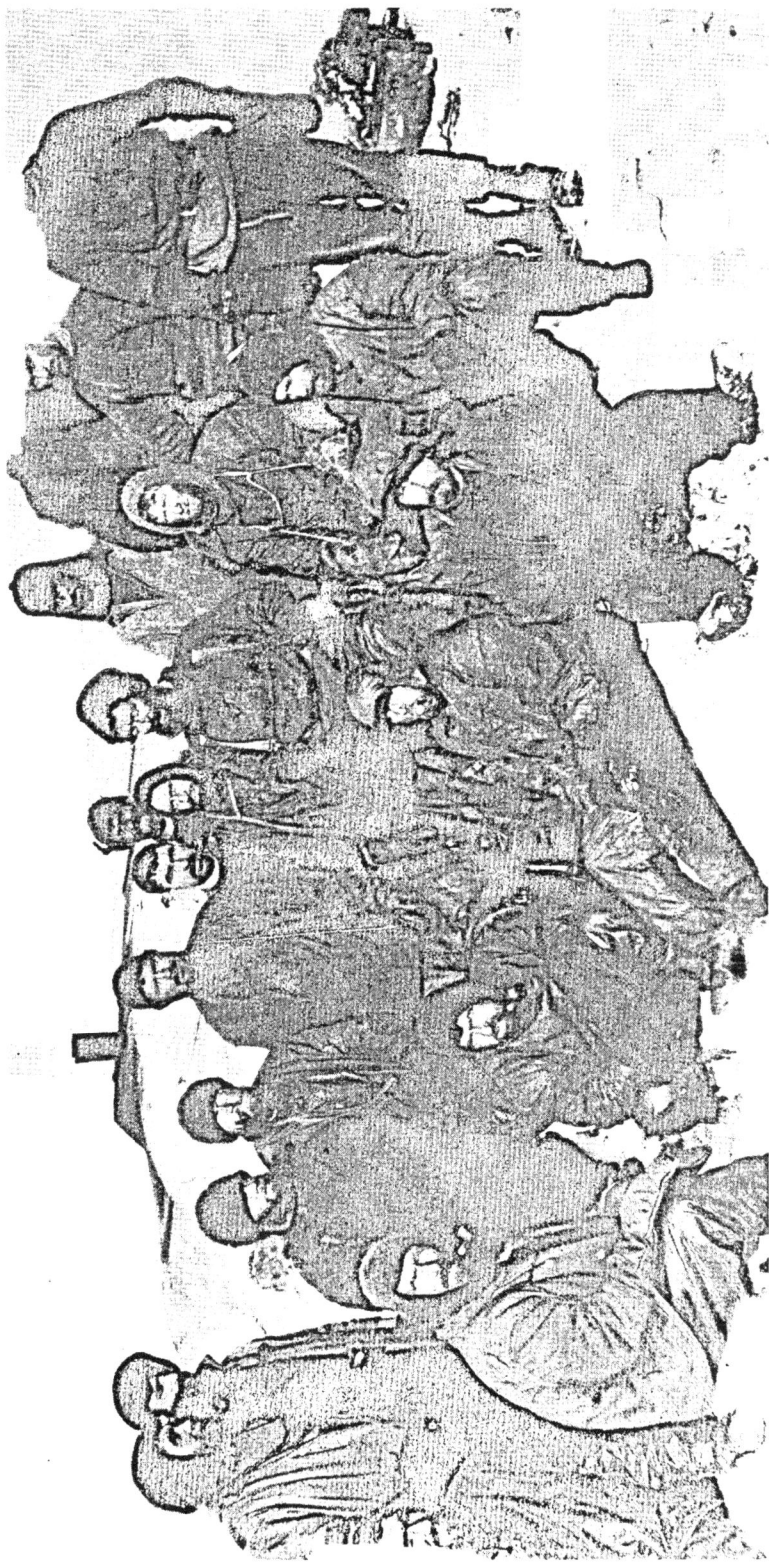

The castaways on Elephant Island. The black smudges on the faces are accumulations of soot and grime.

...y are (Back Row): Greenstreet, McIlroy, Marston, Wordie, James, Holness, Hudson, Stephenson, McLeod, Clark, Orde-Lees, Kerr, Macklin. (Second Row): Green, Wild, Howe, Cheetham, Hussey, Bakewell. (Front): Rickensen (below Hussey). Blackburrow, the stowaway, is missing from the group, being an invalid and confined to the "Snuggery." Hurley took the photograph and consequently is not seen.

graph films were hastily loaded into a boat, all were to be saved at last. In less than an hour the marooned party were all safely on board the *Yelcho*, and steaming North to those we held dear.

As we stood on deck watching the gathering mists veil familiar peaks, there was not a man amongst us who did not feel, mingled with his gratitude, a touch of sadness. We were gazing for the last time upon the land which, though bleak and inhospitable, had taken us to its bosom and been the means of our salvation.

EPILOGUE

THE NEXT THREE MONTHS

I SHALL not attempt to describe our feelings at the reunion with the men who had made, first, the gallant bid for freedom, and then a series of untiring efforts for our release. As we listened to Shackleton's story of the eighteen weeks between their departure in the *James Caird* and their return to pick us up, there was a tinge of envy mixed with our sincere admiration. Theirs was an achievement that, in spite of its almost incredible hardships, every one of us would have been glad to share. Over the cigars that followed our first civilised meal, "The Boss" sketched it in outline; later talks filled in the details.

This was their fourth attempt to effect our rescue. After sixteen days of unspeakable privations, in a tiny crazy boat at the mercy of terrible seas, they reached the iron-bound coast of South Georgia. But the elements were still implacable and gathered in a final effort to defeat them. They were tossed in their cockleshell in the worst hurricane they had ever experienced, threatened with destruction on a lee shore, while searching hopelessly for a possible landing place. At last a narrow passage through foaming reefs was

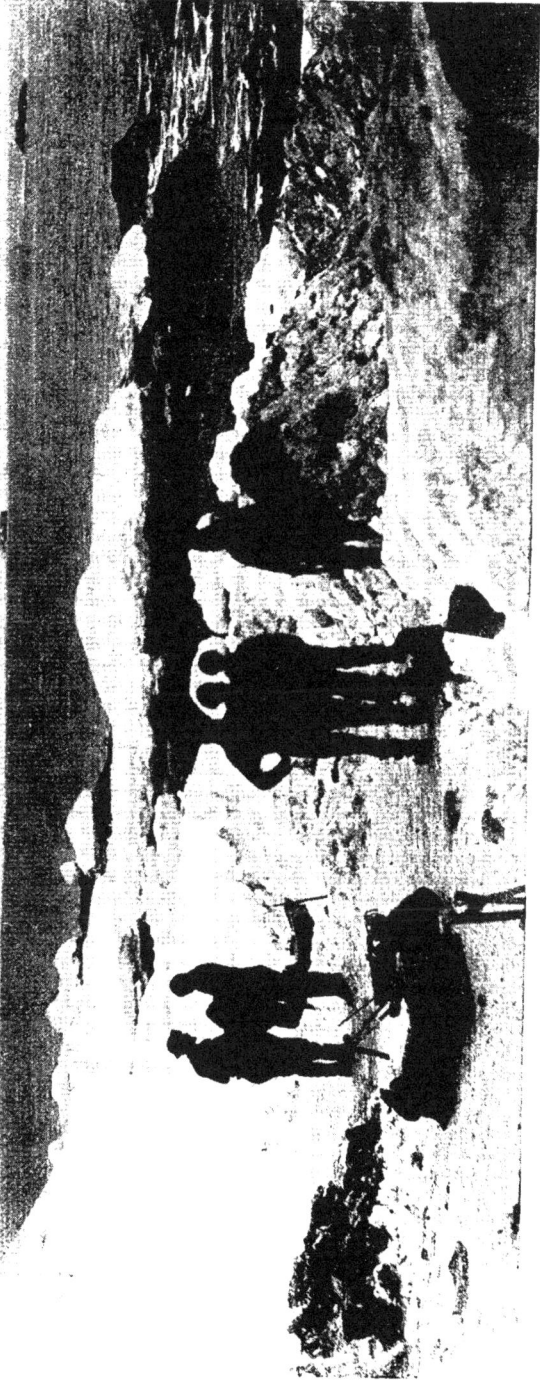

A vessel came in sight.   Wild gave orders to kindle the beacon and soon a goodly pile of penguin skins and seal blubber was sending up a dense smoke signal.

sighted, and thanks to superb seamanship they made it. Seven hundred and fifty miles of turbulent sub-Antarctic Ocean had been crossed in a small boat twenty-three feet long—a boat journey which must ever rank with the noblest achievements in the epic of man's conflict with the sea. They landed, six gaunt, battered, spent, starving, frozen men, more dead than alive.

They were still far from all human aid. Their way was barred by the unmapped mountains and glaciers of the interior. These had always been considered impassable even to strong and well-equipped parties. It was impossible to put to sea again; their boat, badly damaged, could never weather the mad waves which storms were driving directly on to the coast. Yet stricken men on Elephant Island were awaiting relief which they alone could send. There was only one thing to be done. The impassable mountains must be conquered.

Several days were spent recuperating in a tiny cave before they dared attempt the journey. Then Sir Ernest, Worsley and Crean set out on the hazardous enterprise. Enveloped in mists, staggering perilously on the brink of precipices, they won their way doggedly. Their courage was rewarded. They reached the Stromness Whaling Station—woebegone refugees, spectres from the Antarctic, surely the strangest wayfarers who had ever knocked at a civilised man's door.

Of the terrible perils encountered in that climb, Sir Ernest spoke scarcely at all, but from what I afterwards saw I say that nothing but unfaltering loyalty and the grimmest determination to save the lives of twenty-two starving comrades left behind on a storm-swept rock ledge could have produced the desperate urge that impelled them to travel such damnable country by night and day without rest and equipment.

The first thing to be done was to dispatch a vessel to rescue the three men left in a cave on the opposite side of the island. Next, the *Southern Sky*, a steel whaler under the command of our old friend Captain Thom, was commissioned immediately and made good speed for Elephant Island but, after sighting the peaks and approaching to within seventy miles of the spit on which we were marooned, could proceed no farther on account of dense pack-ice. Disappointed but undaunted they returned to the Falkland Islands. Sir Ernest appealed to the various South American Governments.

The second attempt was in a steel trawler generously equipped by the Uruguayan Government. This time the relief ship actually steamed to within twenty miles of our camp. A low fog veiled the sea at the time, otherwise we must have seen the vessel on the margin of the pack-ice which prevented her from reaching us. A desperate attempt to force a way through the ice ended in nearly stripping the blades from her propeller, and, as coal was exhausted, once more our gallant comrades and their helpers were compelled to turn back. Sir Ernest then visited Punta Arenas, and the sum of £1500 was subscribed in a few days by the British residents to send a small auxiliary schooner, the *Emma*, to our rescue. After leaving the Falklands, bad weather was experienced throughout the whole voyage, which lasted a month. Life on board the cranky craft was a feat of anxious endurance, as, buffeted by heavy seas, she tossed about—a mere toy in the Cape Horn gales. Ice was met one hundred miles from Elephant Island, and an attempt to force a way through was given up—the vessel becoming damaged and narrowly escaping being crushed. Limping north through the deep furrowed seas, the little ship returned to the Falkland Islands, in a battered condition. But Shackleton was still determined. He knew only too well the desperate straits of the men relying on his efforts. Each day was bringing them closer to starvation and he dared not delay for the Summer when the seas would be ice free; he must try again in spite of storms and ice and the seventeen hours' daily darkness.

He appealed urgently to the Chilian Government. There was only a small steel vessel, called the *Yelcho*, available. She was quite unsuitable for such a voyage, but on August 25th with Shackleton, Crean and Worsley and a crew of Chilian officers and seamen, she left Punta Arenas on the fourth attempt. This time Providence rewarded them. The sea was calm, and five days later Elephant Island came in view. There was a wide rift in the pack-ice made by a recent gale that allowed the rescue vessel to slip through. Worsley picked out the camping place and the *Yelcho* was run as close in as reefs permitted. A boat was lowered and put off for the shore. The anxiety of those aboard the little boat can be imagined. The leader stood up and hailed Frank Wild, "Are you all well?"

"We are all well, Boss," Wild called back.

"Thank God," replied the "Boss." Then there were cheers and greetings on either side as we recognised our three comrades, Shackleton, Crean and Worsley.

The three days' run across to the tip of South America was a period of new and renewed sensations. To us who had been completely isolated for the most sensational twenty-two months of the world's history, the news we had to learn was staggering. That the War could still be raging in Europe was amazing, but the terrible impression and shock created by its horrors and fiendish scientific developments can scarcely be realised. We looked at the files of illustrated papers aghast.

Our reception at Punta Arenas was something more than a welcome—it was a triumph that extended without interruption through the ten days which we spent in this southernmost town in the world, and through the following six weeks of our journey through the country.

The city was en fête. On the wharf a picturesque

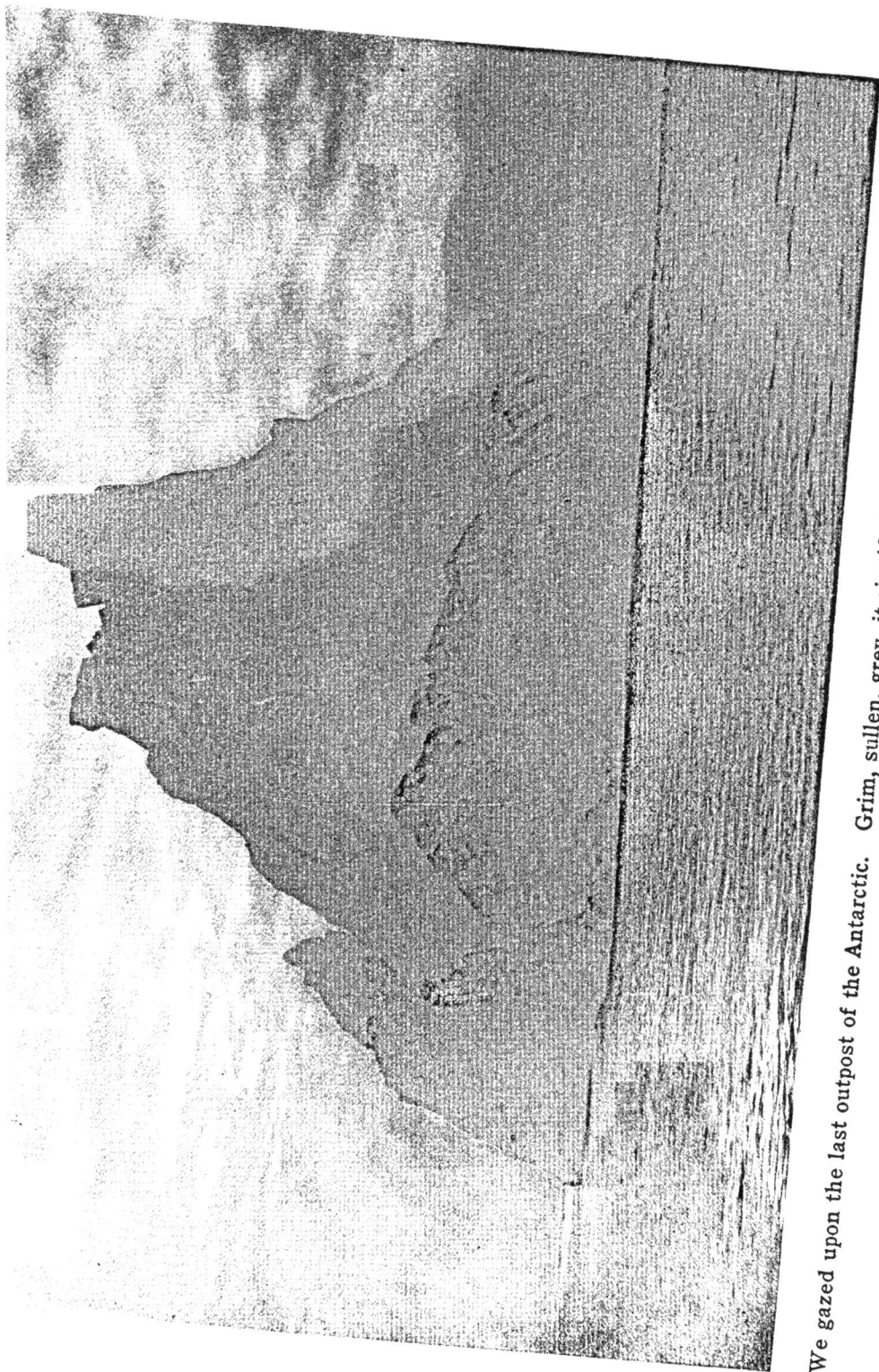

We gazed upon the last outpost of the Antarctic. Grim, sullen, grey, it signified the terminatio
our lives.

and dense assemblage had gathered, prepared to clasp us to its hospitable bosom. On second thoughts, it was content to cheer us wildly—and allow us to pass through its midst down a widening lane; for, in our Elephant Island husks of malodorous blubbery clothes, our beards and hair grown long and bodies unwashed for ten months, we were indeed an unlovely group. Nevertheless, Punta Arenas rose to us. Noble families and families noble in deed if not in rank carried off the rescued ones to their homes, except a quartet of us, who declined all pressing offers and made the chief hotel our home.

Our appearance caused a stampede of waitresses from the hotel, and it was not until the next morning, when assured that the shaved, bathed, and respectable fellows seated at table were actually the wild men of the night before, that the timorous maids would return to duty. And that hot bath! That transforming shave! Those beautiful, grease-free garments which the kind-hearted people had collected for us!

The "wishing game" had been a favourite sport in our Elephant Island shanty. In our sleeping-bags we had often speculated upon the sensation that would most poignantly appeal to our senses when, if ever, we might enjoy creature comforts again. We argued as to what would be the most delightful food, but on one point there was no argument; it would be magnificent to have a bath, for the encrusting grime of that smoky hut had seemed to penetrate to our very souls.

The soaking tub, bars of soap, the tingling shower, the glow-infusing rub-down, the well-nigh forgotten rasp of the keen razor—these would represent to us Paradise regained—and they did!

In many little ways the citizens showed their desire to welcome us. Those who stayed in private homes were made the recipients of almost embarrassing attentions. I remember meeting Wild, the least dandified of men, swanking it in his host's fur coat, and looking like a millionaire. We who lived at the hotel were serenaded by musicians, playing guitars. Motor cars and theatre-boxes were pressed upon us; and our hosts seemed determined to show us that nowhere in the world could such culinary marvels be produced— not even on Elephant Island!

The Governor held a formal reception and a magnificent welcome was tendered to the party by the Magellanes Club. This was a function indeed! The banquet began at 8.30 P.M. and marched in stately fashion through a range of speeches and gastronomic achievements till one o'clock. It eclipsed the most fantastic dreams that had haunted our sleep on Elephant Isle.

Social distinctions were forgotten in this overwhelming wave of hospitality and I saw a greaser (one of the Expedition's firemen) in borrowed finery and diamonds, drinking champagne familiarly with millionaires, and puffing luxuriously the finest cigars with the complacency of a magnate. What a change from filthy, blubber-reeking garb.   Yet how awkward it seemed to have to use knives, forks, spoons and plates again—what a useless lot of things there seemed on the banquet table!

Only the bed-ridden and the blind failed to appear on the wharf when, at the end of ten days, we re-embarked.   To the accompaniment of whistles and sirens, the *Yelcho* pulled out, dipping her ensign to the bunting that waved a thousand compliments and farewells from every masthead in the port and every pole on shore.

Our programme was to push westward through the Magellan Straits, then northward along the Chilian coast to Valparaiso, landing there to cross the Andes, take train to Buenos Ayres, then across the Atlantic to Europe and finally to London.

Let me pay tribute to the boat and crew who had rescued us from Elephant Island.   Built for use as a British trawler the *Yelcho* had, at the time of our rescue, seen twelve years' service—and showed every day of it.   In any kind of sea she behaved like a porpoise. Aloft she looked like a dissipated Christmas tree, and in a blow anchors, chains, deck cargo and a miscellaneous litter maintained an everlasting bumping. Paint had long since disappeared from her hull and one picked the flakes of rust from her plates with uncomfortable speculation.   Yet two days out from Punta Arenas she ran on to an uncharted bank, rose a couple of feet higher in the water, dented her plates badly and scraped over without leaking! It was as well; for though fitted with pumps like all other craft, the pumps differed in one important respect—they would not pump.

And yet after all was she not the instrument of our relief from misery? *Yelcho*, we lift our hats to you—you and your crew and your cook! You were unkempt —but you did us an unforgettable service and we shall ever remember you with affection.

Great hospitality welcomed us at Ancud, Coronel and Concepcion. The good folks, mindful of our past days of privation and want, showered on us pleasures and banquets to such a degree that we became thoroughly over-fed.

Especially was this the case at Ancud where I had the misfortune to arrive on my birthday. A celebration dinner aboard the ship in which the *Yelcho's* chef excelled himself, made us pleasantly happy, and, after the festival, we went ashore to do the sights. Shortly after landing, James and I met a fellow countryman of mine—an Australian. This was an "occasion." Nothing would suffice but we must go and dine and wine with him! We survived this second orgy, when we blundered into a patrol of young Chilian officers who had been scouting the town for us. Not being able to understand the language—after two dinners— we were carried to the barracks and there, to our horror, were ushered into a brilliantly decorated mess room in which the garrison officers were gathered with

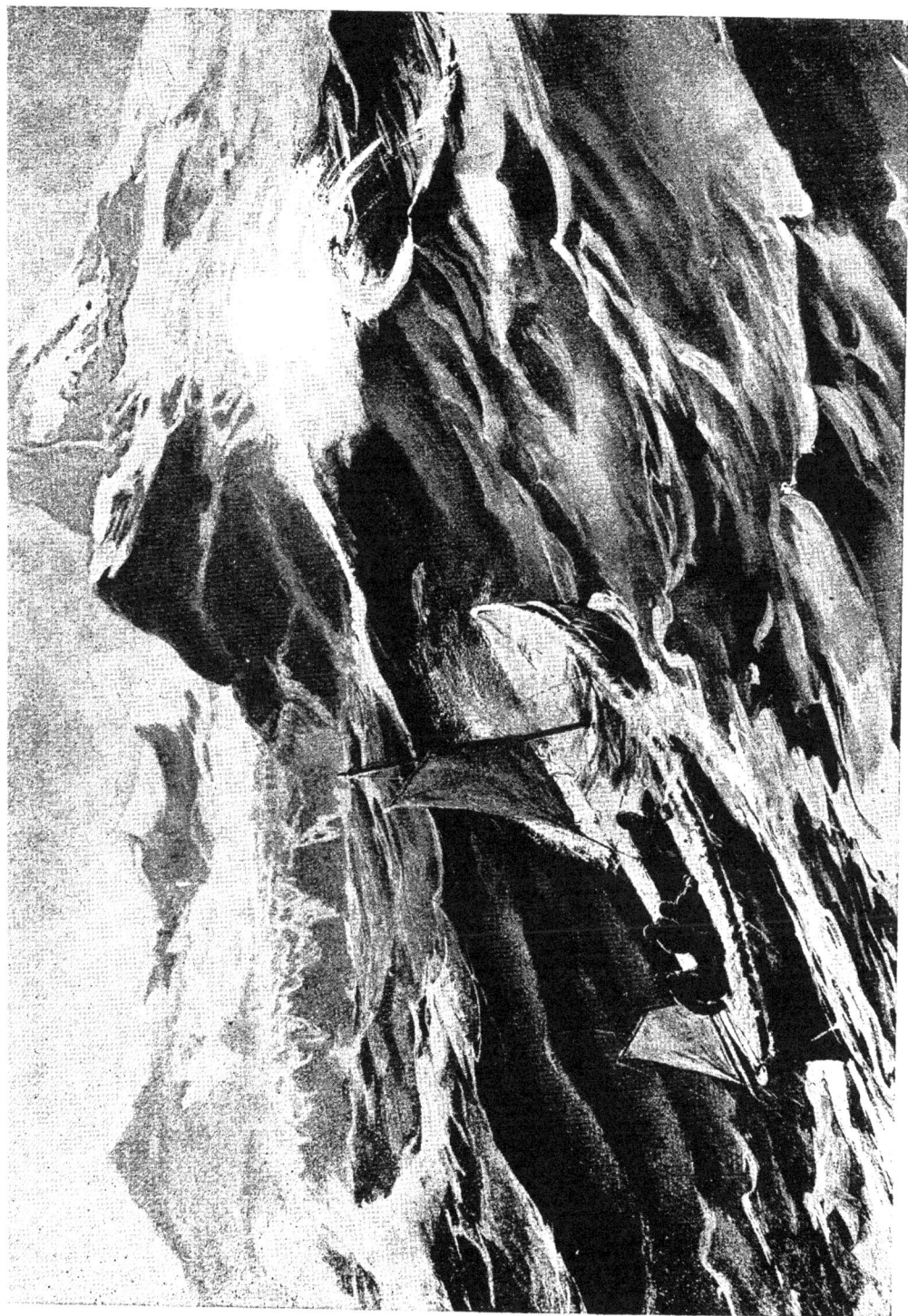

Sir Ernest Shackleton and the remainder of our party
—banquetting! Our excuses availed us not, and, for
the third time, we were compelled to eat and drink—
we could not be merry—and to wade through another
twelve courses! Two weeks ago we were in danger of
death from starvation, now it seemed as if we had
escaped that danger only to die at the festive board.

We left for Valparaiso. If our previous greetings
had been sweetened by the taste of liberty newly
regained, the welcome which was accorded us on arrival
—and later at Santiago—was enhanced by the sense
that something deeper than simple hospitality lay
behind it all. The record of Shackleton's achievements,
and the rescue of his party by a Chilian vessel, had
touched the public imagination and he became an
object of hero worship; but there grew on us a feeling
that it was a tribute, not to us as individuals, but an
expression of friendship towards fighting Britain.

As the *Yelcho* steamed up the lane formed by Chilian
warships everything that could safely float, ferries,
launches and coal barges, followed in her wake. Bands
blared, bunting fluttered, whistles shrieked and the
sailors, massed on the warships, cheered—it was a
supreme day.

At Santiago, the capital of Chile, Sir Ernest delivered his first lecture to a crowded and enthusiastic
audience. A dinner with the President and an afternoon at the races closed our Chilian experiences and
we entrained for the Argentine.

The rail journey across the Andes is one of the most remarkable in the world. A special train had been detailed and I was glad of the opportunity of making a series of pictures, the train stopping when required for this purpose.

The sensation of recognising familiar faces at Buenos Ayres was a keen pleasure and many friends who had waved us farewell when the *Endurance* left this port two years previously greeted us as the train drew in. Again gorgeous hospitality was extended to us, but I was keen to hasten to England.

The homeward journey across the Atlantic promised excitement as the air was heavy with rumours of raiders and submarines; but a succession of violent gales and rainstorms protected us; no submarine could operate in such "splendid" weather.

We safely entered the port of Liverpool.

Now were the dreams of boyhood and the cherished ambitions of youth realised in this my first sight of old England! The endless procession of ships; transports just arrived from India, Australia and Canada crowded with cheering troops; others with contingents outward bound for fields unknown; great war vessels lying at anchor and swift destroyers and submarines— chasers coming and going, were clear indications of the magnitude of the struggle in which the Old Country was embroiled.

As the train carried me to London, the England that I knew without having seen was revealed: the patch-

The "Yelcho" steaming into Valparaiso with the rescued party on board at the termination of her mission of salvation.

work fields of velvety green bordered with brown hedges; the winding canals and reposeful villages, the avenues of birch and oak, russet brown and yellow with the glory of late Autumn.

My first night in London was startling. It was quite impossible to sleep. I found myself contrasting the restricted confines of my bedroom, with the vast open spaces which had been my environment for so long. How secure and comfortable my bed seemed compared with the shivering bivouac on the ice-floes. Suddenly I heard whistles blowing in the streets, a hubbub of voices and an excited shuffle of slippered feet hastening along the hotel corridor. I paid little attention until I was startled by the boom of a distant explosion. Then it dawned on me that an air raid on London was in progress. I raised the window blind and watched the sweeping searchlight beams. Suddenly the rays were all concentrated on one spot and the anti-aircraft batteries nearby began pounding away.

A terrific explosion in a neighbouring street violently shook the hotel. There was a crashing of splintered glass followed by further explosions and heart-rending sounds.

Bitter thoughts came to my mind. This madness was the civilisation that we had been yearning to return to! Far friendlier were the ice-floes even in their cruellest moods. Yet a few weeks later and the Shackleton party to a man had rallied to arms in the fields of France and Flanders.

Emerged from a war with Nature we were destined to take our places in a war of nations. Life is one long call to conflict, anyway.

THE END

Date Due